THE INFECTED

MATT CRONAN

SEVERED PRESS
HOBART TASMANIA

THE INFECTED

ISBN: 978-1-925493-05-4

PART ONE: NEW HOPE

1

Alarms blared overhead as dozens of people crowded together on either side of the laundry facility. A handful of soldiers scrambled back and forth, securing the room's steel doors. Their shouts meshed with the sobs and pleas of panicked workers, creating a discordant orchestra of chaos.

Samantha Albright and Rebecca Young huddled against the wall at the forefront of the crowd. The overhead fluorescents gleamed in Rebecca's wide blue eyes as tears spilled down her cheeks. Sam knelt, so that she was eye-level with the little girl and grasped her by the shoulders.

"What's happening?" Rebecca asked. Her high-pitched voice wavered when she spoke, and Sam struggled to maintain her composure.

"You know what's happening," Sam said. "They've breached the walls."

"It's not a drill?"

"No. It's not a drill."

"Will everything be okay?"

"Yes."

"How do you know?"

"I just do."

Across from them, an old woman clutched a cross in a wrinkled fist and whispered prayers to it. Sam wanted to tell her not to waste her breath. God had stopped listening to them a long time ago. Instead, she looked back to Rebecca, offered the child a confident smile, and wiped her wet cheeks with the soiled sleeve of her coverall.

Outside the facility, a round of gunfire burst through the air and Sam pulled Rebecca to her knees. She grabbed the girl's small hands and squeezed them tight as she fought back her own urges to cry. She hadn't cried since coming to New Hope. That had been a decade ago. Her eyes stung as the backlog of tears threatened to spill over. She pulled Rebecca closer and kissed her on the top of her head.

"It'll be okay," Sam said.

"You promise?"

"I promise." She tried to sound strong, tried to speak in measured tones, but her trembling voice betrayed her.

Two soldiers ran past and positioned themselves at either side of the main entrance. The one on the left side of the door shouted commands to his partner. The patch on his breast pocket had the name 'Horn' stitched onto it. His face was grizzled and hardened.

The other soldier's name was Dennis Freeman. He was 19—five years younger than Sam—and had lived in the same region before the outbreak. His baby-face was far less menacing than Horn's gruff appearance and his finger twitched as it lay against the trigger. Freeman's presence didn't instill the same level of confidence as Horn's.

"I don't want to die," Rebecca said.

"We're not going to—"

Sam's wavering promise was interrupted as a man crashed through the window in the front of the room. Screams erupted from the crowd as the body convulsed on the ground. The man wore the same fatigues as Freeman and Horn. Blood spewed from a gaping wound in the man's neck and showered the left side of the room.

Sam's heart seized as the hot blood splattered across her face. Her eyes slammed shut and her lips pinched together. She let go of Rebecca's hand and wiped the blood from her face with the sleeve of her coverall— careful not to let any get in her mouth, nose or eyes.

Rebecca let out a stifled yelp and Sam's eyes shot open. Her heart lurched at the sight of the little girl doused in crimson. The whites of her eyes were red. Blood covered every entry point. For one long second, Sam sat frozen and horror.

"Sam?"

Sam pressed her sleeve to the girl's face and wiped it away, as she struggled to take a breath.

"It's okay," Sam said. "It's not bad at all."

Rebecca answered with a sob.

The man who had crashed through the window stopped convulsing and lay still. Sam held her breath as the two soldiers took a tentative step toward him. Suddenly, the man shot to his feet. Sam caught the briefest glimpse of his milky-white eyes. He was no longer a man. No longer a living, breathing soul. He was infected.

"What are you waiting for?" Horn screamed as he lifted his rifle.

It was too late.

An inhuman scream ripped through the room and Sam's skin erupted in gooseflesh. A guttural growl followed the scream and the infected man lunged at Freeman. The young soldier tried to backpedal and fired two blind shots as he did. They missed wide and lodged into the wall above the crowd on the right side of the room. The infected man grabbed ahold of Freeman's field jacket and sunk his teeth deep within the soldier's neck. The two collapsed to the ground, and Sam heard the bone-chilling sound of flesh ripping from the young man's throat. Freeman managed a scream which devolved into a nauseating gurgle. Two more gunshots tore through the room and both the infected man and Freeman stopped moving.

Horn's eyes were wide and his skin was ashen. His eyes swept the gruesome scene on the floor and then darted to the group of onlookers covered in blood. He hesitated for the briefest moment and then pulled a white lever next to the door. Sprinklers emerged from the ceiling and drenched the room.

The alarms stopped a few minutes after the shooting. Three Ministry buses idled outside the facility within an hour of the incident. The soldiers forced everyone onto the buses and sent them to the Infection Control Center for testing. The ICC resided in the center of New Hope within spitting distance of the capital building.

Sam covered her eyes as she exited the bus. The pale sun hung high in the air as the group trotted from the bus to the lobby of the small building. She savored the few seconds of warmth it provided before entering through the two glass doors.

Sam took her place in line with the rest of the workers from laundry. They had been exposed to contaminated blood and the ICC would examine them at extensive lengths before rejoining the population. Rebecca stood in front of her. The young girl shivered and clutched her stomach.

"I'm infected," Rebecca whispered as they moved a step forward.

"No you're not." Sam kept her voice low as a soldier walked past them.

"Okay."

"Do you believe me?"

"No."

Sam started to say something but her words fell short. Instead, she squeezed the girl's shoulders, hoping to give her a little comfort. The shaking assuaged, and the girl took a deep breath.

"Next," a voice said. It belonged to a squat woman with short silver hair who sat at a desk at the front of the line. Two soldiers armed with automatic rifles stood behind her on opposite sides of a steel door. They wore stoic expressions but their eyes darted from side to side—scanning for anyone that displayed symptoms of infection.

Roger Farris, a gaunt man in his late sixties, moved from the head of the line to the woman's desk and sat down in the metal chair. Everyone in line took one silent step forward as Roger pressed his face against the retina scanner mounted on the desk. A couple dozen people separated Sam and Rebecca from the woman at the desk.

The testing wasn't new to any of them. Every Friday, the ICC selected a large group of citizens and brought them to the quarantine center. The workers drew their blood and scanned their retinas. Their vitals taken and recorded. In the ten years Sam lived in New Hope, there had never been a breach and no one had ever tested positive.

"No!" Roger screamed. "That's not right." He clambered to his feet and the metal chair flew back and clanked against the concrete floor. The two soldiers approached him, their guns raised and aimed. A third soldier emerged from the rear of the line. Sam's heartbeat quickened and her breath caught in her chest. More soldiers came from the door beyond the silver-haired woman's desk and swarmed upon him.

It took less than ten seconds to secure the man and drag him through the doorway. The heavy metal door slammed shut, but Sam could still hear Roger's muffled screams. A single gunshot echoed beyond the door. And then there was silence.

Before Sam reached the front of the line, the soldiers had taken three more people to the room beyond the desk. Gary DeLaney, Maria Gomez and… Rebecca Young.

They carried the young girl away as she pled for someone to save her. Sam screamed for them to stop and tried to pry Rebecca from their arms. One soldier broke from the group and pinned Sam against the wall.

The small girl clawed at the doorframe as tears poured from her clouded eyes. And then she was gone. Her small body disappeared behind the veil of darkness and the door swung shut. The soldier let go and Sam collapsed to her knees.

"She's a child for god's sake," Sam cried. "You can't—"

The report of the gunshot interrupted her and a gut-wrenching scream burst from Sam's throat. The world blurred and grew distorted. She didn't notice the soldier's hands forcing her to the ground or the pinprick of the needle as it punctured her skin. The light faded from her eyes and darkness swallowed her.

2

The tallest skyscraper on the horizon erupted in brilliant colors of yellow and orange. The flames danced hypnotically as they climbed to the apex of the building and spread to the monoliths surrounding it. Thick dark smoke wafted up from the towering infernos and disappeared into the pitch-black sky above.

Sam stood in a field of unkempt grass and watched the city burn. Long before the outbreak, she had played freeze-tag and hide-and-seek in this field with a boy named David. Before the quarantines. Before the infected stalked the ruins and wastes of the broken world.

The boy lay at her feet, unmoving. His clothes had been torn off of him and on his chest the number zero was seared into his skin. Sam knelt beside him, but when she did, the boy's body disappeared. She ran her hand over the mashed-down grass and felt the warm ground.

Sam stood and turned around. Hundreds of faceless onlookers stood behind her as the enormous blaze swallowed the city. The air grew heavy with ash and soot and Sam tore at the neck of her sweater in a frantic attempt to draw breath. The smoke was suffocating her. She turned around to see if anyone else was affected but the crowd had vanished. A single person remained.

Rebecca Young stood in the center of the field and stared back at her. The girl's pink skin had turned a sickly sallow shade, and the moon gleamed in the milky-whites of her eyes. Sam's heart raced in her chest as the two girls stared at each other in silence. Then the little girl screamed the same inhuman scream as the man who had infected her and a deep chill ran down Sam's spine. And then Rebecca, the girl who Sam loved so much, who she thought of as her baby sister, lunged at her.

Sam woke up screaming. She sprung to her feet and clawed at the empty air. It took a few seconds to realize she was in her own room and safe. And a few seconds more to remember that Rebecca was dead. She had no memory after the execution.

Her eyes scanned the darkened room as her heart continued to slam against her chest and each beat echoed the fear of the nightmare. The fear of seeing Rebecca as an infected. She swallowed hard and the acid filling her stomach burned her insides raw. Outside it was still dark, but Sam had no intention of going back to sleep. Her eyes landed on a handwritten note lying on the small table in the corner.

She crossed the room and picked up the note. Her hands trembled as she struggled to unfold it. The handwriting of the dozen or so words was familiar, and the fear abated as the pain and agony of Rebecca's loss washed over her.

Dax from laundry called me and I brought you home. I'm sorry about Rebecca.

Remember the flowers.

-Jordan

She sat back down on the bed and stared at the note. Cold sweat soaked the sheets, and she noticed the stretched collar of her night shirt. She fingered the scratch marks on her throat and they glistened red when she withdrew them. She wiped them on the white linen and then stared at the crimson spot for a long time. Sam thought of Rebecca and the others and wept until daybreak.

She crawled out of bed when sunlight peeked through the sheer curtain hanging over the lone window in the small room. Her apartment was less than 300 square feet and consisted of two rooms: the main room—that operated as a kitchen, a dining room and a bedroom—and her bathroom. There was no closet, but she didn't have enough belongings to warrant extra storage space. The twin-sized bed, the monitor, the rundown appliances, along with the shelving and fixtures belonged to the Ministry. She could fit everything that she owned into a small suitcase and still have space leftover.

Sam brewed a cup of coffee and sat down at the small corner table. She gripped the ceramic mug in her hands and took a sip of the hot bitter drink. She had hoped the coffee would warm the ice-cold numbness residing inside of her. So far it hadn't. Deep down, she knew it wouldn't. There wasn't enough coffee in the world to fix a broken heart.

The clock continued to move, and when the hour hand found the seven, she took a deep breath and rose from the table to get ready for work. She forced herself into the bathroom and stripped herself of the ragged night shirt. Ice-cold water drizzled down from the rusted showerhead, offering no comfort from the chill in her bones. Then she toweled off, returned to the living area and plucked a pair of coveralls from the dresser. She would have to replace the ones from yesterday.

After she dressed, she picked up the porcelain hairbrush resting on the top of the dresser and dragged the bristles through her long brown hair. The hairbrush was one of the few items she owned outright and one of the few that had escaped the fire. She couldn't remember why she had chosen to bring the hairbrush of all things but she had blocked a lot of the past from her mind.

An alarm sounded and Sam screamed as images of Rebecca's milky-white eyes flooded her mind. She collapsed to the ground and covered her ears. Every muscle in her body trembled with fear and her mind raced at the thought of another breach. The last ten years had been quiet. Too quiet.

Two more ear-piercing bleats followed the first and then a woman's voice came over the intercom. "Attention. Attention. All citizens of New Hope are required to report to the town square at once. This is an official request from the Ministry."

The dread gripping Sam's body eased, and her muscles relaxed. She took a deep breath and got to her feet. She chortled at the gross overreaction to the alarm and caught a glimpse of her reflection. The smile looked foreign on her thin face and its appearance so soon after Rebecca's death disgusted her. The smile faded, and she turned from the mirror. She slipped on her work shoes, zipped up the coveralls, pulled her hair into a ponytail and exited her apartment.

A handful of girls sped toward the stairs at the end of the narrow hallway. The Ministry didn't consider the elevators a necessity and had disabled them. It made the apartments on the lower floors a premium option but no one paid for housing. The citizens worked 70 hours a week and in return the Ministry provided food, clothing and shelter.

Casey Morrison, a red-headed girl that lived two apartments down, bumped into her and offered a quick apology as she continued toward the exit. The Ministry had segregated the single males from the single females, and provided separate housing for couples on the opposite side of the city.

She entered the stairwell last and descended the concrete steps. The footsteps below grew fainter and fainter until hers was the only ones left. It took several minutes to descend the 18 floors to the lobby. She wasn't in a hurry and didn't care if her tardiness upset the Ministry. She didn't care about a lot of things anymore.

By the time Sam reached the bottom of the stairwell and exited into the lobby, she was sure that she would be the last person left in the building. She was wrong. A tall boy her age stood by the revolving glass door.

"Jordan," she whispered.

Her heart skipped a beat at the sight of him and again when he smiled. Bright spots came few and far between after the outbreak, but Jordan was one of them. The weight of Rebecca's death lifted just enough to smile back.

"Thought I was going to have to come get you," he said.

"Sorry," she said.

She crossed the room and wrapped her thin arms around his neck. He responded with a bear hug of his own. She tried to pull away, but he planted a kiss on her lips. Sam melted into his arms and kissed him back. For that short moment, everything was right with the world. Then she pulled away and shook her head.

"We can't," Sam said. "We'll get in trouble. We haven't told the Ministry. If they catch us, they'll throw us into the stockade."

Jordan didn't answer. He pulled her back into his embrace. She didn't stop him. Her cheek rubbed against his and the weeks' worth of stubble he sported scratched against her smooth skin. She didn't pull away from the pain. Instead, she savored the moment.

"I'm sorry about Rebecca."

"It should have been me."

Jordan shook his head. "It shouldn't have been either of you."

"They shot her, Jordan." Sam's voice shook as she said the words aloud. "I heard the gunshot. She was nine years old. She was a child."

Her voice broke, and the tears returned. She sobbed and her knees buckled. Jordan caught her as she fell and guided her to the ground. Sam pressed her head to his chest and balled her eyes out for what seemed like an eternity. Jordan held her close and stroked her hair.

She would have stayed there for the rest of the day if she had a choice but the siren overhead emitted three short bursts as it had before. The female voice boomed through the lobby and repeated the announcement from earlier.

"We need to go," Jordan said. He brushed the hair from her face and tucked it behind her ear.

Sam nodded.

Jordan got to his feet and helped Sam to hers. He wiped her face with his hand and kissed her forehead. She hugged him one more time, then took him by the hand and started toward the front doors. He stopped her right before she entered the turnstile.

"I love you, Samantha."

The ghost of her smile returned. "Remember the flowers."

3

They exited through the revolving door and headed toward the plaza in the center of the city. Sam guessed most of the citizens would already be at the square, but they watched as a few stragglers sprinted past them.

"Why do you think they're running?" Sam asked and let the top of her hand brush his.

"I suppose some people feel they still have something to lose," Jordan said.

Joel Hawkins, a lanky boy with a thick layer of acne, sprinted past them at a frantic pace.

"What's going on, Joel?" Sam shouted after him.

The teen slowed to a stop and turned on his heel. Pocks and craters covered the boy's face and fear resonated from his eyes. Between gasps, he managed, "They caught...six citizens...something about treason...whatever it is...real bad."

"What?" Jordan asked. "Who? Why?" A series of questions cascaded from his lips, but they fell on deaf ears. Joel was on the move again. Not yet at a sprint, but rather a quick jog.

"Who did they catch?" Sam yelled.

The firmness of her voice caused the boy to stop. He turned again and placed his hands on his knees. After a few deep inhales, he looked back to them. "The Ministry caught six and they're accusing them of treason. That's all I can say." Joel motioned toward the plaza. "Can I go now?" The moment's hesitation gave Sam an opportunity to interrogate him further.

"Joel Hawkins, you tell me what you know," Sam said.

Blood rushed into his face, making the skin under the sea of acne glow bright red. The color faded fast, and the boy grew stark white. He looked from Sam to Jordan and then back to Sam. A sudden, intense fear burrowed its way into her stomach.

"Don't know who they caught," Joel said, and then added, "but the

Prime Minister is at the square and he's holding court." This time, he didn't wait for any further questions and sprinted away.

Sam's stomach clinched at the news and she fought to keep her body from doubling over. If the Minister held court at the square, it was so the public could see. The six accused of treason would be tried and made an example. The Minister was the judge and the jury, but he'd bring along an executioner to handle the dirty work. She forced her legs to move, and after a few painful steps, she was at full stride. Jordan kept pace beside her. She said a silent prayer that the Minister was in a gracious mood. It was a fool's prayer; God had stopped listening a long time ago, but she prayed just the same.

Hundreds of people gathered around the enormous stage at the edge of the plaza. Dozens of soldiers, each paired with two ICC workers, guarded the outskirts of the crowd. The ICC officials scanned each citizen as they approached the plaza. The soldiers served as muscle. Sam and Jordan split up, and they each jogged to the closest available group.

"You're late," the soldier said. She was a thin black woman with dark eyes and graying hair. The patch across her breast read Robertson. Her cold gaze fixed on Sam. Sam ignored her and held her wrist out to the ICC official closest to her.

"Nothing's happened yet," Sam said and beckoned to the stage.

The ICC official pulled the sleeve of Sam's coverall back and scanned the barcode tattoo on her wrist. The screen on the device flickered and Sam's picture and name appeared. The official released her wrist and his partner held a portable retina scanner up to Sam's eyes. A red LED light moved from the top of her eye to the bottom and then a green light atop the device illuminated.

"She's good," the official said.

Sam turned to join Jordan when the soldier caught her by the sleeve. "They're watching you."

They shared a long silent look. The soldier's eyes burned with hatred and Sam mirrored it to reflect her own. No love lost between them. Sam had hated the Ministry and its minions from the moment she stepped foot inside of the concrete walls. Killing Rebecca Young had further solidified her disdain for the Ministry. The soldier released her grip but continued to glare. Sam stared for a moment longer and then walked away.

"What was that all about?" Jordan asked when they were out of earshot.

"I'm not sure."

The crowd buzzed as they waited for the arrival of the Minister. Sam caught fragments of worrisome chatter as they pushed their way to the front. The knot in her stomach tightened with each step, and by the time they reached the midpoint, a cold wave of sweat had broken on her forehead. Sam paused and wiped it away with her coveralls.

The stage towered over them and cast a long ominous shadow over the plaza. The Ministry had constructed it after the city gates closed for the last time. During their first year in New Hope, it served as an entertainment outlet for the citizens. They congregated each night as friends and neighbors performed plays and musicals from the pre-infection days. They told stories of a world that no longer existed and sang songs about places and things that they'd never see again. The first year was the only good year Sam could remember.

It took just one song of rebellion and the stage became off-limits to the citizens. It was a brisk autumn evening when Tim Miller, an older man who worked in landscaping, belted out a rendition of Bob Marley's "Redemption Song." Midway through the second verse, the crowd joined in and something electric filled the air. As Tim reached the last line of the song, a soldier rushed the stage and put a bullet through his skull. The old man crumpled, and the crowd watched in horror as blood and gray matter poured from the gaping hole.

That was the moment when the citizens of New Hope first opened their eyes. Freedom and liberty had been surrendered for protection and security. Within a few days of the incident, the government—they would later refer to themselves as the Ministry—started releasing new rules and policies, and within a month, the word freedom was nothing more than a foreign concept.

"Come on," Jordan said and grabbed her hand.

The physical contact snapped her back to the present, and she jerked her hand away. Jordan's face twisted in anguish as if Sam had stabbed him in the heart, but a second later it relaxed and he mouthed a silent apology.

If a Ministry official saw a display of physical intimacy, even a gesture as miniscule as holding hands, then the inquiries would begin. They would be shipped off to the outskirts of town and Sam would be pregnant with Jordan's seed before either of them could raise a hand in protest. Sam had no intention of living on the baby farm and neither did Jordan.

"I'm coming," she said.

They pushed through the majority of the crowd with ease and neared the stage when a hand wrapped around Sam's arm and pulled her in the opposite direction. Her heart leapt into her throat. Thoughts of them being seen by an official flooded her mind, but when she spun around, the fear waned. It wasn't an official that had grabbed her but rather her friend, Abigail Stevens.

The girl was Sam's age and on most days they could pass for twins. But today, Abby's face was swollen and puffy. Her thick brown hair disheveled and the whites of her eyes so bloodshot that Sam wondered how long she had been crying.

"Abby, what's wrong?" Sam asked. She grabbed a hold of Jordan's sleeve to prevent him from moving any further. He stopped, examined the situation, and a concerned expression washed over his face.

"My brother—" Abigail said. Her voice broke and tears rolled down her cheeks. A single high-pitched squeal escaped her before and she wilted into a full-blown bawl.

"What about him?" Jordan asked. "Where's Tyler?"

Tyler Stevens worked in maintenance alongside Jordan. The siblings were a rare anomaly in New Hope. Parent-child relationships didn't exist outside the baby farms. The majority of the citizens were sole survivors of their respective families.

"Where's your brother, Abby?" Jordan's eyes grew wide, and he placed a hand on each of Abby's shoulders. When he asked again, his voice was low. "Where is Tyler?"

Abby didn't answer with words, perhaps couldn't answer, and instead pointed to the stage. Sam turned and through the crowd saw six hooded men. They sat on their knees, their hands and ankles shackled. Tears formed in Sam's eyes and she fought hard to suppress them. She had never been as close to Tyler as she was to Abigail, but the Stevens', next to Jordan and Rebecca, were the closest thing to family she had here.

Rebecca.

An image of the young girl clawing at the doorframe swam to the forefront of Sam's brain and the tears spilled from her eyes. She pushed the thought away and wiped the thought from her mind. This wasn't the time to mourn. At least not for Rebecca.

"Why is he up there?" Jordan asked.

"We were eating breakfast in the mess hall," Abigail said. "We were just sitting there and when I looked up, two soldiers were standing behind him. They said they had proof of acts of conspiracy against the Ministry, and that he was going to be tried for treason. They said he was facing—"

Abigail didn't finish and instead melted into another wave of sobs and tears. But she didn't have to finish for Sam to know why she was so upset. The punishment for treason was execution and just like when a citizen became infected—there were no exceptions. The muttering of the crowd died as the national anthem pumped out of the speakers around the stage and Sam's blood boiled with hatred.

4

Feedback squelched through the speakers and the few citizens who had covered their hearts lowered their hands. Cyrus Poxxal, a man whose dimensions didn't match one another, slid out from behind the velvet backdrop and waddled across the stage. He was a heavyset man who stood just over five feet tall. His long, black mane was pulled back into a ponytail which looked comical considering the lack of hair atop his head. He peered over the crowd through circular wire-rimmed glasses with light blue lenses. They made his fat face appear even meatier and Sam grimaced at the sight of him. He trundled to the center of the stage and then smiled.

"Attention, citizens of New Hope," he said. The man talked through his nose and caused Sam's skin to erupt into gooseflesh. "It's my greatest honor to introduce our wonderful leader. Please give a warm welcome to Prime Minister Carson Troy." He smiled a crooked, yellowed smile and clapped his chubby hands together. Most of the audience members followed suit and applauded. Sam, Jordan and Abigail did not join in.

A thin man emerged from behind the curtain and slithered across the stage. He paused for a moment to sneer at the six prisoners and then addressed the microphone. Cyrus offered an exaggerated bow and Troy waved a dismissive hand at him. Without hesitation, the fat, little man waddled back offstage.

The Prime Minister wore a long, black coat with deep purple trim. Except for his age, he was the polar opposite of Cyrus. Troy was tall and gaunt with a long face and hollow eyes. His salt-and-pepper hair matched the pencil-thin mustache and goatee. He stroked the goatee, delivered a devilish smile to the crowd, cleared his throat and spoke into the microphone.

"Citizens of New Hope," his deep voice boomed from the speakers, "we have traitors amongst us."

A clamorous rumble overtook the crowd and Troy lifted his hand to silence it. The crowd fell silent at once. He stared out into the ocean of onlookers. The population of New Hope was around 8,000 citizens and Sam guessed most were in attendance. The sick and the pregnant would be at home and they'd be forced to watch on their televisions.

"A little over ten years ago, a biological weapon detonated in our nation's capital...on our nation's soil. The government considered the weapon's contents, the RIZ-4 virus, the ultimate global threat, and within two weeks of the detonation, it had spread throughout the world with a 99.9% infection rate. We lost friends and neighbors. Family and co-workers."

His words grew soft as he recounted the horrible story of their past. An image of the burning city flashed in Sam's brain and she shuddered. Jordan grabbed her hand and this time she didn't pull away. The crowd was packed too tightly for anyone to notice.

"Over five-billion people died within the first 48 hours," Troy said. Each word grew more somber and Sam's anger intensified. "We lost more during the quarantines and you, the fine citizens of New Hope, became all that is left of the United States of America," he paused, waiting for his words to sink in and then continued, "us and the infected." Another low murmuring swept through the crowd and this time Troy did not try to stop it. Instead, he waited for the citizens to silence themselves.

His voice intensified. "The Ministry has done its best to protect the great citizens of New Hope from the monstrosities roaming the wastelands. We have committed ourselves to guard the freedoms that this great city holds so dear."

"This is such bullshit," Jordan said in a whisper.

Sam nodded.

"An estimated 10 million of those monstrosities roam what's left of the United States." Troy lowered his voice again. "Ten million. An army of abominations waiting to rip the flesh from your bones."

Sam sighed, her heart heavy in her chest. That part wasn't bullshit and the idea of a childhood friend, or worse a family member, as an infected caused another swell of tears to return to her eyes. This time she blinked them away.

"We have worked so hard to keep you safe," Troy said, now sounding disappointed in the audience. "We have worked so hard, and how do you repay us?" He removed the microphone from its stand and hurried across the stage to where the prisoners knelt.

"You repay us with treachery." He reached the first prisoner and yanked the black hood from the man's head. Donald Robbins, an old-timer that worked in Maintenance alongside Jordan and Tyler, stared at ground. The man didn't acknowledge the crowd and kept his eyes fixed on the stage. Sam squeezed Jordan's hand. He returned a feeble squeeze of his own. She glanced at him and saw the color drain from his face.

"You repay us with disloyalty." His voice had turned venomous. He moved to the second prisoner and ripped the hood away. The second man was Ken Hunter, who worked as a farmer. A sickening cry erupted from somewhere deep in the crowd. Sam imagined it belonged to Ken's wife, Darla. The knot in her stomach cinched and a wave of acid made its way up her throat. Somewhere in this lineup was Abigail's brother.

"You repay us by showing an utter lack of allegiance and devotion for your city." Troy moved to the third man and pulled off his hood.

"Ray Carrol," Jordan said. His voice was cold.

"You repay us by violating the very rules and regulations we have put in place to protect you," Troy said, pulling off both the fourth and fifth men's masks. Derek and Darryl Hoffman were identical twins. The lone pair in the city. They worked as porters. Sam knew them well. They visited the laundry facility daily to drop off chemicals and pick up fresh linens. Their faces were stony and pale.

One prisoner remained.

"You repay us by defiling every sacrifice we have made for you." Troy paused for a moment and the corners of his mouth sunk into a reproachful grimace. He gripped the hood of the last man and snatched it off.

Tyler Stevens.

Abby screamed out something incomprehensible and then melted into silent sobs. The Minister looked in their direction and the scowl curled into a faint grin. It was thin—almost invisible—but it was there and it sickened her.

"These are the men responsible for the breach yesterday," Troy said.

Sam shot Jordan a glance, but he didn't look back.

"These are the men responsible for the death of four citizens."

"It's not true," Abby said. Her voice was so quiet only the people closest to her heard it.

"These men compromised the lives of every citizen of New Hope."

A handful of onlookers jeered at this last statement and then others joined in. Troy had won over the mob and the faint grin appeared once more. After a chorus of boos and hisses, he spat on the ground and marched back to center stage. He placed the microphone back in the stand and plucked a thin, piece of parchment from his pocket. He lifted a hand, and the crowd drew silent.

"On this 14th day of April," he read from the paper, "I, Prime Minister Carson Troy, hereby declare the acts these six men committed as treason. These six men are a reprehensible stain on our society and have proven they are no longer worthy of residing within these city walls. We will punish these deplorable acts in the swiftest of manners as a reminder to the citizens of New Hope that the Ministry acts in the best interests of the people, *for* the people."

Some of the citizens cheered. Sam wanted to vomit.

"Any man, woman or creature that puts the common good of our great city at jeopardy is considered an enemy of the state." As he spoke, four soldiers appeared from behind the thick, velvet curtain. They strutted single file across the stage and lined up behind the prisoners.

"Let the record show, at ten past the hour of eight, on this Tuesday morning, I hereby find these six men guilty of all charges brought forth to me and condemn them to death…by decapitation."

Abby, along with several others in the crowd, screamed and wailed but the chorus of cheers drowned out their mournful protests. After a moment, the cheering softened but Abby's cries remained.

"As New Hope is a free society," Troy said, "if, for any reason, a person wishes to contradict this ruling and can provide ample proof that would acquit these men from their heinous acts, let them speak now."

The crowd fell silent, and Troy's grin widened into a sickening smile.

"Let the record state the citizens of New Hope have acceded my ruling and punishment. Let the executions commence and let God have mercy on their souls." The minster moved from the microphone to the left side of the stage. Cyrus Poxxal emerged from behind the curtain and handed Troy a glass of water. He gulped the contents down but never took his eyes off of the prisoners.

Abigail sobbed and when Tyler Stevens made eye contact with his sister, he began to cry. He sat upright on his knees, his face emotionless, while two of the soldiers unshackled him. They drug him to the center of the stage where a third soldier waited. This one carried a long-handled ax. A fourth soldier wheeled a wooden block from somewhere off stage and placed it in front of Tyler.

The soldier carrying the ax pushed Tyler's head forward until it rested on the block and a deafening silence swept over the crowd as everyone seemed to hold their breaths in unison. Sam looked over to Abby. The girl squeezed her eyes shut and buried her head in her hands. She was about to lose the only family she had left in this world and an abhorrent bitterness pooled somewhere deep inside of Sam. Rebecca's death was still fresh in her mind.

The executioner took his position and lifted the blade of the ax high in the air. The early morning sun gleamed off the sharpened steel blade. Sam gripped Jordan's hand so tight that her knuckles turned a frightening shade of white and her heart slammed against the walls of her chest with the ferocity of a jackhammer.

"Wait!" Sam screamed with such force that her voice cracked midway through. The ax hung frozen in the air and the executioner stared blankly in her direction. A few gasps echoed through the crowd. The songbirds stationed in the trees surrounding the square quit chirping. Silence.

"What are you doing?" Jordan whispered. His voice filled with panic and his grip tightened further around her hand. "Sam, what have you done?"

Sam didn't answer him. The ax wobbled in the executioner's hands. She took a deep breath and screamed again, "Wait!"

Troy's ghoulish grin became a seething grimace as his eyes darted through the sea of faces, searching for the citizen who had the audacity to speak against the Ministry. He sped back to the microphone as his eyes scanned the crowd. There was something strange in his voice when he spoke again.

"Wh-who said that?" he stammered.

Fear.

Sam didn't answer. Terror coursed through her body. She wished she could reverse the hands of time. She wanted to withdraw her plea. Why hadn't she just let the ax fall? Why had she been so stupid?

"Who said that?" Troy asked. The fear had dissipated and a malicious confidence flooded back into his voice.

"Don't say a word," Jordan said. "Samantha Albright, don't you dare say a word."

But it wasn't that simple. She looked to Abigail who stared back at her in alarmed bewilderment. Underneath the perplexed look on her friend's face was a horrifying sadness. It tore at Sam's heart. She couldn't watch in silence as her friend lost a family member.

"Who *said* that?" Troy commanded.

"I did," Sam answered, not trying to mask the terror in her voice.

The crowd parted as if she was one of the infected. Gasps of unbridled horror echoed throughout the mob, but Sam barely registered them. The only thing she heard was her pulse racing between her ears. Jordan remained beside her and grasped her hand so tight that she thought it might break.

"Is there something you would like to say, Miss—?"

"Samantha," she said interrupting the Minister. "Samantha Albright."

"Miss Albright, are you issuing a formal petition against my ruling?" the Minister grinned.

"No."

"Then why, pray tell, have you interrupted my execution?" he screamed into the microphone. His face turned a ghastly shade of blood-red.

Feedback howled through the speakers and Sam pried her hand away from Jordan's and covered her ears. Tears streamed down her face and she cursed herself for acting so weak. Her knees quivered, and she took a deep breath to right herself.

"I—"

"You what?" the Minister interrupted.

"I think a last word should be given to the prisoners." She wiped away the tears from her cheeks and then continued, "They should be able to say goodbye to any family they have left."

Troy stroked his wiry goatee. Sam thought she detected a momentary look of compassion, but the horrible grin returned, and after a moment, he laughed. Sam braced herself and Jordan reclaimed her hand.

"And what does your boyfriend think about this?" Troy asked

Her heart dropped into the depths of her stomach. She tried to let go of his hand but his grip stayed firm.

"I concur, your honor," Jordan said. His voice trembled as he said the words.

"And the rest of you?" the Minister asked the crowd. "Do the rest of you *concur*?" He emphasized the last word, mocking Jordan.

A long moment of silence passed before a woman near the back of the crowd screamed, "Let them speak!" The crowd rumbled with agreements, although none were as brave or as loud as the woman had been. And none were as stupid as Sam had been.

The Minister seemed taken aback by the support of the citizens. But he composed himself, straightened his coat and pulled the microphone from the stand once more. He walked over to Tyler Stevens and grabbed a handful of the man's sandy blond hair. Tyler cried out, and when he stopped, the Minister whispered something into his ear. The Minister pulled away and Tyler nodded his head.

"It seems," Troy's words oozed out of him, "your peers have afforded you the opportunity for one last goodbye." The Minister moved the microphone from his mouth and shoved it into Tyler's face.

Sam reached out and grabbed Abigail's hand with her free one. She gave a reaffirming squeeze, which Abigail returned, but never once took her eyes off her brother. The crowd went silent.

"Abby," Tyler said and paused, tears welling up in his eyes, and then he screamed, "It's all a lie!"

The moment froze and Tyler's last words hung in the air like the smoke from the burning buildings that haunted Sam's dreams. But that moment was just that: a moment—and it passed like all others before it.

With one seamless motion, the Minister dropped the microphone and pulled a dagger from the hitch on his belt. Troy cocked Tyler's head even further and then jammed the dagger's blade deep into Tyler's throat. Sam's knees weakened as she saw the point of the blade reemerge from the back of his neck.

Panicked screams broke through the crowd as they struggled to make sense of the horror that had just unfolded. Blood rushed from Sam's brain and the shouts from the surrounding crowd grew distant and muted. She could see Jordan was still holding her hand but could no longer feel it. On stage, blood squirted from the gaping hole in Tyler Stevens' neck and puddled at the bottom of the wooden block.

"Take the girl into custody! Kill the prisoners!" the Minister yelled. His voice didn't come through the speakers, but Sam could still distinguish it above the roar of the crowd. The only noise coming through the speakers was Tyler gasping for his last breath and the sound of his blood as it gurgled through the hole in his throat. The light in Sam's eyes faded and her knees gave way.

5

Sam opened her eyes. Her chin rested on her chest and the room spun around her. She blinked, and it steadied. She lifted her head and wished she hadn't. Shelves full of leather-bound books covered the walls, and the room smelled of cheap cigars. She slouched in a leather chair in the center of Prime Minister Troy's office. He sat on the opposite side of a large mahogany desk and stared at the contents of a manila folder.

"Where's Jordan?" she asked. Her voice was raspy. She pulled herself into an upright position.

The Minister held up a long, bony finger and continued to scan the stack of pages paper-clipped to the folder. "Quite an impressive show you put on out there, Miss Albright." He glanced up at her, sneered and looked back at the file. After a few minutes, he closed it and clicked his tongue. "Quite a show indeed."

"Where is Jordan?" she repeated. Her head throbbed and her pulse echoed between her ears. The image of the Minister's dagger lodged from Tyler Stevens' throat flashed through her mind.

"Do you know the Ministry's policy on relationships outside of marriage?" the Minister asked. He locked his cold, hollow eyes on to hers and she cringed. "You and your boyfriend are in a lot of trouble, Miss Albright."

"He's not my boyfriend," Sam said.

"I've sentenced him to a month in the stockades," he said. His voice was emotionless.

A wave of guilt rushed over her. Her defiant act would cost Jordan a month of what little freedoms they had left. The stockades would strip him of everything. No clothes, no plumbing, no showers and nothing but bread and water. Her heart ached at the thought it. She had sentenced him to a month in hell.

"What is your affiliation with Tyler Stevens?" he asked.

"I don't have an affil—"

"Don't lie to me," he interrupted. His voice was venomous.

"I'm not lying."

Troy looked deep into her eyes. He tapped a finger on the cover of the folder. "Tell me about Rebecca Young. Our records indicate—"

"Fuck you."

Troy's grin widened into a vicious smile.

"It's none of your business," Sam said. Her throat was tight, and the words struggled to escape from it.

"Everything that happens in the city is my business, Miss Albright."

Sam looked away from him and fought the urge to cry. She had cried enough in the past 24 hours. She refused to let Troy see her as vulnerable.

"It's their fault she's dead, you know?" His voice was soft. "The men you saw today let the creatures through our walls. Why are you protecting him?"

"I'm not." She looked back to him.

Troy's brow furrowed, and he stroked his goatee. "Are the citizens talking, Miss Albright?"

"What? What do you mean?"

"I'm talking about secret conversations." Troy shifted in his chair and his lips turned downward. "Conversations happening out of earshot of my soldiers. Discussions happening in the dark corners of the city. Are they talking?"

The question stumped her and she shook her from head side to side. "No."

The Minister's frowned deepened. He opened his mouth to speak, but a knock at the door stopped him. Cyrus Poxxal stuck his odd-shaped head through the office door. His fat cheeks burned with color.

"What is it?" Troy asked.

"There's something that requires your attention in the…" he hesitated, "um…in the conference room, My Lord."

A chill ascended Sam's spine at the sound of the fat man's voice. It was like fingernails dragging across a chalkboard. She wondered how the Minister could stand hearing it on a daily basis.

"If you'll excuse me." Troy rose from his seat and rounded the desk. He took a step toward the door, paused and then walked to Sam's chair. He bent down and pressed his lips to her ear.

"Think hard about how you want the rest of this conversation to go," he whispered.

Her skin erupted in gooseflesh as the Minister's hot breath seeped through her ear and she struggled to not vomit on him.

"I haven't decided your fate quite yet," he said. He straightened, turned and walked out of the room. The door closed and Sam heard the unmistakable sound of a lock engage.

Blood rushed into her cheeks at the thought of what her fate might be. She took a deep breath and wiped away the tears as they spilled from her eyes. Rebecca was dead. The Minister had thrown Jordan in jail. And now her fate resided in the hands of the most evil son of a bitch Sam had ever met. She had to act.

She stood and rounded the desk. She tried the desk drawers but found them locked tight, and her eyes darted around the room for anything that could be used as a weapon. Nothing. She cursed and looked down at the desk. Printed on the tab of the manila folder was her name. She gave the door another hesitant glance and opened the folder.

The first sheet contained vital statistics: her last recorded height and weight, her hair and eye color, and her blood type. She flipped through the stack of pages until she reached one entitled: Blood Test Results. She scanned through the lines of text but there were no results. Just a list of dates and beside each one the words: Results recorded in main file at Concordia.

"Concordia," she said aloud. The name struck a chord deep within her. She didn't have time to investigate further.

The lock clicked open.

She slammed the folder shut, sprinted around the desk and hopped back to her seat. She hoped the Minister wouldn't notice the skewed files, or her flushed cheeks.

The gaunt man entered and closed the door behind him. Sam's eyes grew wide as the Minster took the small gold key in his hand and locked the door from the inside. Her heartbeat quickened, and she cursed herself for not trying harder to find a weapon.

The Minister glided across the room, but instead of returning to his seat across from her, he moved behind her and placed a thin, hand on each of her shoulders. Sam shuddered at his touch.

"Miss Albright, we find ourselves in quite the predicament," he said in a whisper.

"What would that be?" Sam concentrated on keeping her voice steady.

The Minister massaged her shoulders and the overwhelming urge to vomit returned. The thick fabric of the coveralls, which always felt too hot during the summer months, now seemed paper thin.

"You created quite the scene, Miss Albright. A scene that is now burned into the minds of my citizens." His hands kneaded the muscles in her shoulders for a quick second before moving down her neckline and under the protection of the coveralls.

She wanted to run as the ice-cold skin of his fingertips pressed against hers. But she didn't. Too much was at stake for her to make an irrational decision. Jordan's life hung in the balance of her decisions. And so did hers. She took a deep breath and clenched her jaw shut.

"My advisors tell me this can have detrimental effects on the city." He rubbed the top of her chest and his hands inched lower with every word.

The tears Sam had hidden from him now fell down her pale cheeks. She glanced at the door but knew there would be no escape. Troy had locked the door and even if she somehow got it open, how many soldiers would be waiting on the other side? She closed her eyes as the Minister's hands reached the top of her breasts.

"My advisors tell me there is just one scenario that will reverse the damage you've caused."

"Please," Sam pleaded. "Please don't do this."

"Oh, but you've done this to yourself, my dear." His hands moved even lower, and he cupped her breasts. "Normally, we would begin the coupling process for you and your boyfriend. But you embarrassed me today. And no one embarrasses me."

Sam stood and tried to push the old man away, but the Minister kept a firm lock on her chest. He kicked the chair out from between them and pushed her against the desk. He continued to grope her and bent her over the desk. A bulge protruded from under his coat and he grinded it against her.

"Please," she begged again, no longer able to hide the tears in her voice.

"Shut your goddamn mouth," he hissed and grabbed her breasts hard.

Sam gasped as pain shot through her chest. The Minister's hands pawed at her chest and panic flooded through her. He would rape her. He would kill her. She was sure of it. She squirmed away and faced him. He advanced, and she shoved him hard in the bony chest. He fell back a step and grinned.

"I've called for another town square meeting," he said. "Tomorrow morning, you will show the citizens that your loyalty lies with the Ministry and to me. You will beg me on your knees for forgiveness. And I will show mercy and accept. Tonight, however, you can beg and plead all you want," he paused and eyed her from head to toe, "tonight, I will be merciless."

He took a step forward, but Sam lifted a trembling hand and he hesitated.

"And if I don't?" she asked. "If I don't apologize, then what?"

The Minister's grin widened into a blood-curdling smile. "If you are defiant, if you attempt to embarrass me in the slightest, I'll cut your boyfriend's head off and bury him right next to that little bitch you liked so much."

Troy unbuttoned the long black coat and removed it. It revealed a thin, sickly frame underneath and the outline of the ancient erection he had rubbed against her. Sam gagged at the sight of it. The Minister's face reddened, but the grin remained.

Sam's eyes fell to a glass paperweight, and she picked it up from the Minister's desk. "I won't make this easy."

"Good," the Minister said and advanced.

Sam threw the paperweight, but Troy ducked it and lunged at her. She tried to side step the charge but failed. He grabbed her by the waist and pushed her up against the desk once more. And once more, he pressed himself upon her. She squirmed with all her might but the old man was much stronger than he looked. He bent over her and she cringed as his hot, stale breath blew into her face. She gagged again.

"I will ruin you," he said. One of his hands pawed at her chest and the other slid between her legs. Sam squeezed her thighs together, but the Minister forced his hand higher. She panicked but when the Minister's hand found her groin, everything went red.

She placed both hands on the desktop and pushed. The force was enough to knock the Minister backwards. She spun around and swung her fist. The blow landed and his lip split as her knuckles crashed into his teeth. The Minister reeled, steadied himself and spit out a mouthful of blood.

"I'll kill you," he growled as the grin peeled back into a snarl.

"You'll have to," Sam said.

Sam swung again, but this time the Minister was ready for it. He caught her by the wrist. She swung with her other arm and he grabbed it as well and then pulled her into him. Sam tried to pull away and Troy head-butted her. Sam's knees weakened and something warm oozed from her forehead.

"With pleasure, my dear." He pushed his mouth to hers and buried his tongue deep inside. It was like a diseased worm rooting its way to the back of her throat and Sam coughed hard. It forced him to pull away.

"After I use you up," he said, the heavy exhale of his breath swarming around her, "I'll execute you in front of your worthless scab of a boyfriend and then I'll screw your corpse in front of him." He flashed a wide crooked smile and then kissed her again.

The intrusive tongue wriggled in Sam's mouth and she seized the horrific moment. She bit down and sunk her teeth deep into the thick, slimy muscle. The metallic taste of blood filled her mouth and hot liquid poured into her mouth but she refused to let go. Troy managed a muffled howl and tried to pull away from her. Sam clamped down even harder and as he screamed into her, she buried a knee into his groin. She opened her mouth, and the Minister crashed to the ground.

Sam spat a large crimson blob onto the floor and turned toward the door. Before she could take a step, a hand wrapped around her ankle. Her momentum carried her forward, and despite putting her hands out to break the fall, her head hit and bounced off of the hardwood floor. Stars filled her vision, but the adrenaline coursing through her forced them away. She kicked with her free foot and landed a blow square in the Minister's bloody mouth. His grip relinquished, and she managed to get to her feet. She stumbled to the door and her heart sank as she tried to turn the knob. She had forgotten.

The Minister cackled as he stared up at her. Blood poured from his mouth as he did and streamed down his chin. Sam ran back to Troy's crumpled body, and when he reached out to grab her, she evaded him and then kicked. The toe of the steel-toed boot collided with her target and a chill ran up her spine as she heard the sickening crunch of the blow. Troy fell motionless.

Not willing to succumb to a trap, Sam kicked again for safe measure. This time her boot found his gut and the Minister's mouth shot open. Blood spewed from his mouth along with part of his tongue. Sam held her hand over her mouth to keep her from vomiting. She squatted down beside him and sunk her hand into the breast pocket of his coat. Her fingertips touched the small golden key, and she fished it from his pocket.

Sam stood, turned toward the door and then turned back again. She could still feel his hands groping her body and again she saw red. She kicked Troy in the crotch and spit the remnants of the blood in her mouth onto his face.

"May God have mercy on your soul, Minister."

She bolted to the door and then shoved the key into the lock. It turned without restraint and the lock clicked open. She took one last look behind her and realized she had not only signed her own death warrant but Jordan's as well. Probably many more. Anyone that had ever associated with her. Tears stung at her eyes, but she fought them back. The emotional breakdown would have to wait. She took a deep breath and exited into the hallway.

6

Sam made it down three flights of stairs before the alarms sounded. They were the same ones that rang when the infected had breached the walls. Long and whooping. Above her, doors slammed open. She hustled down the last two flights and burst through the steel door at the bottom of the landing.

The midday sun blinded her, and she covered her eyes as she stepped out into the courtyard. A handful of soldiers ran past her and mounted the stairs to the building's entrance. She pressed her palm to her forehead and fixed her eyes on the sidewalk. When she reached Main Street, she took off in a sprint toward the stockades.

The men's stockade was an old police precinct on the East side of town, three miles from Ministry Headquarters. Sam darted down side streets and alleyways, being careful not to be seen by the passing soldiers who all hustled toward City Hall. Toward the Minister. They'd soon be alerted of her indiscretion and sent to the stockades to hunt her down. She imagined fat, little Cyrus Poxxal stooped over the Minister's crippled body and declaring a full-blown manhunt. Her lungs burned and her muscles ached, but the thought of being captured and executed caused her to run faster.

Sam rounded the corner of Elm and Second and spotted three soldiers emerge from the doorway of the stockade. She ducked into a grouping of ancient elms and oaks and watched as they took off in a jog toward the city. They disappeared out of view and Sam turned toward the building to think about her entrance strategy.

She had almost decided on a point of entry when a giant hand covered her mouth. She let out a muffled scream as a second hand wrapped around her waist. Her feet left the ground and her assailant carried a few feet farther into the woods.

"Hush," a man said. "I ain't here to hurt you."

Sam stopped screaming as the man lowered her. The man released his grip and Sam turned toward him. Her face lit up as she eyed the giant man standing behind her. Cole Porter smiled back at her.

"You scared the living daylights out of me," Sam said.

"Sorry, Miss Sam," Cole said. "Didn't mean to scare you. Figured you'd show up here. Heard a buncha chatter on one of the soldier's walkie-talkies." He pulled a greasy rag from the back pocket of his coveralls and offered it to her. "Your head's bleeding. Did you know that?"

"Yeah." She took the rag and pressed it to her forehead. "But you should see the other guy."

Cole's eyes widened. "Did you kill him?"

"Not yet." She pulled the rag back and stared at the bright red patch of blood on it. "But the day's not done."

One of Cole's meaty fingers shot to his lips, and he pointed toward the building's entrance. A blond-haired soldier popped his head up from behind the glass double doorway and Sam's muscles tensed. The man looked in either direction and then disappeared into the building.

"Have you seen him?" Sam asked as her muscles relaxed.

"Naw. Not since they hauled him away from the plaza." Cole's voice lowered even more. "But you're here to bust him out, ain't ya?"

Sam nodded.

Cole stroked his thick, bushy beard and sighed. "Best we go around to the back and get 'em." He pointed toward the rear of the building. "I got a key to the door, and no one uses the hallway back there."

"How do you have a key?" Sam asked.

Cole smiled. "Been in maintenance ever since they shut the gates. I got a key to just about anywhere you want to go."

"Do you have a key to get us outside?" Sam asked. "Outside the walls."

"Naw. But I know someplace we can lay low until we figure it out." Cole looked toward the street and then back to the stockades. "We need to get going."

Sam nodded, and they started toward the rear of the building. They stayed as low as possible as they crossed the empty lot of overgrown weeds and brush, but Cole stood close to seven feet tall and was a hard person to miss. She prayed no one would see them as they neared the stone building.

In the distance, the bleating alarm halted and Sam's heart jumped into her throat. What little time remained for this rescue attempt was dwindling. She quickened her pace as she rounded the corner of the building and Cole fell in line behind her.

"Thank you," Sam whispered as they reached a set of stone steps at the rear of the building.

"Don't thank me yet," Cole said. He stepped past her and descended the steps. "Door at the bottom leads to the holding cells."

They reached the landing and Cole dug into the pocket of his coveralls and fished out a massive ring of keys—all assorted shapes and sizes. He picked a small silver one from the bunch and shoved it into the lock. He turned it and the door opened.

Cole took a step forward but Sam grabbed him by the sleeve. "Why are you helping me? If the Minister finds out, he'll kill you."

"Ain't got time to explain," Cole said. "Jordan's a friend of mine and I could leave it at that but..." His voice trailed off.

"But what?"

"Someone wants to meet you when we're done here."

"Who?"

"I'll tell you after, Miss Sam. I just need you to trust me for right now. We're running out of time."

Sam's brow furrowed but nodded in agreement. Cole was right. It had been half an hour since she escaped City Hall. The soldiers knew about the attack. The longer they waited, the lower their chances of success would be. Cole disappeared through the doorway and Sam followed.

They tiptoed down a narrow hallway toward a frosted glass door at the end. Overhead, emergency lights illuminated the corridor in a dull glow. The walls, once white, were now yellow and covered in mold. Portraits of police officers lined the walls. Photos of ghosts hung frozen in time. Sam shivered as she passed them. She felt like they were watching them.

They reached the end of the hall and Cole pointed to the top of the door. Someone had scrawled the word 'Inmates' into the wood just above the frosted glass. Sam nodded, took a deep breath and threw open the door.

Six jail cells lined either side of the room. Two soldiers stood in the middle and stared at them wide-eyed. Sam gasped as they both raised their weapons in unison, but Cole Porter pushed past her and punched the closest guard in the nose sending him reeling backward. He snatched the muzzle of the rifle of the second man and forced it to the ground. The gun flew from the soldier's hands and clanked on the concrete floor. Cole seized the disarmed man by the collar of his field jacket and tossed him into the empty cell and then he slammed the iron door shut.

"I'll take care of them," Cole shouted. He dug his free hand into the pocket of his blue coveralls and retrieved the heavy key ring. He tossed them to Sam and then buried his boot into the nose of the soldier lying crumpled on the ground. Sam shivered at the sound of the crunch.

She ran past three cells before she reached Jordan. He stood at the barred door and covered himself with his hands. Sam blushed at the sight of his naked body. Except for a secret kiss or holding hands, they had never been intimate with one another. They had never even seen each other outside their Ministry-issued coveralls.

"Are you okay?" Sam asked as she fumbled through the keys. She avoided making eye contact but also focused on keeping her gaze above his waist.

"Well," Jordan said, "I'm standing naked in a prison cell and I'm pretty sure those alarms have something to do with you and your busted forehead."

Sam gave him a half-grin as she plucked a key from the mass and shoved it in the lock. She tried to turn it, but it remained steadfast. "The alternative to the situation is," Sam said as she pulled the key from the lock and scanned through the others, "is me being raped and executed in front of you."

"Did he put his hands on you?" Jordan asked, his voice trembling.

Sam bit her lip and locked her eyes on the keys. The thought of the old pervert rubbing against her brought a fresh set of tears to her eyes. She blinked them away and said, "It's not important. What's important is getting you out of here."

She needed to touch him. To hug him. She needed to be wrapped up in his embrace. To feel his flesh against hers. It would be the only thing that would make her feel okay again. The only thing that could wash away the lingering touch of Troy.

"Tell me."

"Yes," Sam whispered. She drew in a painful breath. Her hands trembled as they rooted through the many keys. "Dammit. Why are there so many keys?"

"I'll kill him."

Sam picked out another key that looked like it might fit and slid it in the keyhole. She turned the key, and the lock clicked open. The door swung open, and she threw her arms around his neck. She didn't care that he was naked or that an entire army was hunting them. She kissed him on the mouth and he returned it, although he didn't remove his hands from his groin.

"I love you," she said. She could no longer fight the tears and they streamed down her face.

"I love you, too." His eyes were also wet, and she wiped them away with the sleeves of her coveralls.

"I hate to break up a tender moment such as this," Cole said from behind them, "but we got about two minutes to make haste."

The two guards lay motionless in the cell near the door and Cole had stripped one of his clothing. He tossed the fatigues into the cell. Jordan caught them with one hand and his cheeks turned bright red. Sam turned away and Jordan slipped into the stolen clothes.

Sam placed the heavy ring of keys back into Cole's hand and wrapped her arms around his neck. He bent down and Sam whispered into his ear, "Thank you."

The three of them backtracked out of the stockade and fled across the field behind the station. As they reached the edge of the woods, Sam turned and saw a bevy of soldiers approaching the building.

"Run," she said.

They sprinted until the woods gave way to the rear of an old neighborhood and then they slowed to a stop to catch their breath.

"Where are we going?" Jordan asked.

"Edge of town," Cole answered. "Someone wants to meet you two?"

"Who?" Jordan asked.

"You'll see," Cole said "For now, you two catch your breath. I'll check our six and make sure no one followed us." The giant stepped back into the woods, and after a few seconds, Sam lost sight of him.

She sat down on the street and pressed her palms against the hot, faded blacktop. It burned her skin, but the pain was welcome. They were still alive. Jordan squatted beside her and wrapped a hand around a cluster of weeds sprouting up from the cracked pavement.

"This place is creepy," Sam said.

"I grew up in a neighborhood just like this," Jordan said. He uprooted the weeds and tossed them aside. "I can't remember the name of the town."

Sam furrowed her brow as she tried to remember the name of the city she lived in before the quarantines. She could see the burning city, but that was all. "I can't either."

"It's weird."

"I can't remember my parents' faces. Can you?"

"No."

The abandoned houses surrounding them peered out from behind thick foliage and a shiver ran down Sam's spine as her eyes fell upon a pink tricycle in the front lawn of the adjacent yard. Children once played here. Families once lived here. In the distance ahead, she could see the concrete wall encircling the city.

"What's happening to us, Jordan? It's like we're all stuck in someone's nightmare and everything is fading."

"If it's a nightmare then I wish the son of a bitch would wake up." He reached out and tucked a strand of her hair behind her ear. "But then we wouldn't have each other and that would truly be a nightmare."

Sam smiled and turned as she heard footsteps behind them. Cole emerged from the woods and squatted down beside them.

"I doubled back," he said and withdrew handkerchief from his pocket. "Laid down some tracks goin' the opposite way. Any of them can track worth a hoot shouldn't be too fooled, but I know most of them soldier boys and they ain't hunters." He wiped his brow with the napkin and then tucked it back into his coveralls. "You two think you gotta couple miles left in those wheels of yours?"

"I think we can manage," Sam said.

Cole nodded and stood. Jordan stood as well and offered a hand to Sam. He pulled her to her feet and squeezed her around the waist.

"We're going to be okay," Jordan whispered.

"I hope so."

They jogged to the front of the neighborhood and turned right toward the west side of the city. Cole moved fast for his age and Sam struggled to keep up. Her adrenaline levels had spiked during the escaped, making her body numb to pain and fatigue. Now, the muscles in her thighs and calves quaked with every footstep and her forehead throbbed to the rhythm of her heartbeat. Her lungs burned with each shallow breath she managed.

Sam counted each footstep as it smacked the pavement, trying to force her mind away from the events of the day. She had sealed her fate in the Minister's office and sealed Jordan's as well. The Minister would execute them. Cole would be executed too if the soldiers caught him helping two fugitives. A wave of nausea swept through her and she stopped in her tracks.

"What's wrong?" Jordan asked.

She tried to answer but panic prevented her voice from reaching her lips. An image of Jordan kneeling on stage to be executed flashed through her mind and she vomited onto the worn down pavement.

Jordan pulled her hair away from her face and she heaved again. It had been almost a full day since she had eaten and threw up liquid. Water and stomach acid. It burned her throat and nose and splashed as it struck the ground.

"Miss Sam—"

Her stomach clenched again, and she wept as she threw up again.

Inside, a mixture of terror and sorrow ravaged her heart and soul. Everything was her fault.

"We have to keep going," Jordan said.

"Okay," Sam said through tears.

"We ain't got much further, Miss Sam." Cole said. "Just hang in there a little longer." He panted but not as hard as Jordan or herself. Sam wondered how the old man could be in such better shape than two youngsters half his age.

She nodded, dried her eyes on her sleeves and straightened.

"Where are we going, Cole?" Jordan asked.

Cole looked around as if he were making sure the coast was clear and then whispered, "The ol' train yard down on Elm. Gotta bring you to 'em. Let 'em tell ya the story. Let 'em tell ya the truth."

"Bring us to whom, Cole?" Jordan took a few steps toward Cole. He poked a finger into the old man's chest. Cole dwarfed him by a foot and at least 100 pounds. "Are you setting us up? Is this a trap?"

"Jordan, calm down," Sam said. Her voice came out weak and fragile and she cursed herself. "He helped get you free."

"Why? Why are you helping us?" Jordan asked. His words came out tough but Sam could see the fear in his eyes. "Who the fuck wants to meet—?"

Cole threw a jab so quick that Sam barely saw it. It caught Jordan in the mouth and he took a couple of steps backward. Sam gasped. Jordan's eyes widened and his hands wrapped around his jaw. He didn't go down, but his knees buckled and he took an awkward step forward.

Jordan spit a mouthful of blood onto the blacktop. "What the hell, Cole?"

"I ain't no traitor and I don't appreciate you accusing me of one," Cole said. "And you ought not to speak like that in front of Miss Sam or any matter of fact. Didn't your parents' teach you any manners?"

"Who are you taking us to see?" Jordan asked. His brow furrowed, but he stayed out of striking distance.

"You don't know them," he said.

"What does—?"

"Listen here," Cole interrupted. "We can stand 'round here with our thumbs up our keisters," he pointed back in the direction they had come from, "wait till one of those soldier boy's catches and skins us, or we can get on with the gettin' on."

Sam pulled Jordan back to her side and spoke in a whispered hush. "We don't have a choice, Jordan. If it's a trap then we're already caught. Besides, I trust him." At this, Sam detected the faintest of smiles behind

Cole's thick beard.

Jordan seemed to consider her plea and then nodded his head. He turned back to the big man and extended a hand. "Sorry, Cole."

"Aw, you ain't got to say sorry to me," Cole said, "but you need to apologize to Miss Sam."

Jordan nodded and turned to Sam. He didn't apologize though. His eyes grew saucer-wide, and he raised a trembling finger. Sam spun around and her heart dropped as her eyes fixed on a squadron of soldiers marching down a cross street. They didn't seem aware of their presence...yet.

"Let's go to the train yard," Sam said. She turned and saw Cole had already taken off in a sprint in the opposite direction. Without hesitation, Sam and Jordan followed in his footsteps.

7

A sea of rusted rail cars stood atop broken-down strips of iron. The town had abandoned the train yard long before the infection took place. It reminded Sam of the rest of New Hope. A city of ghosts forgotten and left to rust.

The sun beat down on them from its perch, high and the cloudless sky, as they weaved through the corroded boxcars. Cole led them through the maze as if he had done this a hundred times before. They reached the end of a line of cars and he made a left and then at the next intersection a right. Never a misstep or a moment of hesitation.

"Shit!" Sam yelled. A giant opossum had hissed at her as they passed an open boxcar. It hunkered in a bed of rotten hay and its pitch-black eyes darted from Sam to Jordan as it bared a vicious set of teeth.

"Sorry," Cole said. "Forgot about her. She won't hurt ya as long as ya keep your distance."

Sam pressed herself against the adjacent boxcar as they passed. The animal stuck its head out of the door and watched them until they made another quick turn.

"Any more surprises heading our way?" Jordan asked.

"None of the four-legged sort," Cole said.

"That's a real comfort," Jordan said.

The word struck a chord with Sam. *Comfort.* When would they ever be comfortable again? They would be on the run for the rest of their lives. If they escaped to the outside world, they would live in fear of the infected. Her breath caught in her chest. What had she done? She had ruined their lives.

"I'm sorry," she whispered to Jordan. "I'm sorry for speaking out—"

Jordan shushed her and reached out his hand. She took it and their fingers intertwined. His hands were rough, but they comforted her. Sam's were the same although not to the same degree. Not even close. Maintenance was hard labor. He squeezed her hand, and she returned it with a gentle smile. Maybe she had signed their death warrants but maybe an end to all this wouldn't be too bad. They had no plans to repopulate the Earth, what was their purpose?

"I love you," Jordan said.

"Remember the flowers," Sam said back.

"Yes, remember the flowers."

Sam didn't remember any flowers, and neither did Jordan. "Remember the flowers" was nothing more than a code phrase they had created when they first started…whatever it was they did. Sam didn't know what to call it. Date? No, they'd never been anywhere. They weren't *going steady* or *going out* or whatever else it people called it before the infection. Soul mates? Yes. Their souls belonged to each other, in this life and the next.

"We're here," Cole said as they reached a steel door at the end of the lot. It had been built in the side of a large concrete wall that stood 15 feet high and stretched 50 yards to the right. To the left was a large gate made up of rebar that crisscrossed from top to bottom. The gate covered a giant tunnel that once led in and out of the city. When Ministry erected the city walls around New Hope, they blew up the interior of the tunnel to keep the infected from coming in. And to keep the citizens from going out.

Cole fished the ring of keys from his pocket. He inserted one into the lock on the steel door and pushed it open. Beyond the door was a lightless corridor, and without hesitation, the old man disappeared into it. Sam looked at Jordan, who offered her a nervous smile. She returned it and they followed Cole into the darkness.

"Keep straight," Cole's voice echoed around them. "Keep your hands out in front of ya and keep straight. You bump into a wall and ya done got yerself twisted up. Just holler and I'll come back and straighten ya out."

"Where are we going?" Jordan asked. His voice boomed through the hallway. He followed with a much quieter, "Sorry."

"Fifty yards," Cole said. "We're halfway now."

"But where?" Sam asked.

Cole didn't answer.

As creepy as the darkness was, it provided a refreshing break from the heat. She wiped the sweat from her brow and winced as the sleeve of the coverall rubbed over the forgotten wound on her forehead. The pain returned in a slow, agonizing throb that spread out through her head like a wildfire.

The sound of gears and cogs turning filled the air, and the headache was forgotten. Sam froze in place and she reached blindly to her side. She found Jordan's hand and squeezed as tight as she could. He squeezed back, and they stood there in the darkness. Sam held her breath as the noise grew louder and louder around them.

The gear sound stopped and there was a loud click followed by four short bangs. A stream of light cut through the dark tomb and Sam shielded her eyes as they adjusted to the bright fluorescents ahead of them. Cole stood a few feet ahead of them in a doorway that mirrored the one they had entered.

"Sorry," he said. "Should have warned ya." He chuckled and proceeded through the doorway. Sam and Jordan followed with no further questions. There didn't seem to be a point. Either they would die here, under the ground, or later in the town plaza. The question had become 'when' not 'if.'

Sam's eyes took a moment to adjust as they stepped into the illuminated room. The thin layer of carpet underneath their feet was pale green and covered in spots of mold. The far wall was glass from floor to ceiling and a long wooden table sat in the middle with a dozen leather chairs surrounding it. Sam jumped at the sight of two people sitting at the end of it. One was a man whom she had never seen before. He wore a Ministry-issued black coat with blue trim. The other person at the table was a female soldier. The same female soldier from the plaza.

"What the hell is this, Cole?" Jordan asked. His voice shook with anger. He had betrayed them. Cole joined the two at the end of the table a wide grin covering his traitorous face.

"Sit down," Robertson said. Her voice was just as cold as it had been in the plaza.

"Make me," Jordan said.

Robertson stood but the man in the black coat touched her arm. The soldier hesitated and then sat back down.

"It's alright, Jordan," the man in the black coat said. He sat at the head of the table and offered a slight grin. He was Cole's age but was much thinner and not as tall. The little hair he had left was gray and cut short and his voice was soft when he spoke. "We're not here to hurt you."

"What are you here for?" Sam asked.

"To talk to you," the man answered. "To talk to both of you."

"Why?" Sam asked.

"Because the two of you deserve an explanation and I would like to be given the opportunity to provide it."

"An explanation?" Jordan asked. "For what?"

"For everything," the man said. He smiled and beckoned for them to sit.

No one moved.

"I won't bite," the man said.

"And your lap dog?" Jordan asked and motioned toward Robertson.

"Boy, if you don't sit your ass—" Robertson snapped.

"That's enough, Jeanette," the man in black interrupted. His voice remained calm but firm. Robertson fell silent and a half-cocked smirk edged her lips. "Sgt. Jeanette Robertson is on our side," the man said. "She is here to assist in what comes after..." he hesitated, "...assuming you are receptive to what I have to say."

"To your explanation," Sam said. It wasn't a question.

"Yes," the man said.

Sam took a seat at the opposite end of the table. Jordan hesitated for a moment as he stared down Cole. Their betrayer never stopped grinning, and after a few awkward moments, Jordan joined her at the table.

"My name is Holden Deckard, and I work—" the man said and stopped himself. A faint smile crossed his lips and then continued, "Correction, I worked for the Ministry as a biogenetic engineer."

Holden picked up a glass of water in front of him. He lifted it to his lips and took a large drink. Sam's mouth felt like sandpaper and she longed for the liquid as it disappeared into Holden's mouth.

After a few gulps, he sat the glass down and his cheeks flushed. "How rude of me. Cole, please bring our guests some water. And please get Miss Albright a rag to clean her wound. I believe there's a first-aid kit outside of the mechanical room."

Cole nodded and exited a room through the door opposite of them. There was a long moment of silence as they waited. Holden continued to smile and Robertson continued to glare at them.

"So how about you give us this explanation?" Jordan said after a full minute had passed.

Holden took another sip of water and cleared his throat. "You have been lied to," he said and placed the glass back on the table. "We want to tell you the truth."

Sam's pulse quickened, and she swallowed hard, "What truth?"

Jeanette Robertson shifted in her seat, but her face remained stony. Sam wondered if she had ever smiled in her entire life and wondered what it would look like if she did.

"The official statement released by the United States government was that they had developed the RIZ-4 virus in secret as a response to the increasing threat of nuclear war. They thought of it as an endgame, only to be used under extreme circumstances."

Sam and Jordan both nodded. The same story revolved around the quarantine center after the outbreak. Then the government shipped them to New Hope where the stories continued. When the statements stopped being released and communication from the government ceased, the gates guarding the city had been closed.

Cole reentered the room carrying two glasses filled with water. He set them in front of Jordan and Sam. "I'm gonna go check the yard," he said and placed one of his giant hands on Sam's shoulder. He squeezed it. "I put the rag in the room in the back, along with the rest of the first-aid kit." Holden nodded in approval and Cole disappeared into the dark hallway.

Sam picked up the glass of water and took a sip. It was the greatest thing she had ever tasted. She took a big gulp and then another. Her body longed for her to finish it all, but she forced herself to return the glass to the table.

"There's plenty more," Holden said.

Sam hesitated for a moment and then drained the rest of her water. Jordan's glass remained untouched.

"Drink it," Sam said.

"I'm not thirsty," Jordan said.

"Please."

Jordan shot her a look of contempt but drained the contents of the glass.

"Would you like more?" Holden asked.

"No," Jordan said.

"It's not a problem. We have plenty—"

"Just get on with the damn story," Jordan interrupted.

"Please calm down," Sam said. "They're here to help us."

"You don't know that," Jordan said.

"And you don't know that they're not."

"Actually," Holden interrupted, "we're not here to help you. Truth be told, we need your help."

"Then let's hear what you have to say," Sam said. Underneath the table, she took Jordan's hand in hers and squeezed. She didn't want to fight with him. She needed him now more than ever. But she also needed to hear what Holden Deckard had referred to as 'the truth.'

"According to the official statement," Holden continued, "a North Korean insurgent stole the virus and detonated it in the main terminal of the Hartsfield-Jackson Atlanta International Airport. Within the first week, more than half of the population had been exposed to the virus. By week two, the media reported a 99% kill rate. And by the 19th day, the only ones left outside the quarantine centers were the abominations the virus created."

Holden stared into each of their eyes, perhaps waiting for a response. When one didn't come, he continued. "What if I told you the virus wasn't stolen?"

"What do you mean?" Sam asked. Her words were raspy and her palms were sweaty. She wiped her hands on her coveralls.

"The RIZ-4 virus never fell into the hands of the North Koreans or anyone else," Holden said. "Our own people detonated the bomb."

"But why?"

"Population control." Holden leaned forward. "There was no third world war. We were facing a global crisis. Global warming, peak oil, deforestation, pollution, fracking...the world was on life support. We had exhausted all of our resources. A secret organization made up of the extremely wealthy decided the only way to save the planet would be to kill off its number one predator."

"Humans," Sam said.

"Yes," Holden agreed.

"That's a load of crap," Jordan said. "The government would never sign off on something of that magnitude. They would never kill their own people."

"But they did," Holden said. "The official kill order came from the President herself. You'd be surprised what money can buy. The men and women involved offered not just riches but protection from the virus."

Sam's throat grew even drier and her head spun as she tried to process the words.

"What do you mean herself?" Jordan asked. "There was never a female president."

Holden grinned but there was no humor or friendliness in the smile. "This is the point where I will ask you to take a leap of faith with me. Close your eyes and think back to the day the quarantine team took you away from your homes."

Sam closed her eyes and did as he instructed. Her mind wandered to the burning buildings, and she pictured standing in the field on the edge of town. The overgrown grass itching at her legs. David's crumpled body lying at her feet. His skin gray and already decomposing. The number seared into his skin.

"Soak in every detail," Holden said, "no matter how much it hurts."

Tears streamed down Sam's face but she didn't wipe them away. Instead, she concentrated on the memories. They appeared even clearer. Men in yellow biohazard jumpsuits walked toward her. They scanned her retinas and put her on a bus. The field igniting in flames. David still there, helpless. Sam opened her eyes.

"You can both remember that night, correct?" Holden asked.

"Yes," they said in unison.

"Now close your eyes again," Holden instructed.

"Is there a point to all this?" Jordan asked.

"Yes," Holden answered.

"Well, what is it?"

"Close your eyes and you will see."

Sam did as he asked and closed her eyes again.

"Clear your mind," Holden said, "and try to remember a day before the virus. Any day. Birthday. Christmas. First day of school."

Sam searched her memories but nothing remained except blurred and distorted images. She shifted in her chair and concentrated harder.

"I played with this boy in a field by the city," Sam said. "His name was David. We used to play games in the field." Her heart ached at the sound of his name. The image of his body flashed through her mind and she opened her eyes. "He died during the infection."

"But you can remember him before the infection? You can see yourself playing tag with him?" Holden steadied his voice. "Think as hard as you can, Sam."

Sam closed her eyes again. She pictured David in the field, but the only memory that came to her mind was the one of his lifeless body curled into the fetal position. She thought harder, confident the memories would flood back into her mind. But nothing came. Sam shook her head and opened her eyes. "I can't see them but I know we played them."

Holden nodded as if he understood and looked to Jordan whose eyes were still clamped shut. "And you, Jordan? Do you remember anything before the event?"

"I helped my father work on his car," Jordan said. His voice shook when he spoke and Sam squeezed his hand under the table. He didn't squeeze back. "Every weekend," he continued, "he would take me to the garage and we would work on the motor."

"And you can see this, you and your father?"

"No."

Jordan opened his eyes. A single tear rolled down his cheek. Sam's heart broke at the sight of it. She had never seen Jordan cry before. He was always so strong, so tough. He was her rock. His face had grayed and his palm was sweaty.

"You know these things to be facts, though?" Holden asked. "Playing tag in the field? Working on the car with your father? In your mind, you hold these as truths?"

"They are truths," Jordan said.

"Tell me what your father looked like, Jordan," Holden said.

Jordan didn't answer.

"Sam, who did you live with before the infection?"

"My mother," Sam answered.

"Describe her."

Sam squeezed her eyes shut, but again, there was nothing but a blank slate. A deep panic swelled in her chest as she grasped for any mental image of her mother she could find.

"What color hair did she have?"

Nothing.

"What color were her eyes?"

Again, nothing.

"What color was the car, Jordan?" Holden asked.

"I don't know."

"How tall was he?"

"I don't know."

"What did he—?"

"I told you, I don't know!" Jordan screamed. The outburst caused Sam to jump in her chair. The questions had shaken him. He buried his head in his hands and Sam ran the fingers of her free hand through his thick brown-black hair.

"It's okay," she whispered.

"No," Jordan said. "No it's not."

"As I told you before, I am a biogenetic engineer and before I came to New Hope I worked in a city called Concordia."

The name of the city echoed in Sam's brain and her stomach knotted. She thought back to the words in her file, 'Results recorded in main file in Concordia.'

"It's a city a hundred times larger than this one," Holden said, "located in the middle of the country."

"Bullshit," Jordan blurted out. "Everyone is dead, infected or lives in this city. There were no other survivors. No other cities, or towns, or villages. New Hope is the last beacon of light left in this hellhole."

"And how do you know this?"

"That's what they told us," Jordan said.

"The Ministry has told you a lot of things haven't they?"

Neither Sam nor Jordan responded to this. The Ministry had told them *everything* for the last ten years: what to eat, what to wear, what to do and especially what to think. The knot in her stomach grew tighter.

"Concordia gave you the memories of the fires and the men shipping you the quarantine centers. All the vague memories that you know as fact are all lies. They implanted a biochip into your brains. It controls your thoughts. Suppresses the old ones."

Sam's head swam. She closed her eyes again, as tight as she could, and tried to envision her mother or her father. Anything besides for David's cold, dead corpse lying in the field. She concentrated on remembering the city before it was burning, but there were no memories to back up the facts she knew.

"That's impossible," Sam whispered.

"What's going to seem even more impossible is the event you two remember so vividly—the infection—happened over 300 years ago."

There was a long pause. Sam tried to comprehend the words: 300 years ago. She couldn't. It didn't make sense. None of this did. "You've lost your mind," she said.

"I wish that was the case," Holden said. "But I assure you, I'm very much in control of my facilities."

"But why?" Sam asked. "How?"

"Your DNA is resistant to the virus," Holden said. "It possesses a certain genetic makeup we can neither identify nor duplicate. The weekly blood samples are collected to produce an anti-viral drug that's then administered to the citizens of Concordia."

Silence.

"The actual kill percentage of the virus fell more in the 97 percent range," Holden continued. "A large majority of survivors were cryogenically frozen and are reactivated as others from around the country pass on. The—"

"You're a liar!" Jordan slammed both his hands down onto the wooden table. "What would be the point? Why put on this charade? Why erase our memories and force us to live out in this Hell on Earth? Why not just keep us in the lab and milk us like cattle?"

"Because we're their science experiment," Robertson said. Her cold words sent chills up Sam's spine.

"New Hope, along with several other facilities around the country, is functioning as a giant science project," Holden said. "The primary purpose is blood cultivation but the secondary initiative is to test how far humans can be pushed. Where is the breaking point in mankind?"

"No—" Jordan started but Holden continued.

"Everything is monitored and recorded. The foods you eat, where you sleep, what you do. They're all controlled experiments. They harvest the data and implement it into how the citizens of Concordia live their life.

The goal of the science project is to use the data collected to create a utopia in the center of Hell."

"It's not true," Jordan said.

"These science experiments have been happening since long before I was born. I've watched them since I was an intern in the Ministry's Science department. I've seen the horrors your people are subjected to." Holden's voice was grim and when he finished he sighed.

"You've seen the horrors?" Jordan asked. "Try living through them. Try watching everyone you love get taken away from you. Try living in a shit-box like New Hope."

"I can't imagine the struggles you've suffered," Holden said.

"No, you can't," Jordan said.

"That's why I'm telling you this," Holden continued. "The six executed today were working for me."

"The ones that let in the infected?" Sam asked.

"They didn't let in the infected," Holden said. "I did."

8

A deafening silence swallowed the room. The revelation caused Sam's insides to ache. Rebecca had died because of him. She struggled to stay in her seat. Her blood boiled and every muscle fiber yearned to rise out of her chair and rip out Holden Deckard's throat.

"The recruits' job," Holden continued, "was to infiltrate New Hope's data warehouse and collect as much evidence as possible. The majority of Concordia's citizens aren't aware of this facility's existence, and the purpose of the resistance is to pull back the curtain. Expose the dirty truth behind it all. The Ministry caught them hacking into the computers and I needed a distraction to obtain the information they'd collected before—"

"A distraction?" Sam asked. Her hands trembled with anger. "That distraction cost the life of a little girl. Did you know that?"

Holden looked down at the table and frowned. "Robertson made me aware of the child's death along with several others." When he looked back up, his eyes gleamed wet. "Was she important to you?"

"Very," Sam said.

He nodded. "I am sorry. I don't take the tragedy of the girl's death lightly. Or any of the others. I did what needed to be done to ensure that we can move forward."

"Her name was Rebecca," Sam said.

"Yes," Holden said.

"Say it."

"I'm sorry?"

"Say her name," Sam demanded.

"Rebecca," Holden said.

There was a long pause as the two stared at each other.

"Maybe we should take a break," Robertson said. "It's getting late. We can resume this in the morning."

"Why would we stay here?" Sam asked. "We're done as far as I'm concerned."

"Where are you going to go?" Robertson asked. "There's a whole city looking for you. Orders are to shoot on sight."

"We'll take our chances," Sam said.

Sam rose from the table and Jordan followed suit, but Cole stepped in-between them and the door.

"Miss Sam," Cole said, "what if I asked you to stay? Just tonight. And listen to the rest in the morning? You do that and if you still wanna leave, I'll help you get out of the city myself."

"Cole, I—" Sam started.

"I helped you get Jordan out," Cole interrupted. "All I'm askin' is you hear the man out."

"That's not fair," Jordan said. "Rebecca died."

"Ain't got time for fair," Cole said. "And everybody in this room is sad about that little girl. I can guarantee that. Wasn't no one's intention to get anybody hurt. That infected boy wasn't supposed to make it to the city. The soldiers at the gate shoulda seen him. Shoulda pulled the alarm a lot sooner."

"It doesn't make it better," Sam said.

"Naw," Cole said. "I reckon it doesn't. But neither will runnin' away from this. This thing is bigger than all of us."

Sam gritted her teeth together. She wanted to run out of this place, but where would she go. How long did she have on the outside before they caught and executed her? If she stayed, she'd compromise everything she believed in, but if she left, she'd be putting Jordan at risk as well as herself.

"I'll stay the night," Sam said. She turned back to Holden and Robertson. "You have two hours tomorrow morning to say whatever you have to say and then we're leaving."

"Thank you," Holden said.

"Don't thank me," she said. "Thank Cole."

They excused themselves from the group, and Sam and Jordan followed Cole into the offices beyond the conference table. He stopped at a small office toward the end of the hallway and opened the door with one of the many keys on the massive key ring.

"I know you two ain't married." Cole said. "But I don't suppose no one here is gonna mind you shacking up tonight. Unless, you two want separate rooms and that ain't no problem either."

"One room is fine," Sam said.

He pointed down the hall, back toward the conference room. "Washrooms still work. Tapped into one of the Ministry's water lines a few months ago when Tyler and his crew got recruited. Ain't got no soap or toothbrushies—"

Sam snorted at the pronunciation of toothbrushes and Cole's face flushed. "I'm sorry Cole," she said. "I wasn't trying to hurt your feelings. Toothbrushies…it's cute." The red in Cole's cheeks deepened, but a smile widened across his face. No damage done.

"I set a couple MREs on the table in your room," he continued. "Found a bunch of 'em at the hospital locked in one of the supply closets. Don't taste great, but they'll keep the meat on your bones. Laid the first-aid kit next to 'em."

"What's an MRE?" Sam whispered to Jordan.

"Meals Ready to Eat," Jordan whispered back.

"Why do you think there was a bunch stored at the hospital?" Sam asked.

"Don't rightly know, Miss Sam," Cole answered. "Got Holden all confused too."

"How are they still edible?" Jordan asked. "There's no way they would've kept for 300 years."

"They ain't that old," Cole answered. "These were made in Concordia. At least that's what it says on the packaging."

"But it doesn't have a date?" Sam said.

"No," Cole said.

"Do you know what year it is?" Sam asked.

Cole stroked his thick gray beard and shook his head. "Naw. Holden said it's been about 300 years since the fall. That would put us at 2332. Can't be entirely sure though."

"About anything it seems," Sam said.

"Or anyone," Jordan added.

"I know you're mad at Holden," Cole said. "I would be too if I was in your position. But he's playin' for the right team. I can promise you that much. He'll tell you the rest tomorrow. You'll see."

"I hope so," Sam said.

"You will."

Cole turned and walked down the hallway and disappeared out of sight. Jordan ran his hand through hair and shook his head. "What the hell is going on?"

Sam shrugged.

"How you holding up?" he asked. Gently, he pressed his thumb against the cut on her head. It stung, and she winced at the pain. He pulled his hand away from the cut and rested it against her cheek.

"I don't know," Sam answered.

It was the most honest answer she could give. The executions in the plaza seemed like a lifetime ago. Holden's revelation about their past coupled with everything else...was she dreaming? None of this could be real. Could it? She felt numb. Empty.

"I'm glad you're here with me," she said.

"Me too," he said.

They took turns going to the washroom. The water drizzled down in freezing spurts, but she was grateful for every drop. She grimaced when she pulled back on the dirty coveralls and sweaty undergarments.

They met back in their sleeping quarters and Sam took a seat on the floor against the far wall. Jordan brought over the first-aid kit Cole had left and one of the MREs. He squatted down beside her.

"What do you make of all this?" he asked.

He pressed an alcohol wipe to her wound and Sam cringed as the pain shot through her forehead.

"Sorry," he said, recoiling his hand.

"It's fine," she said through gritted teeth. "Just get it over with."

He pressed the wipe to her forehead again. Her head throbbed, but the pain was duller than before.

"I don't know what to make of it," Sam said. "Those things they said in the conference room, none of it seems real. How could they erase all of our memories? How does no one know about any of this?"

Jordan removed a bandage from the tin box and opened it. "We only know what they want us to. We're their puppets."

The words sent shivers down Sam's spine.

"If there's a chip in our mind suppressing our old memories then maybe there's a way to disable it. We can be fixed."

"We're not broken," Sam whispered.

"You know what I mean."

"I know."

Jordan placed the bandage over the cut and then kissed the top of her forehead.

"I'm sorry," Sam said.

"Don't—"

"It's all my fault."

"No, it's not," Jordan said. He sat down beside her. "None of this is your fault. It's theirs." He pointed at the corner of the MRE where 'Concordia' was printed in big bold letters.

Sam nodded but didn't speak. They sat in silence as Jordan opened the MRE. It consisted of a package of beef enchiladas, refried beans, crackers, cheese spread, and two cookies. They read the heating instructions, fumbled around with the packaging and then decided they weren't hungry after all. They split the two cookies and the package of crackers.

Cole was right. They tasted horrible. The cookies were dry and the crackers stale. When they finished, Jordan retrieved two glasses of water from the washroom.

"We should get some sleep," he said after they refilled their water glasses.

"Sleep sounds good."

There were no blankets or pillows or sheets. They stretched out on the hard wooden floor and Jordan wrapped an arm around her waist. He pulled her body close to his, her back to his chest. She rested her weary head onto his outstretched arm, and she asked him if it was okay.

"Are you okay?" Sam asked.

"Wouldn't have it any other way," he answered.

"You can't be comfortable."

"I've never been more comfortable."

Sam felt the same way. They'd never been this close, yet their bodies locked together like they had been designed for that sole purpose. Sam turned so she could look at him.

"Jordan?"

"Yes?"

"I love you."

"I love you too."

She kissed him deeply. His lips were warm and full. Why couldn't there have been a lifetime of these kisses?

"Remember the flowers," Jordan said as he pulled away.

"I will."

A moment of silence passed and Sam felt herself slipping toward her dreams. Effigies of enflamed towers etched their way across the back of her mind. She forced herself to keep her eyes open. To not drift off before she had a chance to say what she needed to.

"In case we don't wake up," Sam said, "I want you to know that I've loved you since the day I met you. And whether that was ten years ago, or twenty, or 300, that feeling's never changed. If I could do it all over again, I would let you—"

Jordan interrupted her with a kiss. She melted into his arms and he pulled her closer. The kiss was sweet and rough and the best of her entire life. He pulled away and smiled and then they fell asleep in each other's arms.

Sam didn't dream of the burning city. Moments after they dozed off,

Cole Porter burst into the room. He was yelling, but it took Sam a moment for her brain to catch up to the current situation. The unfamiliar place. Cole's thick southern drawl. The shouting. Everything was foggy.

"Gotta go now!"

His words clicked and panic rushed through Sam's body.

"Now!" he yelled.

They scrambled to their feet. Sam's head throbbed again, worse than when she had nodded off. She touched a hand to her head and felt it was puffy and swollen.

"What's going on?" Jordan asked.

"We got word the Minister is sendin' the transport out early. After it leaves, they're lockin' down the city for good. 'Til they find her." He nodded toward Sam and her head throbbed harder as her pulse quickened.

"What transport?" Sam asked.

"The blood truck," Cole said. "They take the samples to Concordia every week. Leave in the middle of the night when everyone's asleep. They're sendin' off the latest samples and they ain't openin' the gates again until you two are dead. It's our only shot of getting' you two out of here alive."

"What are we waiting for?" Jordan asked.

"But..." Sam started but her voice trailed off. The news that Rebecca's death was the result of Holden's ill-thwarted plan was still fresh on her mind.

"If we stay, they'll kill us," Jordan said. "At least this way we have a chance and I'm not ready to lose you."

She hesitated for a moment longer and then said, "Okay."

They followed Cole back to the conference room. She expected to find Holden and Robertson waiting for them but the room was empty. A small fire erupted in Sam's guts.

"Where are they?" she asked. She didn't try to mask the panic in her voice. "Where are Holden and Robertson?"

"They went on ahead," Cole said as he jerked open the door leading back to the train yard. "There's a whole mess of soldiers guarding the gates. They're getting in position. Didn't want to put you two in any more danger than necessary."

The knot in her stomach clenched tighter as she stared into the pitch-black darkness beyond the doorway. This was it. No matter what happened, they had spent their last night in New Hope. By sunrise, they would be dead or traveling through the wastelands. She swallowed hard and plunged into the lightless hallway.

Cole led them back outside and through the train yard. They sprinted to the main road and jogged away from town and toward the city gates. Sam said a silent goodbye to their old lives as they passed her apartment unit. The few belongings she owned would be destroyed. The life before the infection—real or not—was gone forever.

They ran for a long time as they crossed through the city. The full moon hung low overhead and bathed their path in its soft light. In the distance, the huge steel gates came into view.

Cole broke from the road and jogged to the concrete wall that extended around the city. They followed him and huddled together when they reached it.

"We'll hug the walls the rest of the way," Cole whispered. "Gotta keep outta their sights." He pointed up to the top of the wall toward the gate. Through the darkness, Sam could see two men standing on top of it. Both carried long rifles.

"Snipers," Jordan said.

"Yeah," Cole said. "Robertson said they're aiming to kill on sight so stay close behind me. I move, you move. I stop, you stop. I tell you to run—"

"We get it," Jordan said.

"Good," Cole said. "Now let's move."

Sam's shoulder scraped against the wall as they closed in on the gates. Cole walked in front of her doing the same. She focused on keeping her breaths steady and slow, but inside, her heart pounded against her chest and she wondered how no one else heard it.

Cole held up a hand. They stopped and hunkered in the tall grass. The two massive steel doors were ahead of them. They reached far into the night sky. Sam wiped a sweaty hand on the leg of her coveralls and almost screamed when Jordan reached out and grabbed it.

"Sorry," he whispered.

She nodded. She was too afraid to say anything. Her knees shook under her weight. She wanted to cry. She wanted to go back to the train yard offices or even better, back in time before she had gotten them in this mess.

Cole pointed at his eye and then to the guard shack sitting a few yards in front of the gates. They focused their attention on it and Sam's heart jumped into her chest. Robertson emerged from the shadows on the opposite side of the guard shack. She sprinted toward it and disappeared into its innards.

Sam waited, unable to breathe. The light in the window illuminated and then extinguished. They looked to Cole who nodded.

"This is it," Jordan whispered.

Before Sam had time to answer, two headlights cut across the horizon. She heard the low rumble of the engine and then saw a box truck trundle down the main road. She couldn't believe it. It had been a decade since she had seen a car or truck in operation. Much longer if what Holden said was true. She stared at it in disbelief.

"When it pulls to a stop," Cole said, "we go fast. You two head to the rear of the truck, Holden'll be waitin' in the back for ya. Me and Jeanette'll overtake the driver. We'll be outta here before they know what hit 'em."

"What if things go bad?" Jordan asked.

Cole pulled a revolver from under his coveralls and cocked the hammer back. "Let's hope it don't come to that."

Sam nodded.

The three of them turned back and watched as the truck neared the guard shack. Gears creaked and moaned as the gates opened. Sam marveled at the dark unknown of the outside world.

"I love you," Jordan whispered.

Before she had a chance to return the sentiment, the brakes of the truck squeaked and Cole whispered, "Go."

The three of them raced toward the truck, and Sam's heart jackhammered in her chest as they neared it. Cole broke apart from them and ran toward the cab of the truck and Jordan and Sam sped toward the back.

They reached the guard shack and Robertson exploded from it. She lunged toward the driver-side door, a pistol clutched in one of her hands. Cole flanked the truck from the other side. Sam lost sight of them as she reached the rear of the truck.

"We made it," Jordan said and flipped open the door latch. He pulled up on the handle and the door rattled up the tracks.

Sam's heart caught as the contents of the truck were revealed. Holden Deckard knelt at the edge of the truck—bound and gagged and screaming muted pleas. Prime Minister Troy stood behind him, knife in hand and a sinister sneer coating his face. Two soldiers, armed with assault rifles, stood on either side of them. Moonlight gleamed from the tip of the blade as it pressed against Holden's throat.

"No!" Sam shouted.

Without warning, Troy dragged the blade from ear to ear and Holden's eyes widened. A thick, red mist spewed from the gaping wound and doused Sam and Jordan as they watched in shock. The fear in Holden's eyes turned to a vacant stare and then his body lurched forward and crashed into the dirt in front of them.

Jordan tugged at her arm and she stumbled. Everything seemed far away. Panic engulfed her, and she realized this would be their final day on Earth. Desperation crashed over her as Jordan pulled her from the rear of the truck.

"Get dem!" the Minister screamed. His words were distorted and Sam tasted his blood in her mouth.

"Cole!" Sam screamed. They ran down the length of the truck toward the open gates and Sam picked up speed as she snapped out of the shock of the events unfolding around her. And then her heart dropped. A flat, open desert surrounded them. Nowhere to run and nowhere to hide.

Robertson emerged from the front of the truck, the butt of a service rifle pressed into her shoulder. The muzzle of the gun was directed right at Sam and she squeezed her eyes tight. It was over now. Robertson had betrayed them.

"Get down!" Jeanette shouted and Sam felt Jordan pull her to the side.

Sam opened her eyes. A harsh orchestra of gunfire exploded through the air as Robertson squeezed the trigger of the semi-automatic rifle. Sam turned briefly and watched as the two soldiers flanking the Minister flailed backward. The Minister ducked back behind the truck as Robertson continued to fire.

"Come on," Jordan yelled. He pulled her by the hand. She forced herself to turn back to the desert and sprinted toward it.

An alarm pierced through the air and giant halogen lights atop the city walls illuminated. More shots fired from the snipers perched along the wall. Patches of dirt exploded on either side of them as they ran into the darkness of the wastelands. Sam screamed out but continued to run as fast as she could.

There was a moment of silence and then a single burst of gunfire. Sam felt her arm jerk back. She turned back, terrified the soldiers had caught up with them, or that someone had grabbed Jordan, but no one else was in site.

"Jordan?" Sam asked.

And then she saw it. A tiny red dot had emerged on his chest.

"I'm sorry," he said.

"Jordan, I—"

Jordan's face turned pale, and the dot expanded to the size of a saucer. He fell to his knees and then on to his back.

"Jordan!" Sam screamed as she fell down with him.

She pressed her hand over the red circle. It had tripled in size, and Sam's heart broke as she felt the warm liquid ooze from underneath the field jacket. Her eyes filled with tears and she screamed a guttural, primal cry up to the heavens.

"Sam?" Jordan asked. His face was gray and his eyes looked hollow.

"I'm here," Sam sobbed.

"Did we make it?" he asked. "Did we make it out of the city?"

Sam looked around at the expanse of nothingness surrounding them. Tears poured from her eyes. "Yes," she said. "We made it."

More gunfire sounded in the distance. She prayed for the next bullet to come and find her. To take her to the same place Jordan was going. She sobbed at the thought of him leaving her. She bent down and kissed his lips. They should have been warm and full. They felt cold. Sam sobbed harder.

The truck roared to life and rolled through the city gates toward her. Sam barely noticed.

"You have to go," Jordan said.

"I won't leave you," Sam cried.

"You have to."

"No."

"If you stay," Jordan said, "then all of this is for nothing." His voice was weak and strained. He lifted his hand, wincing as he did, and Sam grabbed a hold of it. She squeezed as tightly as she could.

"Please don't make me go."

"Sam?" Jordan asked.

"Yes?"

"I remember," Jordan said. "I remember the flowers. They're not what you think. They're real, Sam. They're bad. Remember them."

"What do you mean?" she asked.

Jordan didn't answer.

The truck squelched to a stop beside her and she heard Cole screaming from inside of the cab. She looked to Cole and then back to Jordan. Life had escaped his eyes leaving them dark and blank.

"No!" she wailed.

"We've gotta go!" Cole screamed.

Sam closed Jordan's eyes with her fingertips and whispered one last goodbye to him. She kissed his lips and breathed in the smell of his skin.

"Now, Miss Sam!"

There was a discordance of noise coming from everywhere around her. Rounds of gunfire erupted in the distance. Cole screamed for her to get in the truck. She whispered that she loved him and told him she was sorry. She got to her feet and clambered into the cab of the truck.

The tires spun, and then caught traction, and they sped toward the heart of the desert. Toward Concordia. Away from Jordan. In the rearview mirror, she watched as the city of New Hope grew smaller on the horizon until finally disappearing. The wastelands stretched out in front of them. Hundreds of miles filled with the infected. And somewhere past that, Concordia.

Sam curled up into a ball on the passenger seat of the truck and wept for Jordan. She wept for Holden and Robertson, for Tyler and the rest of the prisoners that had been executed. She wept for Rebecca.

After a while, her eyes grew tired and heavy. In the driver's seat, Cole rambled on about the disaster they had survived, but his voice seemed distant. Sleep was coming to take her and she only hoped it wouldn't take her back to the burning city. She hoped it would bring her to Jordan for one last kiss.

PART TWO: LOST ANGEL

1

The Ferris wheel stood in the middle of the deserted field like a giant sentinel watching over the city below. Years ago, the steel structure was painted in vibrant shades of yellow and orange and trimmed in thousands of white lights that would flash through the pitch-dark night like a beacon guiding lost travelers home. Now, it served as a cruel reminder of a pastime that would soon be long forgotten. A thick layer of rust and decay covered the massive spokes and the cogs and gears of its innards. The steel bucket cars squeaked and groaned as they swayed back and forth and provided a chilling melody that echoed through the night sky.

Sam marveled at the ancient relic. The blood-red moon hung low behind the structure and cast long shadows across the field. Somewhere in the woods beyond, dogs barked and growled. Soon the entire tree line would be ablaze and they would be screaming.

Sam glanced to her side and saw Jordan standing beside her. Without speaking, he wrapped his big hand around hers and together they stared up at the distant memory of Sam's childhood. A childhood that happened long before she ever met Jordan. A memory he had never been part of before tonight.

"You're not supposed to be here," Sam whispered.

"I know."

Sam turned toward him and smiled. Jordan returned it and pulled her into his arms. She buried her head into his strong chest and took a deep breath. He smelled of bath soap with the slightest tang of motor oil and the familiarity of that scent, *his scent*, brought tears to her eyes. She pressed her cheek deeper into his chest and felt the soft cotton against her skin. Beneath the white tee, she heard the thrumming of his beating heart.

After a long time, Sam lifted her head, just enough to turn it away from the Ferris wheel, and then nuzzled back into his chest. The field was flat for a couple hundred yards and then broke into a steep hill that led to the city. Fire and ash draped the skyline.

"How is this possible?" Sam asked.

"It's not," Jordan whispered. "None of this is real." He wrapped his arms tighter around her shoulders and the strong embrace warmed her heart. But the warmth lasted for only a moment. Despite the insufferable temperatures, an underlying chill resided in the hot breeze. It carried Jordan's words through the night air and they replayed in her head, over and over.

None of this is real.

None of this is real.

None of this is—

"You died," Sam managed, as a single tear slipped from her eye and rolled down her cheek. "I couldn't save you. I wanted to—"

Her voice broke as more tears streamed down her face. She took a deep breath of the smoky air and it caught in her lungs. She forced it out, her chest heaving, and managed a tearful, "I wanted to, but I couldn't."

"It's okay," he said. "It's not your fault."

She pulled away from him altogether and turned back toward the giant wheel fixing her glassy eyes upon it. She tried to hold back the next wave of tears fighting their way to the surface but her efforts were futile. A river of tears burst forth from her eyes and she collapsed to her knees as an empty shell of the girl she once was. She sobbed as she mourned her best friend, and he knelt beside her and gently caressed her back until she stopped crying and there was nothing more than the ominous groans of the Ferris wheel.

"You have to go on," Jordan said, helping her back to her feet.

"I won't. Not without you."

"You have to, Samantha. You have to do it for me."

She said nothing. In her mind, the journey no longer mattered. She didn't want to live in a world without him. Concordia had taken Jordan and Rebecca away from her and now the only thing she cared about was reuniting with them.

"You can't afford to think like that," Jordan said. "Too much depends on you."

"How did you—?" Sam started.

Jordan shook his head, "I didn't read your mind." He smiled and then added, "I'm not real, remember?"

She nodded.

"They'll come for you," Jordan said after a long moment had passed.

"I know," Sam whispered. She wiped the tears from her face and took a deep breath. The hot air burned her lungs.

"What will you do if they catch you?"

"I don't—"

Jordan grabbed her by the wrist and spun her towards him. "What will you do, Samantha?"

She didn't answer. Instead, she pulled away and stepped past him, toward the city. Less than a mile away, everything she ever knew burned in hopes to control the spread of the virus. All the love and joy she had ever experienced was nothing more than a pile of ashes.

But that wasn't real either.

None of this is real.

"We need to go," Jordan said. The reflection of the flames danced in his eyes.

"Go where?"

"To the city."

He reclaimed her hand, and this time she didn't pull away. They started toward the city, making their way through the tall grass. They had made it halfway through the field when Sam stopped in her tracks. Jordan tugged at her sleeve but she didn't budge.

"What's wrong?"

"What about David?"

She gazed down and lying at her feet was the naked and crippled body of the boy. David, her best friend, the boy she played hide-and-seek with, the boy who shared her first kiss with, he was dead. He had contracted the RIZ-4 virus the day before and was now dead and lying face down in the dirt with a number burned into his flesh.

"We can't take him with us." Jordan jerked on her hand to continue, much harder than before, but Sam's feet remained planted.

David's symptoms presented just as the news reports said: bloodshot eyes, fever, legions, and sudden hair loss. In the tall grass, he was nothing more than an effigy of himself. Open sores pocked his skin, and his thick brown hair had begun to come out in clumps.

"I can't leave him," Sam said. She yanked her hand away and bent down to scoop up the boy's body, but Jordan snatched her wrist preventing her from touching the corpse.

"He's one of them, Samantha," Jordan said. "He's *infected.* You know what that means."

"He's all alone."

"I know. But he'll be coming back soon and I suggest we're not here when he does."

He kept his tone even but the words still cut her to the bone. A furious abhorrence towards him bubbled in the pit of her stomach. "None of this is real, remember? Not you, not David and not the goddamn virus! You're dead, Jordan Riggs. You left me in this fucking hellhole. You don't get to tell me what to do here."

She regretted the words the moment they left her lips. The venom residing in them wasn't meant for the love of her life. Hot blood filled her cheeks and even in the pitch-dark of the night, she was sure that he could see her blushing.

Jordan turned away for a long moment. Sam thought she could detect tears forming in his gray-blue eyes and it tore at her heart to know that she caused even a millisecond of sadness. But when he turned back to her, there were no tears. Instead, a polite smile touched his lips.

"I'm sorry," Sam said, not giving him a chance to speak.

"It's okay," Jordan answered. "This is a difficult situation for all of us." His words sounded disconnected from the loving expression he wore on his face. He continued, "We have to leave your friend here and I have to show you what's in the city. It's vital to your survival."

Jordan extended his hand and this time she accepted it, and he led her away from the field and away from David. They walked toward the burning city of steel. She hesitated once as they reached the edge of the field and turned back to the spot where the dead boy lay in the deep grass. Sam said a silent goodbye and then followed Jordan into the city.

The half-mile walk seemed to take only a minute, the travel time unrealistic, furthering the proof that this was a dream. But it was a dream where Jordan lived. One where his heart still pumped in rhythmic, steady beats. It was a dream that she didn't want to end, despite the increasing volume of screams from the buildings towering over them.

Jordan led her past burning building after burning building. They stopped at the intersection of 21st and Smith Street. The street corner was familiar like she had stood on it a million times before. She was close to home. Much closer than she had been in a long time.

"Do you know where we are?" Jordan asked.

"I think so."

The shouts and pleas of help from the windows above became more and more distinguishable from one another. Sam heard the wails of a little girl in the building ahead.

"Help me," a woman in the adjacent building screamed out. "I'm not one of them. I'm not infected."

"Can we save her?" Sam asked Jordan.

Jordan shook his head. "She's already dead."

"I know."

Sam's flesh erupted in gooseflesh as an explosion of fire ripped through the apartment building and the woman cries fell silent.

"I can't go on," Sam said. "I need to wake up."

"Not yet."

"How much further?"

"Not much."

"Okay."

Jordan started toward the heart of the city, but Sam found herself unable to continue. She attempted to take a step forward but couldn't lift her foot. She tried to take a step with the other foot but nothing happened. Her legs refused to listen to the commands of her brain. Jordan hadn't seemed to notice that she was no longer with him.

"Jordan," Sam called out after him. "There's something wrong."

He didn't look back.

She leaned forward as far as she could without falling over but couldn't lift her foot even a millimeter off the ground. "Move goddamn you." She looked back to Jordan who was now far ahead of her.

"Jordan," she called out again, this time a bitter sense of urgency prevalent in her voice. A hot ball of panic formed in the pit of her stomach and spread through her body.

"Jordan Riggs!" she yelled.

But Jordan didn't turn back or even hesitate. He was too far away from her. Swallowed by the darkness.

"Don't leave me here!" Sam cried out.

She pawed at her leg with both hands trying to lift it from the ground. Her nubby fingernails dug into the bare skin and she clawed at her flesh. It remained planted to the ground. She tried the other one to no avail and then shrieked as her foot sank into the blacktop.

"Please come back, Jordan!" This time she screamed with all of her might, straining her voice until it was nothing more than a raspy gravel. It didn't matter how loud she screamed though. Jordan was gone. She had lost sight of him. He had left her and now she was all alone.

She continued to scream and tear at her legs. Blood trickled from the claw marks. Above, the towering infernos roared louder and louder. It drowned out the screams of the people trapped inside and then her own screams. The temperature sweltered and bulged and Sam felt the intense heat of the flames kissing her skin like the sun on a hot summer's day.

In the distance, just past the point where she had watched Jordan disappear, the slightest of movements caught her eye. She breathed a sigh of relief knowing Jordan had realized that he left her. He was coming back to save her and he would free her from the blacktop, from this city, and from this horrible nightmare.

The thing in the distance screamed. It was a high-pitched, inhuman scream and Sam's skin to erupt in waves of gooseflesh. The tiny hairs on her arms and the back of her neck stood on end. It wasn't Jordan returning for her. She stood frozen as she watched whatever had made the horrible scream begin to move toward her.

Sam's heart slammed against the walls of her chest in what seemed like a desperate attempt to flee her body. She didn't blame it. A thick layer of concrete covered both of her feet. She tried to keep her legs still, but they shuddered uncontrollably.

The blistering temperatures of the fire plummeted, and a chill ran up her spine. The roar of the fire along with the screams from the burning buildings faded to silence and the only thing Sam heard was the faint sound of footsteps which grew louder by the second.

"JORDAN!"

The *thing* in the distance had grown double in size, now as large as two men in both height and width. It thundered toward her and fired off another scream, this one louder and more ferocious. Sam shuddered as the concrete continued to rise past her ankles.

"Jordan, please come—" She choked up midway through the desperate plea. An intense fear ran rampant through her body. It coursed through her veins and gnashed at her organs. She wanted to wake up from this horrible nightmare. Why wouldn't she wake up?

"Sam."

Her legs broke free of the concrete at once and she spun toward the voice. Jordan stood beside her and a grave look covered his face. She grabbed his hand, still wary of the creature in the distance, and tried to pull him back toward the field. She needed to get them to safety, but Jordan didn't move.

"We have to go!" Sam screamed. "Something's coming." She pointed toward the beast but it was no longer there. Her eyes darted around the empty landscape trying to fix in on the horrible creature.

"Sam."

"It was just there."

"Sam."

She looked to Jordan. The air warmed and silence gave way to distorted, muted screams from the buildings above them. It was as if they were standing under an unseen protective bubble protecting them from the elements.

"Something *is* coming," Jordan said. His lips drooped into a frown.

"What's coming?" Sam asked. "What was that thing?"

"You are the light, Sam." Jordan's eyes looked even more hollowed and his skin was a pallid, putrid shade of gray. "You are the light and David is the key." He pointed toward the heart of the city and Sam's stomach lurched as the awful scream of the creature ripped through the night sky.

"Look at it," Jordan instructed.

"I won't," Sam said. She shook her head. "I'm too scared."

"Please," he pleaded, "look at it for me."

Hesitantly, Sam glanced in the direction he pointed, but instead of finding the hideous monster, she saw something else. David stood in the middle of the road, holding a bloodied teddy bear in one hand and bundle of schoolbooks in the other.

"Oh my god," she whispered.

The boy was far away from them, almost the same distance the creature had been when Jordan appeared. He stood motionless in the middle of the street and his clothes hung around the rotting flesh underneath. Sam's heart split in two at the sight of him.

This was all her fault.

The burning city.

David.

All of it.

"Sam," Jordan said

She turned back to him. A crimson dot appeared in the center of his chest. Sam's heart dropped, and she pressed her hand over the wound.

"You have to remember the flowers," Jordan said. "The flowers are the answer to all of this."

The blood spread beyond her palm and she pressed harder against his chest.

"No," she pleaded. "Don't do this. Don't leave me again. I don't understand."

"Sam, you have to wake up now," Jordan instructed her, but his voice sounded foreign. "You have a job to do."

Sam barely heard what he was saying. She placed her free hand over the one on his chest, but the blood continued to expand.

"Please don't go."

"You have to wake up."

"I don't—"

"Wake up, Sam!"

Her eyes flew open.

She no longer stood in the burning city but rather sat shotgun on the cold leather seat of the truck. Cole Porter's monstrous arm latched across her shoulders and pushed her back against the seat. He shouted something, but Sam didn't understand.

The words didn't make sense but the hysteria in his voice and the frightened look in his eyes caused a chill to run up Sam's spine. She looked forward and fifty yards ahead, bathed in the headlights of the truck, was an infected. Its once human body was nothing more than a skeleton covered in a shell of rotten flesh and tattered clothes. Snow white hair jutted wildly from grayish-black skin and the creature's open mouth revealed a set of broken, blood-stained teeth.

Sam screamed.

Cole jerked the wheel and the dark landscape filling the windshield pivoted around them. The headlights spun from the faded asphalt and spilled onto sand and cacti. Her brain, still foggy from the remnants of the nightmare, searched for an answer to what was happening. By the time she understood, it was too late.

The moment of clarity seemed to freeze and stretch out for an eternity. Sam looked at the speedometer which read sixty-five, to Cole's face which was twisted in fear and disbelief and then back to the horizon which spun around them. Her brain registered one fleeting thought: she wished she would have put on her seatbelt. The moment that seemed like it would never end finally did and the passenger side tires lifted from the ground.

The truck crashed hard on the driver side and Sam slammed into Cole. The glass windshield of the box truck fractured into millions of spider-legs and then shattered as the truck skid across the desert floor. She closed her eyes and prayed for all of this to be over. Instead, the truck slid for a second longer and then flipped into a death-roll at breakneck speed.

Another moment of clarity struck Sam. This one even odder than the last. She found herself floating over the wreckage. Below her, the crunching sound of metal echoed through the night sky. Above, the stars grew closer and closer and Sam smiled. She was on her way to heaven to be reunited with her lover.

She took a deep breath of the brisk air as she stared at the vast expanse of twinkling sky above her. "I'm coming, Jordan."

And then her ascension stopped, and much to her dismay, she started to fall. The twinkling stars faded as she plummeted toward the ground. The air grew hot and thick. And then there was nothing.

When Sam opened her eyes again, the world was blurry and distorted. Her ears rang and her body numbed to non-existence. The first rays of dawn dotted the horizon, and she fixed her eyes on the purple and pink streaks cutting through the black sky. It was beautiful

Somewhere in the distance, inaudible shouts broke through the silence. She couldn't move her head, but focused her eyes on the crumpled shell of the truck. It was lying upside down, a hundred yards away from her. The frame rocked back and forth as black plumes of smoke rose from its engine.

Sam strained her eyes and saw what was causing the strange movements. The truck was surrounded by a half-dozen decomposing bodies. The infected had found them and they were trying to get to Cole.

She gasped in terror and when she did, explosions of pain rocketed through her. The cloudiness resurfaced to her eyes and everything grew dark again. She tried calling out to Cole, but couldn't. The pain too great. The unseen injuries too severe.

She resigned herself to giving into the darkness engulfing her and hoped Cole's death would find him quickly and without suffering. The possibility of reuniting with Jordan made all this less painful and their journey to Concordia dissolved into a distant memory. And if death was a way out of this godforsaken world, then Samantha Albright would welcome it with open arms.

2

The horrific images of the last 48 hours played on a never-ending loop. Holden Deckard's revelations, Prime Minister Troy emerging from the back of the truck. The firefight. Jordan. The truck spinning out of control. Rewind. Watch again. Rewind. Watch again. Sam begged for it to stop, but no end came. And then somewhere from far, far away there were voices

"We have to get her the fuck out of here, Doc."

"I'm aware of that, Eric."

The images faded and blurred and Sam fought to pull herself from the wreckage of her mind. She struggled to open her eyes but failed. The memory of Jordan lying on the ground, blood pouring from his chest, flashed through her mind. She tried to scream but couldn't.

"Has your team searched the wreckage?" Doc asked.

"No," Eric said. "Can't get to it. Too many of those brain-dead bastards to get close. Whatever was in the back of that truck has got them all worked up. We found this one about 50 yards from the site. We cleared the truck long enough to get the big guy out, but they swarmed and we had to fall back."

The image of Jordan faded, and another one appeared in its place. Holden, eyes wide and throat slit, spilled out of the back of the truck. Sam pushed the terrible thought away and tried to grasp what Eric had said. They got the big guy out. Cole was alive.

"Were you followed?" Doc asked.

"For about a quarter of a mile. One persistent bugger. No worries though. Xavier put a bullet through its head."

"Suppressed round, I hope."

"Of course."

"And you scanned the area for others before entering the compound?"

The voices grew louder. Clearer.

"You trying to tell me how to do my job, Doc?"

"No. My concern is the safety of my patients. Nothing more."

"Uh-huh. Why don't you leave the military operations to me and focus on getting these two *patients* the fuck out of here?"

The voices were crystal clear now, but so was the pain. Sharp pain pierced her body with each breath. She tried giving herself a quick assessment, letting the pain dictate her ailments. They had shoved a tube down her throat. Her lungs expanded with each hiss of the machine. Why didn't they let her die? Why did they save her?

Another breath. Another wave of pain.

Broken ribs.

Another breath. She held it for a moment. Her lung burned.

Possible punctured lung.

Another breath. Her chest ached.

Broken heart syndrome. Pre-existing condition.

Another breath.

"Where do you think they came from?" Eric asked.

A long pause.

"I'm not sure," Doc said. "It's hard to imagine the big one has missed any meals. This one is malnourished, but not like someone that's survived in the wastelands their whole life."

"They haven't been out there long. They had a goddamn truck for fuck's sake. A truck, Doc. I mean have you ever even seen a—"

"No," Doc interrupted. "Only in the archives. It's quite puzzling."

"Did you check the patch on the girl's coveralls?"

"Yes. Cross-referenced the maps from the old world. There's not a New Hope within 500 miles of here. Hope Valley was the closest thing I could find."

"Keep looking," Eric said. "The General will start asking questions soon."

"He already is," Doc said. "He was down here earlier."

"Why the fuck didn't you tell me?"

"You wanted me to stay out the military operations, remember?"

"Hardy fucking har, asshole. What did he want?"

"Well, it seems he's taken an interest in this one."

Sam's body tensed, and no longer fought to open her eyes. The urge to cough swelled inside her chest and her body trembled as she tried to fight it.

"You blame him?" Eric asked. "She's got a pair of tits on her that I would give my left nut to squeeze. They're real too. None of that silicon shit like you use."

An unseen hand ran up her thigh and stopped just short of her groin.

Her stomach tightened and another wave of pain rocketed through her. She relaxed as much as possible but the thick layer of blanket that covered her leg felt paper thin.

"Tactful as always. Of course, I expect nothing less from you."

"Fuck you, Doc."

The hand rubbed up and down her thigh for only a moment before disappearing.

"Getting back to your original question, I do understand the General's attraction to her," Doc answered. "Aesthetically, her features are welcoming. She's quite exotic compared to the girls here. The General's sexual preference has always been to covet the fruits for which he hasn't tasted."

Sam cringed. A thick bubble of disgust and revulsion swelled in her stomach. Images of Troy pressing himself against her flashed through her mind.

"Coveted or not," Eric said, "you know he's not going to be happy that you're using this many medical supplies to keep a couple of stragglers alive. Especially the morphine."

"Would you rather I let them die?"

"No sweat off my back, man. How I see it, they're two more mouths to feed and we got way too many mouths as it is."

"Your compassion is overwhelming."

"Compassion has nothing to do with it. It's about survival. Always has been, always will be."

"Survival of the human species? Or just yourself?"

"Fuck you twice, Doc. There's plenty of trim to go around in this shithole. And the way upper-management keeps spreading its seed around, we'll have a workforce for decades. Hell centuries if we get the farm up and running again. Just because the General gets a hard-on for some piece doesn't mean we need to run through the pain killers like there's a morphine factory down the street."

"I think you're lacking the bigger picture, Eric."

"Which is?"

"These two drifters might have information on the state of the world up-top. What if there are more of them? What if the conditions outside have gotten better? We could leave this place. Start again."

"You haven't been outside lately," Eric scoffed. "There are more of those fucking mouth-breathers now than ever before. It's like they're multiplying or something."

"Perhaps they are."

"Exactly. Which means we don't have the goddamn resources to keep these two afloat. Patch 'em up and send 'em on their merry, Doc. If the General wants to get his tip wet in the process then so be it. Hell, I might even take a stab at his leftovers. But we have to move fast."

"I wouldn't be too hasty to discard these two like garbage. At the very least, the big one looks like he might have certain skills that could be—"

"Exploited," Eric interrupted.

"Utilized is the word I was looking for."

"I know all about the Midnight Runner project, you piece of shit. Trust me, exploited is the word that fits."

"Doc! Doc!" This was a different voice. One that spoke with a mixture of excitement and fear in his voice.

"What is it, Nelson?" Doc asked.

"The other one…he's awake."

A sense of relief washed over Sam. Cole was alive. He was awake. Relief passed and fear took over. Eric's words echoed through her head. *Exploited.* They didn't have much time and these people obviously didn't have their best intentions at heart. They had to leave and fast.

"Eric, meet me in the other's room. Nelson, inform the General." Doc's voice sounded closer to her now and Sam focused on steadying her breath. She heard footsteps fading away and assumed it was Nelson and Eric leaving to complete their assignment.

She was unsure the intentions of the men that watched over her. Eric's were obvious but Doc's seemed less clear. She couldn't trust him as an ally. Not yet. She pinched her eyes close as another set of footsteps approached.

A machine near her head beeped and a warm liquid flooded into her veins. The urge to sleep resurfaced at once and the pain ebbed. A comfort washed over her that begged her to sleep but her curiosity kept her from drifting into the darkness. She had to see her savior.

She dared to slit her eye. Between the dark lashes of her eyelid, she saw the needle sticking out of her arm and a piece of transparent tape holding it in place. Dozens of wires and tubes ran from her to unseen machines surrounding the bed. They had inserted a feeding tube into her stomach and a catheter between her legs. A dull panic washed over her, but the drugs flowing into her veins counteracted it at once. She was slipping.

She turned her head ever so slightly and caught her first glimpse of Doc. At first, it was only the back of a white lab coat, but as he turned, she saw the monster the man truly was.

His skin was nearly translucent and had been stretched and pulled tight. An unnatural small nose pierced the center of his face. His ears had been pinned back. Toxic green irises, set in unnatural oblong-shaped eyes, darted back and forth across the room.

Sam squeezed her eye closed again and fought the urge to scream. She focused on keeping her breaths steady and her heartbeat under control. As she waited for the malformed doctor to leave her side, she prayed the machines monitoring her vitals wouldn't give her away.

She squeezed her eyes even tighter. The darkness enveloped her and pulled her back into sleep. She felt herself falling once again and found the endless loop of nightmares that awaited her.

3

"Wake up, lady."

Sam's eyes shot open. She gagged as the long plastic tube slid from her throat. She attempted to scream, but a small hand wrapped over her mouth. Sam looked wide-eyed at a girl, no more than 14 years old, staring down at her.

"Shhh," the girl hushed her. "Please, lady, be quiet."

Sam struggled, twisting her head to the left and right, but the girl gripped her face tighter.

"I'm not going to hurt you. Stop."

Sam fought for a moment longer and then calmed. The girl loosened her grip and after a moment removed her hand altogether. Sam took a deep breath, and when she did, every muscle in her body ached. She tried to look at the girl but her eyes wouldn't focus.

"Cole?" Sam asked.

"Is that your friend?"

"Yes. Where is he?"

"I'm not sure. We'll find him though. This is going to hurt. Don't scream."

"What's going to—?"

Sam clamped her jaw together to fight the urge to scream. A guttural moan emitted from somewhere inside her throat and her vision blurred even more. She looked down and saw the rubber end of the feeding tube dislodge from her abdomen. The girl covered Sam's mouth just in time to mute a scream. Once the scream subsided, Sam gaped at the deep hole in her torso.

"Sorry," the girl said. "I'm so sorry." She released Sam's mouth and picked up a piece of gauze lying between Sam's legs. She positioned the gauze over the hole and placed two pieces of surgical tape over it.

The pain shooting through Sam's stomach abated, and she looked up to the girl. Surgery distorted her face but not to same extent as Doc's.

Her lips were two sizes too big and her forehead seemed rippled like something had been inserted underneath it. She wore silver studs in both cheeks where her dimples would be and a silver ring through her eyebrow. Her eyes were wide and an obscene purple color. They matched her tinted hair.

"What's your name?" Sam asked.

"My name is Alexandria," the girl whispered. "But you can call me Alex. What's yours?"

"Sam."

"Sam, we need to go before the doctor gets back."

She was discombobulated but still detected the urgency in the girl's voice. She rubbed her eyes trying to clear the fog away from her mind. The needle from the I.V. pulled at her skin and she winced in pain. "Why?"

"Because I think they plan to kill you. I overheard one of the soldiers say that the General was coming for you in the morning," Alex said as she helped Sam into a sitting position. "He said the General had taken a fancy to you, but they vetoed letting you live here."

"So they'll kick us out?" Sam asked. Her throat was raw from where the breathing tube had been and it hurt to speak.

Alex shook her head. "They won't let you leave."

"Then why wouldn't they just let me die in my sleep?" Sam asked. "Inject me with some lethal dose of something and turn off the machines?"

"Because the General will want to have his fun first." Her words were ice-cold and brought a chill to Sam's flesh. "We need to get out of here before that happens."

Sam, with Alex's aid, twisted her legs over the bed and looked down at the floor. She regretted the decision at once. The checkered tiles spun and her stomach lurched.

"Do you need my help with that?" Alex asked. She pointed to the tube disappearing under the hem of Sam's hospital gown.

Sam shook her head. She wrapped a fist around the rubber tubing and pulled. Tears filled her vision. She had to tug hard and grunted as it tore from her body. Her muscles trembled and stars formed in front of her eyes. She handed the tube to Alex and tried to steady herself.

"Are you okay?" Alex asked.

"I'm going to puke," Sam managed.

The sentence had barely left her lips when Sam was no longer looking at the floor but rather the inside of a trash can. The muscles contracted in her stomach with each wretch. Each time she heaved, it felt like she was being cut open and ripped apart.

"Kill me," Sam cried out in-between vomiting and trying to catch a breath.

Alex pulled Sam's long brown hair away from the mess and held it behind her back. "If we don't hurry, they will kill you," the tiny voice whispered. "But they'll do things to you first. Horrible things."

The nausea subsided after a moment and Alex removed the bucket. She came back with a moist towel and wiped Sam's mouth. Then she removed the tape from her arm and pulled out the I.V. needle.

Sam's head pounded and her body ached with a blinding ferocity. It hurt to breathe. It hurt to move. It hurt to blink. Every movement was the most challenging of her entire life. She wished that she would have died in the wreckage. Anything would be better than this.

"Who is Jordan?" Alex asked.

Sam's jaw fell open. "How do you—?"

"You said his name a lot in your sleep."

The sound of his name brought another round of tears to her eyes. The painful throbbing of her heart returned. It hurt because it was as broken as her body. The bullet that pierced his heart had also shattered hers.

"It doesn't matter," Sam whispered. She stared down at her bare legs sticking out from the paper nightgown. They dangled over a white and black checkered floor. Beside her, the machines that had been keeping her alive hummed and beeped. "He's gone now. He's safe from this place."

"That's good," Alex said. Sam shot her a look and the girl's purple eyes grew wide. "Not good that he's dead, but good he's not in this place. This is not a good place."

"Where are we?" Sam asked.

"An underground city called Lost Angel," Alex said. "Before he died, my dad told me that there's a sign right above us and that's where they got the name. But we can't go up-top to see it because of all the," she dropped her voice to a whisper and said, "halfways."

"Halfways?"

"The dead people that aren't really dead."

"The infected."

"Is that what you call them where you're from?" Alex asked, her eyes wide with excitement. "Where are you from? People are saying you and the other must have come from a bunker like this one, because people can't survive out in the world by themselves. Where is your bunker at? And what's the rest of the world like? I bet it's bad." The more the girl talked the faster the words spilled from her mouth and the more prevalent the nausea became.

Sam held up a feeble hand. "One question at a time."

"Sorry." The girl's alabaster skin turned rosy. "It's been a long time since I've talked to anyone other than the President. They don't let us talk to anyone. Well, besides for who picks us. But mine only wants to talk about boring stuff. And gross stuff. Sorry. I'm talking too much again."

"It's okay," Sam assured her and attempted to slide out of the bed. Alex came to her side and slipped an arm around her. Sam hesitated and then shifted her weight to her feet. The room faded and turned a vacant shade of white. Sam grabbed ahold of Alex's shoulder and squeezed with all her might. After a moment, the feeling passed, and the world came back into view.

"Where are you from?" Alex asked.

"New Hope."

"How far is that from here?"

"I don't know." Sam winced as she took a shaky first step. "Not far, I think."

"President Gates says there's nothing left of the old world."

Sam thought of those same words come from Prime Minister Troy's mouth and how the citizens of New Hope had believed that lie. The Ministry convinced them to live in fear of the unknown because of the infected. She thought of Concordia. The queasiness turned bitter. "There's more out there. Much more than this."

She took another step and stumbled. Her knee slammed onto the hard tile and Sam cried out in pain. Alex caught her before she went down and lifted her back to her feet. She was weak. So much weaker than she had ever felt. The wreck had ravaged her body. It scared her to be this weak.

"Where are we going?" Sam asked. She gritted her teeth together as she took another step.

"The chair by the door."

Ten feet from her, a chair leaned against the far wall of the room. It looked to be miles in the distance. Sam groaned. Alex patted her on her bare back and nudged her forward.

The touch on her bare skin made Sam realize that the paper thin night gown was leaving her backside exposed. She tried to grab one of the rear flaps, but the pain in her shoulder stopped her. Her cheeks turned red hot.

They shuffled across the room at a snail's pace. Each step was a challenge, but each successful inch forward was a tiny victory. Every time she could place one foot in front of the other, she was that much closer to reuniting with her friend. She had to go faster. Eric and Doc's conversation echoed through her mind. The thought of him being *utilized* made her skin crawl.

"Where do you think Cole is?" Sam asked.

"I'm not sure. They moved him a week ago."

"A week?"

"You've been out for a long time."

Sam's blood ran cold. "If you had to guess where he was?"

"One of the surgical wings."

"Why there?"

There was a long pause and then Alex said, "They do experiments here. Bad ones."

They reached the chair and Sam collapsed into it. Alex crossed the room to the wardrobe next to the bed. For the first time, Sam caught a glimpse of Alex as a whole. The young girl's face was not the only thing that had been operated on.

The girl's breasts spilled from a tight t-shirt with a low-cut neck. They were much larger than a budding teenager's should be and accentuated by her freakishly thin torso. The girl's rear was proportionate to her breasts, but judging by the size of the stick-thin thighs poking out of the short skirt, they had manipulated that as well.

In the faint illumination of the overhead fluorescents, Sam could see tiny scars running up the girl's bare white legs. Her pallid skin was fair. Not like the doctor's translucent skin but rather a child who had grown up sheltered from the sun.

Alex turned and caught Sam staring at her. Her big lips curled downward in an almost-frown and her brow furrowed.

"You know far too much about operating rooms," Sam said. "Don't you?"

Alex blinked and her eyes gleamed. She took a breath, blinked again and thick streams of mascara ran down her face.

"It starts after we're picked," Alex said. Her voice quivered when she spoke. "They want us to look like the girls from the magazines. The girls from the old days."

The words caught Sam off-guard. "What does that mean?" she asked. "What does it mean to be picked?"

Alex shook her head and buried her face in her hands. Sam wanted to go to the girl, to comfort her, but knew that without help, she wouldn't make it two feet across the room.

"On our twelfth birthday," the girl began, her hands still pressed against her eyes, "they give all the girls a choice. We can continue to work the mines down below, or come up here and..." The girl's voice trailed off.

Alex let out a loud sob and shook her head. After a moment, she straightened and wiped her eyes with her bare arms. The dark mascara smeared across her cheeks.

"And what, Alex?" She had forgotten about escaping and about Cole. Her blood simmered and somewhere, deep inside of her, a fire ignited. She already knew the answer. She could see it written all over the girl's face. But she braced herself anyway.

Alex removed Sam's sneakers from the bottom drawer, set them on the ground and straightened.

"We do a *different* kind of work up here," she said. "But they don't tell you that when you're 12 years old. They don't tell you about all the surgeries you have to go through or how you'll never see your family again."

Alex pulled Sam's blue coveralls from the closet and turned toward her.

"They don't tell you that your new job will be permanent baby-maker and that you have to pretend like you like it when some old man pushes his stuff inside of you every night."

Sam's mind spun like the wheels of a car stuck in snow, desperately trying to gain traction. The thought of this happening to anyone was blood-curdling. Her thoughts drifted to the baby factories in New Hope. At least the Ministry gave them a choice. Here there were no choices, and they were doing it to children. It was reprehensible. Unforgivable.

"All you know when you're 12 is that you don't want to work in the mines anymore. Anything is better than working 18 hours a day in the pitch-black until every muscle in your body turns to jelly and soot covers every inch of your body. You do that for the first seven years of your life and by the time you're of age, coming to the upper levels is the greatest thing you've ever heard of."

Alex crossed the room with the clothes and helped Sam to her feet. She pulled the paper gown over her head and Sam fought the instinct to cover herself. If this teenager had to be subjected to the horrors she spoke of then she could withstand a few seconds of humility without complaining.

"I'm sorry," Sam said. The pathetic apology was all she could manage. She wanted to tell the girl that everything would be alright. But she wouldn't do that. Sam had first-hand experience that sometimes things didn't work out that way. Sometimes things would never be okay again.

A feeble smile appeared on the young girl's face and she held out the sleeve of the coveralls. Sam turned her body as far as she could and forced a trembling arm into the sleeve.

"Will you take me with you?" Alex asked.

"What?" Sam asked. She barely remembered where she was heading to begin with. The original quest seemed so far removed and the loss of Jordan had buried almost every intention of completing it.

"If I help you escape, you and your friend, will you take me with you?"

"You don't even know where we're going," Sam said as she slipped her other arm through. "Hell, I don't even know where we're going. Plus, it's dangerous out there. There's more than the infec—halfways we're running from. Worse things."

"There can't be anything worse."

"You'd be surprised."

"Please," the girl pleaded, "I won't slow you down."

Alex's voice was thick with desperation. Images surfaced of Prime Minister Troy trying to force himself on her, shoving his repulsive tongue down her throat, and pressing his ancient boner against her. Even now, miles away from New Hope, she could still smell his rotten breath. And then she thought of Alex and how she dealt with worse every day. Some old man having his way with her. *Raping her.* The words forced Sam back to the present.

"Okay," Sam said.

"Really?" Alex asked.

"Really."

"What about my brother?" Alex asked.

"You didn't say anything about a brother."

"I'm saying it now."

"Alex—"

"He's 18 and strong and smart. He'll be useful."

Sam's face screwed up as if this request was more torturous than the pain wreaking havoc with her body.

"Please," Alex said.

Sam sighed but her lips curled upward. "Anyone else?"

The girl shook her head from side to side.

"Fine."

Alex's cheeks reddened and her eyes darted to the floor. "Thank you."

"Don't thank me," Sam said. "We're not out of here yet."

Alex nodded and knelt down. Sam placed her weight on Alex's back and lifted her bruised leg. Tears gathered in her eyes and her muscles trembled as she slipped her leg through the cuff of the coverall. Alex guided Sam's foot back to the ground, and the tears spilled down her cheeks.

"One more, okay?" Alex asked.

Sam nodded but didn't answer. It hurt too much.

She zipped up the coveralls by herself and then slumped back into the seat. She had no idea how they would escape this place, when the simple action of getting dressed had exhausted nearly all of her energy.

"You are very beautiful," Alex whispered as she placed the old sneaker on Sam's foot.

Sam's cheeks flushed at the offhanded compliment.

"I used to be beautiful once…before the surgeries," Alex continued. "There aren't any women you're age that haven't been altered."

"You are beautiful." Another wave of tears threatened, and she cursed herself for being so emotional. This was something new to her. She had grown used to Jordan's criticisms that she wasn't emotional enough. Silently, she blamed the morphine.

"I will be," Alex said and slipped on Sam's other shoe. "One day, I will be beautiful again. Somewhere out there, out in the up-top, I'll find someone to reverse what they've done to me." The young girl paused for a long moment while she finished tying Sam's shoes. When she pulled the knot tight, she looked up at Sam and asked, "Do you think there's a doctor out there? Someone who can make me beautiful again?"

Sam nodded. Holden had mentioned multiple cities operating through the United States. At least one of them had to possess some sane, upstanding citizens. The answer brought a coy smile to Alex's face and her puffy lips curled upward as far as they could.

"Are you ready?" Alex asked.

Sam nodded.

Alex stood and helped Sam out of her chair.

"I can't go fast," Sam said.

"Don't worry." Alex took her place in the crux of Sam's arm. "I know all the secret hiding places. I can keep us from us being seen."

"Okay." Sam took a deep, painful breath. "I'm as ready as I'll ever be."

"Good," Alex said, and twisted the doorknob. "Everyone should be asleep. We'll find your friend first, and—"

Alex pulled the door open and took a quick step back. A man stood in the doorway, towering over the girls. He wore an olive-green military uniform that sported dozens of medals and ribbons. Sam's breath caught in her throat as the tall man flashed a set of pearly whites and took a step into the room. She didn't need Alex to tell her that this was the General.

"Ladies," the General said, "where might you be going at this time of night?" His features weren't deformed like Doc's or Alex's. But his olive skin didn't have a single wrinkle or blemish either. He lifted the military cover revealing a thick mane of perfectly styled jet-black hair. It matched the neatly trimmed mustache and bushy eyebrows.

Sam didn't care about the man's flawless skin or perfect hair. The dread filling Alex's eyes told her everything she needed to care about. The General was bad news. She wanted to run, but the pain prevented her from even moving. Panicked, she did the only thing she could think of and screamed as loud as she could, "Cole!"

The General's smile screwed into a frown. "That's a poor way to introduce yourself."

Sam opened her mouth to scream again but the General, with his perfect hair and perfect skin, threw a perfect jab and caught her right between the eyes. Sam's knees turned to rubber. A sharp pain rocketed through her as the back of her skull bounced off of the tile floor.

Far away, Alex's helpless screams grew fuzzy and distorted. The fluorescent light flickered and faded. Sam closed her eyes, but this time the dark nightmares didn't find her. This time, she didn't dream at all.

4

Sam woke from the dreamless slumber, not in the hospital bed, but rather one of incredible extravagance. A four poster bed draped in a sheer white canopy, the posts made of a rich, dark wood, each engraved in complicated patterns of shapes and lines. The mattress was soft and conformed to her body. It was a definite upgrade from the flimsy cot that she had slept on for so many years in New Hope.

White satin sheets, the kind reserved for government officials in New Hope, covered her naked body. The thought of the creepy doctor or the General undressing her made her skin crawl.

The room surrounding her echoed the same luxurious taste as the extravagant bed. The owner had hung elaborate are all over the walls. Everything from extravagant portraits of people Sam did not recognize, to more eccentric pieces like a statuette of two copper hands, palms facing the ceiling, which balanced a stainless steel heart wrapped in barbwire.

A six-foot tall armoire stood to her right. It looked like the best place to start the search for her belongings and Sam took a deep breath as she prepared for the hunt. She was almost too terrified to move. Afraid that the pain of being thrown from the truck was lying in wait and would pounce on her the moment she shifted the slightest inch.

She exhaled, expecting the shooting pangs from the self-diagnosed broken ribs and punctured lungs to wreak their havoc, but instead she was met with nothing more than a dull ache. She reached her arms under the covers and placed them on her ribcage and received the same result. Hesitantly, she slid through the sheets toward the edge of the bed. The intense agony that she expected never came, which led her to wonder how long she had been unconscious. The fresh track mark in her arm suggested another I.V. It could have been hours or days.

The sheets were smooth against her legs as she slipped through the bedding and her heart sank. Her hands darted to the appendages once covered in fine dark hair and found they had been replaced by hairless ones. They felt foreign to her. Her fingers ran up and down her calves searching for one iota of proof that these were her legs but they couldn't find a single follicle.

Sam hadn't shaved her legs in over a decade. She remembered that it always seemed like a chore and her mother had encouraged her to wait—

Her thoughts shifted.

Her mother.

It had been eons since she was able to dredge a memory of her mother out from the dark shadows of her brain. She focused, grasping for a detail, something specific that would bring the woman out of hiding, but the memory faded as quickly as it had resurfaced. Sam sighed, disappointed that the elusive thought wouldn't become something more substantial and continued toward the armoire.

She reached the edge of the giant bed, sat up and draped her legs over. Below her dangling feet was a Persian rug that spread out the entirety of the bed and a bit more.

Persian rug...Mahogany...Four poster bed. The words bounced around her head. Remnants of her past life. Echoes of buried memories.

She shook her head.

She had no idea at this point if these were things from a previous time in her life or rather manufactured memories implanted for some unknown reason. Either way, she didn't care. The only thing she cared about was getting out of this freak show. Her mission was to rescue Cole and Alex. Find the brother. And then get the hell out of Dodge. Everything else wou—

"I'm glad to see you're awake."

Sam's heart jumped into her throat and she spun to see a small woman standing in the doorway. The pain resurfaced and rocketed through her abdomen. Sam pushed it aside and dove back under the covers.

"Oh, don't be modest, darling," the woman called out to her. "I've seen all your bits and pieces. I mean honestly, who do you think shaved those two bushy cacti you call legs? Or that shrub between your legs?"

Sam swallowed hard as her fingers reached down and touched smooth skin. Her throat tightened and the nausea returned. Sam sunk lower in-between the covers. Her mind raced as she clutched the bottom sheet.

Why had they done this to her?
What else had they done to her?
Where was Cole?

"Are you still there, dearie?"

Sam peeked out from the safety of the sheets.

The woman in the doorway took a small step forward and her face emerged from the shadowed doorway. She had suffered the same fate as the doctor and Alex. Her face stretched upward, making her eyes wide in appearance like she was in a state of permanent surprise. A thick sheet of lip gloss covered her ballooned lips and dark shades of pinks and purples plastered her eyes and cheeks. The makeup clashed with the pale skin and made her look more like a crazed clown than a woman.

The woman's figure had been altered much like Alex's had. Humongous round breasts and a butt that stuck out way too far. A pencil thin waist and two thin sticks for legs. In contrast, the woman dressed in more moderate clothing than the young girl. The green dress she wore was form fitting, but not an inappropriate length or cut.

"If you keep staring at me like that, I'm going to charge admission." The woman's sing-song voice had the same southern drawl as Cole's.

"I'm sorry," Sam whispered.

"Oh, you don't have to be sorry, hun," the woman said, "not unless you plan on staying in bed much longer. Then you're going to have something to be sorry about."

Sam removed her head from the sheets.

"That's better," the woman cooed. "We've got a lot to do to get you ready for the General's dinner tonight. Hop up out of that bed and get your skinny little behind into the shower. Chop chop."

Sam didn't budge from the protection of the covers. "Who are you?"

The woman moved closer and into the soft glow of the room. Her light accentuated her facial features, revealing deep wrinkles despite being pulled to what looked to be its maximum tautness. Heavy bags loomed under the layers of makeup and the neon pink hairdo looked much thinner than it did in the dark.

"My name is Gretaleene Rivers, General Soto's Chief Fashion and Beauty adviser, at your service, darling. But you can call me Greta."

Sam said nothing.

The old woman frowned. "I also do a little interior design, do you like the room?"

"Where's Cole?"

"The big ape with the giant hands and hairy back?" Greta asked, a playful tone in her voice. "He's getting ready himself."

Sam couldn't help but smile, just a little. Not only at her friend being okay—alive at the very least—but also at the comparison. It fit and it made her miss him even more.

"Now, Ms...."

"Samantha. Samantha Albright," then added, "but you can call me Sam."

Greta smiled at this. "Well, Sam, it's such a pleasure to meet you. And now that we've gotten the rigmarole of all these pleasantries out of the way, how about you be so kind as to march your little fanny into the restroom and get in the shower. If we don't get a move on, you'll be late for supper. And one thing the General does not tolerate is tardiness."

Greta took a step toward the restroom and then paused. "Well two things, tardiness and insubordination. Make a note, dear." She walked the rest of the way to the restroom and stopped in the doorway. She raised an eyebrow, "Are you coming?"

"The girl," Sam said. "What happened to her?"

"What girl?"

"Alex." Sam watched as the polite smile faded from Greta's mouth.

"What about her, dear?" Her voice was cold and the words bitter.

"Will she be joining us at dinner?"

There was a long pause as Greta seemed to mull the question over. "No," she said. She didn't wait for Sam to ask any more questions and entered the restroom.

"Can I at least get a bathrobe?" Sam called out.

"I've already told you," Greta called from the restroom, the cheery tone resumed. "I've seen the goods. Now, hurry and get in here. We've got a lot to do to make you fabulous and I don't like working against the clock."

A couple minutes later, Sam reveled in the hot water as steam fogged the frosted glass door. This wasn't the two minute shower she had grown accustomed. The stone-inlayed shower was far removed from the New Hope models with the piss-poor showerhead shooting sporadic bursts of freezing water. Instead, she stood under a gold-plated showerhead and the water was as hot as she could stand it. It rained down, turning her olive-colored skin pink, and Sam wished it would wash away all the pain and horrible memories. She wished it over and over until Greta knocked on the glass door and demanded her to hurry.

After the shower, Sam wrapped herself in a cotton towel, perhaps the softest that she had ever felt, and took a seat at the vanity. In the mirror, she stared at a stranger. The bruises on her face were an ugly shade of yellowish-purple and the spot where the General had hit her was still swollen. The memory of the General's giant fist colliding with her face replayed in her mind. Sam gritted her teeth and ran her fingers over the bruise.

"I swear, dear," Greta said, as she combed the tangles out of Sam's hair, "it's like you've never even heard of a brush."

"It's not a priority where I'm from."

"And where is that? Where did you and the Neanderthal come from?"

"New Hope," Sam whispered as the image of the burning city flashed in her mind.

"Is that the name of the bunker your people are in?"

"We're not from a bunker," Sam said. "We're from the up-top."

Greta stopped brushing and looked at Sam through the reflection of the mirror. The woman's lips sunk into a frown. "Don't be silly, dear," she whispered. "No one's from the up-top. Not anymore."

"I'm not being silly. We're from a town, one not too far from here. It's surrounded by concrete walls and no one's allowed to go in or out because of the—"

"The halfways?" Greta interrupted.

Sam remembered Alex calling them that...the infected. She nodded her head.

"Well, I never."

Sam swallowed and asked a question that she was only half ready to hear the answer to, "How long have you been here, Greta?" She held her breath and waited for the answer. Before Holden Deckard and Jeanette Robertson, before the mass execution in New Hope, she would have thought the number to be around 10 years, the underground bunker a result of pre-planning. She hoped it would be close to a decade. Hoped this was all just a misunderstanding.

"All my life, dearie," Greta chuckled.

Sam's heart dropped. She bit her lip, terrified to ask the next question, still wanting this to all be a horrible nightmare. "How long has this bunker been here?"

Holden had told them it had been 300 years since the RIZ-4 weapon detonated and the burning city and David were just implanted memories. She knew, deep down, that Holden hadn't lied. But still, in that moment she held hope for something, anything, less than three centuries.

"Oh, your guess is as good as mine." Greta ran the brush through Sam's hair and then paused, the bristles still intertwined. "It all depends on who you ask, I suppose. The General says a thousand years or so. But when I was young, my folks led me to believe that it was much, much longer than that."

The world seemed to disappear from underneath and Sam gripped ahold of either side of the chair to keep from dissolving with it.

A thousand years.

Perhaps, much, much longer.

"Are you okay, dear?" Greta asked. "You've gone pale."

"I think...I think..." Sam's voice trailed off and her eyes grew blurry.

Greta yanked the brush down and Sam snapped back to reality. Tears swelled in her eyes. It was less the pain of the brush and more that she had no clue about the world around her. Greta had pulled hard and it hurt.

"Sorry, dear." She ran the brush through the same spot. "A little tangle was all."

"It's okay," Sam heard herself say. Her voice sounded as vacant as the two glassy eyes staring back at her in the mirror.

Greta didn't say another word. Instead, she worked the brush furiously through Sam's thick brown hair. Sam's head yanked back hard with each brush-stroke and she wondered if she had angered Greta talking about the up-top.

Greta brushed and trimmed Sam's hair. Then she wrapped pieces of it in aluminum foil coated in some sort of creamy substance that smelled like cat piss and dried it with a hair dryer. It burned, but Sam didn't complain.

Her eyebrows were waxed along with her underarms and a subtle layer of makeup was applied. Sam didn't protest, but she was terrified that the result would be clown-like—or worse Greta-like. But the final result wasn't bad at all. Sam stared at herself in the mirror, the bruises under her eyes were invisible, the swelling barely noticeable.

Greta removed the foil pieces and revealed subtle strands of crimson intertwined with her normal brown. It was like she was staring into the eyes of a stranger and as much as she hated to admit it...she looked beautiful.

Her heart sank at the thought. She was supposed to be heading to Concordia, supposed to be rescuing her friend, not playing dress up, and every passing moment was an injustice to both Jordan and Cole.

"What's wrong, dear?" Greta asked. "You look upset. Don't you like my work?"

"It's not that. You've done a wonderful job."

"Then what, dear?"

"I need to find Cole and we need to be on our way."

"But you just got here. Why so eager to leave?"

"We're on a journey to a town named Concordia," Sam said. The words sounded foolish to her, but she continued anyway. "It's a city at the center of the country and—"

"Well," Greta interrupted and then gave a nervous laugh. "I'm sure after dinner the General will help get you back on track."

"Do you really believe that?"

The old woman glanced around as if someone else was in the room with them. After a moment, she bent down and whispered in Sam's ear. "If you get the chance, run."

"Greta?" Sam asked, but was answered by a firm tug of her hair.

"Of course I do," Greta said. "General Soto's a wonderful man."

Sam understood at once. They were being monitored. She bit her tongue. She had more questions but knew asking them would only put Greta in a difficult spot. Instead, she remained quiet as Greta finished the touchups.

"There," Greta announced. "Not too shabby if you ask me."

"I agree," Sam said.

"Now, stand up, dearie," Greta instructed and Sam did as she asked.

Greta crossed the tile floor to the closet across the room and removed a short black dress, a pair of heels, and a fresh pair of undergarments. Sam protested but the old woman shook her head.

"Put this on," Greta said. "I'll give you a moment."

Sam took the clothes and Greta left the room and closed the door behind her. She stared at the foreign reflection for a long time before removing her towel. In the mirror, Sam gawked at the bruises covering her body. Remnants of the vicious wreck. How long had it been now? Two weeks? More? Sam didn't know. Time seemed to be an illusion.

The faintness of the bruises suggested it had been at least a week and a half. Ten days since the last time she spoke to Jordan. Since the last time he held her. Tears stung at her eyes, but she forced them back. She had to stop crying. There was no time for weakness.

She pulled on the undergarments. They weren't the traditional pair of Ministry-issued cotton panties and bra. These were lace and satin. These were the type of undergarments that were meant to be seen. She blushed as she caught a glimpse of the thin string disappearing into her backside. And again at how far the bra pushed up her breasts.

Sam's skin turned to gooseflesh as she thought of the General and his unknown intentions. But if she was honest with herself, she knew damned well what they were. The underwear was a dead giveaway but so was the conversation with Alex about how the men treated the girls here.

She stepped into the black dress and pulled the straps over her shoulders. It was a short, black cocktail dress—incredibly short. It hugged her waist and her breasts spilled out of it regardless of how much she adjusted the neckline.

Six-inch shiny black stilettos accompanied it. Sam shoved her foot into the narrow opening of the first shoe and then the second. They were uncomfortable and Sam felt awkward wearing them. She couldn't remember ever wearing anything other than the grimy pair of tennis shoes. These would make escaping that much more difficult.

She looked herself over once more in the mirror. She shuddered as the word *prostitute* flashed through her mind. Seeing the final product and knowing deep down what the General had in mind…she would have settled for clown.

Clumsily, she exited the bathroom where Greta was waiting for her. She stood next to the uniformed man with the perfect skin and perfect hair. He offered a wide smile and Sam's gut instinct screamed to return to the safety of the bathroom. Lock the door and barricade it.

Instead, she approached him.

"You look breathtaking," he said. He offered a slight bow, took her by the hand and then raised it to his lips. "Allow me to formally introduce myself. My name is General Alistair Soto." He kissed the back of her outstretched hand.

Despite the growing urge to knee him in the groin, Sam offered a terse smile and said, "Your fist looks like it's healing nicely, General."

5

The two sauntered down the hall of the complex followed by two armed guards carrying automatic weapons. Sam held onto the General Soto's arm, partially for balance but also because he had insisted. The heels clicked and clacked and each step echoed down the marble hallway.

"I do apologize for the rude welcome," Soto said.

"I have no interest in your empty apologies, General," Sam said. "The only thing I want is to see my friend and then be on our way."

"In due time, my darling. But first a tour of our great city and perhaps an exchange of pleasantries along the way."

The General guided her down elaborate hallway after elaborate hallway. The green and gold marble floor had been buffed to a mirror-like shine and Sam blushed as she caught a reflection of herself in the revealing costume. After years of being resigned to the thick coveralls in New Hope, she felt naked in anything else.

They strode past an endless parade of fine art, each piece framed in elaborate gold and hung to the polished stone wall. Mixed in were countless portraits of more men and women Sam didn't recognize. More decorations. More wall art. More posturing. Sam stopped paying attention to the brash pieces as they proceeded farther into the labyrinth of corridors, but something else had caught her eye.

At first, she had dismissed the small security cameras suspended in each corner. But upon reaching the end of the fifth or sixth corridor—she had lost track at this point—the frequency of the red dots tracking them was too much to overlook.

"You have a problem with privacy?" she asked and nodded to the camera in front of them.

"Our predecessors installed the cameras to help protect the citizens of Lost Angel," the General said. "Not to impede on their privacy."

"Protect them from what?"

"I think the easy answer would be the halfways." The General stopped in the middle of the hallway and Sam did the same. "If one of those monstrosities somehow breached our walls, we would be able to track it. We'd be able to hunt it down and exterminate it before it did any damage."

"Is there a hard answer?" Sam asked.

The General frowned and then nodded. "The hard answer is we put them in place to protect the citizens from themselves."

"Why would you need to do that?"

"For many, many years, we have lived in this bunker, sheltered away from the creatures of the up-top. A select few of my staff patrol the entrance to keep the monstrosities away, but the vast majority of the citizens are restricted to the bunker. Such restrictions can take a toll on a person's psyche. It makes people act of character. Drives them mad. Makes them hunger for unattainable things."

Sam cringed. "What kind of things?"

The General looked her up and down and then smiled. She wanted to vomit.

"We don't have many problems from the lower levels but the citizens near the top, the more well-to-do citizens, sometimes get an itch that they need to scratch. They grow restless from time to time.

"The cameras allow me to keep a watchful eye over the compound. I do this to protect them. And to keep some citizens from visiting with our patients." The General paused and flashed a shit-eating grin.

Sam's blood boiled. He had been watching her room. He had seen Alex try to help her.

"And of course," he continued, "to offer a helping hand when one is needed."

"And who watches you, General? Who watches the watcher?"

The General chuckled and turned away from her. The corners of his mouth drooped into a frown and his eyes stared at the wall ahead of them. "Shall we go?"

Sam knew that she was close to pushing the wrong button and backed off from further questioning. The two resumed their walk, the guards following a few feet behind, and departed from the labyrinth of brash and gaudy hallways.

They reached a large steel door reminiscent of a submarine hatch. Sam placed her hand atop of the wheel lock, but the General stopped her.

"Please, allow me." He placed a hand on each of her bare shoulders and moved her aside. "This is a man's work."

His touch sent a wave of goose pimples up her arm. A Molotov cocktail of repulsion and ire burst open in the pit of her stomach. For a moment, she saw nothing but the color red and her muscles tensed as if preparing to strike. She forced a deep breath and then another and the anger faded.

The General rotated the wheel and the sound of the door unlocking boomed through the hallway. Beyond the door was a metal platform surrounded by a rock wall. It was her first glimpse of anything resembling an underground bunker. The platform opened to a set of metal stairs descending into an abyss of darkness.

General Soto navigated Sam down the staircase. As they descended, the warmth of the higher levels disappeared leaving nothing but the cold hug of the narrow rock walls. Sam clung to the steel railing as she fought to steady herself after each step. Close to a hundred steps later, they reached the landing of the stairwell and Sam found herself staring at a massive cave-like opening.

It took a few minutes for her vision to adjust to the low-lit cave. Electric lanterns hung every few feet, but the darkness swallowed the little light they produced. She tripped over something and the General caught her before she hit the ground. She squinted and saw thick cables, bundled together, running down the length of the cave.

"The backup generators," the General said, "are kept on the bottom floors of the mines. The lower level crew's responsibility is to keep them maintained in case our main power source is ever severed."

"Main power source?" Sam asked.

"Above us is a field of solar powered generators," the General said and paused again. Sam followed suit and stood beside him. "There are 75 total generators and over half are in perfect working order. We consider them to be a gift from our ancestors."

"And the other half?" Sam asked. She didn't really care but figured that it was best to engage the General. She would play the role of the cooperative, friendly guest until the opportunity to escape presented itself and she hoped that would come sooner rather than later.

"Mechanical failures," the General said. "While our forefathers left us with instructions to repair the machines, the parts to maintain them are scarce to say the least. As their operations cease, we've torn them down to keep the others functioning."

Sam eyed the two guards. They stood a dozen feet back and were carrying on their own conversation. The service rifle of one of the guards lolled in his grip, and for the briefest of moments, Sam wondered if she could grab it before being overtaken.

"But as time passed and we've evolved as a society, we've reached a better understanding of how the old technology works. Now, we hardly have any breakage in the working generators and we are repairing some of the broken machines that have lain dormant for years. There are a few we'll never be able to fix. They need parts that can't be recreated and we can't risk any men to scavenge parts inside the old city."

"The old city?" Sam asked, her attention still focused on the soldier's rifle. Inside, she debated with the primal urge to rip it from his hands. The margin for error was small. Where was the urge coming from, though?

"Lost Angel," Soto said. "The original Lost Angel. It was a massive city before the infection. Its skeletal remains can be seen on the horizon if the day is clear enough. Warehouses, old homesteads, gargantuan buildings. We've foraged the outlying areas, but the majority of the city is crawling with halfways."

"You have weapons," Sam said. "Can't you fight them off?"

The General gave a belly laugh. "Our records show that we lost a good number of military during initial explorations of the city. That was eons ago, but I still won't risk any more men to find out if those soulless imps have moved on. Not worth it in my opinion. Of course, that's why they've reelected me so many times. Because of the sanctity I hold for human life."

Sam wondered if Soto had any idea of how asinine he sounded. She thought of Alex and Greta. The fear in both of their eyes. She wondered if he believed in the sanctity of human life or perhaps he meant huMAN life. Sam thought the latter was more likely.

"Shall we continue?" Soto asked.

"Yes," Sam said. "I'm anxious to see Cole."

"All in due time, my darling. All in due time."

They continued down the invisible path and surged deeper into the pitch-black. The lanterns gave way to runs of wired lights strung down the length of wall. Although there were hundreds of the tiny twinkling bulbs—two strands running down the length of each wall and another draped from the ceiling—the darkness was still overwhelming. After a few more feet, they stopped once more. Soto pointed and through the darkness Sam saw the outline of a door.

The steel door was the same gray color as the cave wall and would easy to overlook if the lower strand of lights hadn't stopped and then picked back up on the opposite side. The General placed a hand on the doorknob and paused.

"This is the cafeteria for the higher levels of the mines," his voice echoed off the stone walls. "The workers don't interact with anyone other than the mine foremen and each other. I'd like to apologize in advance for any…staring."

The General didn't wait for a response. Instead, he turned the knob and opened the door. Bright fluorescent lights spilled out into the dark cave and Sam shielded her eyes. The General left her side and entered the room.

Sam followed Soto through the doorway and into a large room. It reminded her of New Hope's mess hall. Dozens of 12 foot wooden tables littered the room. Sam's heart dropped at the sight of the hundred or so people seated around them. Not just people. Children.

Sunken eyes stared at her as she entered. Hollow cheeks. Bloated bellies. They were all malnourished. All covered in dirt and soot. Their clothes consisted of torn rags that hung from their bodies.

"Oh my god," Sam whispered.

"It's impressive, isn't it?" Soto asked. "We've built quite the workforce over the years."

Sam's eyes scanned the crowd. The children ranged from five to 15 and while the majority of the children looked to be boys, there were a handful of girls sprinkled throughout the crowd.

"The barracks and common areas reserved for the older workers are down below, closer to the generators. We've found the steep incline becomes an issue as the adults turn 30."

"And they work down in the mines their entire lives?" Sam asked. Her voice shook as the blood running through her veins turned icy.

"Yes and no," the General said. "The average life expectancy of a mineworker is around 40 years of age. In the rare instances they make it to 50, they are rewarded by being allowed to live on the higher levels and continue the rest of their days as our servants. Maids, butlers, cooks, that sort of thing."

Sam was dumbstruck by the hundreds of eyes that all stared back at her and searched for something to say as the General continued.

"The workers are divided into multiple teams down here. The smarter ones are placed on a mechanical team that services the generators. There's also an excavation team known as the diggers. And a specialized team that handles a multitude of different operations. The foreman—"

"Stop," Sam said.

The General turned toward her and frowned. "I'm sorry?"

"I just…I don't understand," Sam said. "How are there so many kids?"

"Ah, yes." The General lowered his voice and turned to Sam. "The girls are given a choice when they turn 12. They can continue to work in the mines or they can live atop with the military and royal families. They offer a different service."

Sam understood fully what Alexandria had told her.

"They will have children until they can no longer. Our hopes are that each woman can mother at least 10 to 12 children. From birth, the male children are monitored and given a series' of aptitude tests throughout their first five years of life. We select the brightest to continue the bloodlines. Those that exhibit leadership skills are selected for military duty, and those that display adeptness for mathematics and science will join the ranks of our science and medical departments. The rest of the children will join the workforce in the mines."

"Why are you showing me this? Why are you telling me these horrible things?"

"Horrible?" Soto said. He looked taken aback. "This is how we survive, my darling. How we've been able to sustain life for all these years. I assumed you would be interested in this. Just as I am interested in how you and your friend have survived...and where you came from."

Sam didn't answer this, nor did she look at the General. She couldn't. Just being next to the man made her sick. Everything about this place was appalling. Her heart broke as she looked into the gaunt faces of the children. Some still stared back, although most had returned to the bowls of slop that sat in front of them.

Her eyes connected with a young girl with sad, desperate eyes. She thought of David and how his body had rotted away to almost nothing. These children weren't much better off.

"Let us go, my dear. I believe a feast awaits us in the dining hall." Soto placed his hand against her lower back and rubbed his thumb back and forth against her bare skin. A wave of revulsion flooded through her.

He led Sam from the room and back out of the mines. Climbing the staircase proved to be just as difficult as the descent and Sam dreamed of the moment when she would be able to remove the heels.

They reached the top and trundled back through the maze of hallways. Sam thought they were headed in a different direction but she couldn't be sure. Everything looked the same. The gold and green marble floors. The gaudy wall art. The cameras.

The doors lining the hallways changed and the rich, mahogany doors turned golden, each etched in beautiful, elaborate designs.

"This is where our royalty are housed," General Soto said.

Sam walked by his side in silence, her arm still intertwined with his as he had insisted, and still hating every moment of it all. The effigies of the children had burned into her retinas and her heart ached for them.

As they continued to walk down the hall, a young girl burst from one of the golden doorways. The General let go of Sam's arm and advanced on the girl. She was naked from head to toe but Sam recognized the headful of lavender hair.

It was Alex.

She locked eyes with Sam for a moment and then straightened as the General approached. The girl's purple eyes darted to the floor, and she pressed her bare backside against the wall.

"What do you think you're doing?" Soto asked.

Alex shook her head, but her eyes remained fixed on the floor. Violet locks from the girl's disheveled hair covered her face. Heavy, black streaks of mascara ran down her cheeks, and her bare chest heaved up and down. The girl was barely a teenager. Far too young to be naked and crying in a hallway. Sam's blood boiled with hatred for this place.

"Answer me," the General said.

But Alex didn't have to answer. The golden door burst open again and this time a man wearing only a pair of crusty yellow briefs exited into the hallway. His gray hair was as prevalent around the crown of his head as it was in his ears and nose. He wore a thick golden chain around his neck and the extravagant medallion at the end rested in a thick tuft of chest hair. He had dyed his skin an awful orangish-brown color, and it amplified the deep wrinkles covering his body. Sam's stomach knotted up at the sight of him.

"Ah, General Soto," the old man wheezed. He smiled to reveal a set of teeth that were as white and straight as Soto's. Too white. Too straight. "It's so nice to see you this evening." The man spoke with no sign of embarrassment, not even the slightest shred of shame as he stood half-naked in the middle of the hallway.

The General's heels came together and his spine stiffened. "President Gates, it's always a pleasure," Soto said as he brought his hand a perfect 45 degree angle towards the brim of his hat. Gates offered a half-ass salute in response and the General lowered his arm. He then motioned toward the girl. "Is there a problem here?"

Gates laughed and shook his head. "Heavens no, General." The old man walked over to Alex and grabbed a handful of hair. Her eyes grew wide, and the man yanked down hard. She shrieked in pain.

"No!" Sam screamed.

Both General Soto and President Gates looked at her in astonishment.

"Don't hurt her," Sam said.

She attempted to run to the girl, but Soto took a step to his side and blocked her path. He grabbed her by the arm and marched her back to the guards. One of the soldiers seized her from behind and the other shoved the cold steel barrel of his gun in her face.

"You won't say another word," Soto seethed. "Not one more fucking word or I'll rip your spine out of your goddam throat. Do you understand me?"

Sam didn't answer him.

He grabbed her by the chin and squeezed her cheeks together. Sam moaned as excruciating pain shot through her.

"Do you understand me?"

"Yes," Sam said.

Soto's grip relaxed. His lips, which had peeled into a nasty sneer, relaxed as well and then curled into a twisted smile. He took a deep breath, unfurrowed his brow and spun around on the balls of his feet.

"I believe the question at hand," Gates said, a large clump of curls still wrapped in his fist, "is do *you* have a problem?"

Alex's head was cocked at an abnormal angle and Sam worried that her neck would snap. She struggled and tried to go to the girl, but the guard's grip tightened around her arms. Sam relaxed as she thought of a way to escape. A rear-kick to the groin of the guard behind her, perhaps? Then she would drop to the floor and sweep the legs of the one beside her. But the gun shoved in her face would be a quick end to any exit gone awry. Her thoughts halted and for a nanosecond she questioned where it had come from.

"Of course not, sir." Soto looked humbled. His eyes scanned the marble floor, and it became clear that while he might be in charge of the commoners, he wasn't the one pulling the strings in Lost Angel. He was the royalty's puppet. Their singing, dancing, mustachioed enforcer. And President Gates, the old man sporting wood in the yellowed briefs, was the monstrous puppeteer working the marionette.

"The girl is the outsider we found on the up-top," Soto continued. "I haven't had a chance to break her in yet."

"Well see that you do," Gates grinned. "And I will do the same. The younger ones always take a bit longer to tame." He flashed another toothy grin at the General and then yanked the young girl's hair again. Instead of a scream, Alex emitted the tiniest of yelps. "See? Better already."

Without another word, the old man led Alex back through the golden door and slammed it behind him. Sam's skin turned to gooseflesh, and she made a mental note of the golden plaque next to the door. Room 491. She was helpless to act now, but she would return for Alex. She would return or die trying.

General Soto nodded. The guard released his grip and pushed her away. Sam stumbled, trying her best to balance on the foreign heels but then collapsed. Her knees slammed hard against the stone floor and an ocean of stars filled her vision. Luckily, or perhaps not, the stars faded at once.

Instead of passing out, she watched on her hands and knees as the General's polished black shoes approached. Each step echoed off the marble with a maddening ferocity. She waited for his hand to wrap its way into her hair. To be pulled up like the young girl was moments ago. Instead, the General extended a hand to her. She hesitated and then she took it.

Soto helped her back to her feet. On shaky legs, Sam straightened her dress. Her cheeks flushed as she felt the hemline bunched up above her waist and then turned to see the two guards ogling her backside. She lowered her gaze to the floor and unbunched the dress. She was embarrassed and scared. She didn't want to be seen as a victim.

"I'm sorry," the General said. He placed a finger on the under her chin and lifted her face. Sam lifted her head and met Soto's gaze. "Things have gotten out of hand. Do you accept my apology?"

Sam didn't answer. She cringed when he lifted a lock of hair from her face and tucked it behind her ear.

"Let's go to the dining hall. We will feast and you can tell me all about the place that you come from. New Hope was it?" His voice was almost friendly now and the acidic feeling in Sam's stomach increased tenfold. General Soto turned away from her and began marching down the hall.

"What about that girl?" Sam asked. Soto stopped and turned back toward her. "What about Alex?"

"That girl is doing her job," he sneered. "She's doing her part to make sure that Lost Angel continues to thrive."

"And the surgeries?" Sam asked. "Does that help keep Lost Angel *thriving?*"

The General's lips curled into a queer smile. "We have a certain look we try to maintain here. Practices our forefathers began long ago. Traditions that must continue. The men up here, they want something nice-looking to keep them warm in their bed."

"They're children," she said. "You sick fucking bastard." The rage boiled over and she couldn't stop herself. "You're surgically modifying children and then turning them into sex slaves. These men are raping your children and you sit back and let them."

Soto's smile faded, and the sneer returned. And then he charged her.

She backed up as fast as she could but the heels prevented any sort of retreat. Before she took her second step backward, the General's hand wrapped around her throat. He slammed her against the wall and Sam's skull bounced off it with a nauseating thud. Soto tightened his grip and then lifted her off the ground.

"Those *children* are given a choice," Soto said.

Sam barely heard him. She dangled on the edge of consciousness. Her feet hung inches from the floor and she kicked at her aggressor. He evaded them and then pressed his body against hers and she was unable to kick again. Her lungs screamed for air and her eyes bulged. Her heartbeat thrummed between her ears and the world faded.

"They can choose to work in the mines or they can choose to keep the men happy." The General's mustache pressed against her ear. "That's the way it always has been and the way it always will be."

As Sam struggled to take the smallest of breaths, her brain flashed on Prime Minister Troy's noxious tongue wriggling in her mouth. The ancient boner grinding against her. The General's doing the same. Pressing against her. She tried to pull away but couldn't move.

"I can't breathe," Sam managed.

He stared at her for what seemed like an eternity and then his grip loosened. She managed to touch marble and her windpipe expanded. Air flooded into Sam's lungs and the stars faded away from her vision. She coughed in agony as her lungs inflated.

"My men have needs," Soto said. He removed his hand from her throat and pressed it against her cheek. "Itches that need to be scratched. And these needs, these itches, *must* be scratched to keep balance and civility. These girls serve a purpose."

"A wet hole to fuck?" Sam hissed. "They're childr—"

The General slapped her hard across the face. The bitter taste of copper filled her mouth and she spit a mouthful of blood onto the floor. He grabbed her by the neck again and pushed her head against the wall.

"These children," Soto seethed, "as you insist to refer to them, choose that lifestyle and are *deeply* rewarded by it. They become mothers and they raise children of their own." The General lowered his voice, but the hot breath against her ear remained.

Soto's free hand slipped under the hem of her dressed and his fingers slid up her thigh. "We all have *needs*, my dear."

"Fuck you," she said.

"In due time." He traced his fingers up her thigh and to the thin silky underwear. He rubbed against the almost non-existent barrier and pressed his groin against her hip.

Sam's mind raced. The guards' had their guns trained on her. Even if she could escape from Soto, how far could she make it down the hall before getting shot?

"Relax," the General said. "We'll have our time after dinner. I'll show you first-hand how these *children* are rewarded." He placed his tongue against her neck and gave an exasperated breath. The slimy muscle traveled from the base of her throat and up her cheek leaving a trail of hot saliva behind.

"I promise you—" Sam said but stopped.

Her teeth clamped together and her stomach balled into a tight knot as the General kneaded his fingers harder and deeper into her groin. She managed a breath, despite the chokehold, and said, "Before the night is over... I will kill you."

His fingers stopped squirming, and he removed his hand. He lifted the two fingers to his mouth and licked them. His lips curled into the trademark nauseating smile and he said, "Delicious." Then he turned away and resumed his march toward the dining room.

Sam stood against the wall, fighting the overwhelming urge to cry, until one of the guards poked her with the barrel of his gun. She turned and followed the General—the soldiers on her heels. And as she walked down the hall, the General's reproachful touch still lingering between her legs, she promised herself to make him hurt before she killed him.

6

Soto unlocked the heavy double doors at the end of the hallway and swung them open, revealing a magnificent dining room. It was the polar opposite of the dilapidated chow hall in the mines. Track-lighting hung from the ceiling and illuminated the stained glass windows lining each wall.

A long dining table sat in the center of the room. Sitting at the end—squeezed into a tuxedo two sizes too small—was Cole Porter. Her friend. Her fellow refugee. The only thing left in the world that she recognized

"Cole!" Sam squealed.

She ran to him as fast as the heels would allow and threw her arms around his thick neck. She squeezed tight, afraid that if she let go he would disappear like Jordan or David. Like the memories of her mother.

The General followed her into the room and took a seat at the head of the table. The two guards took a spot on either side of the door. She thought she heard the door lock as it closed, the *click* echoing against the stone walls of the dining room, but didn't know for certain. In this moment, she didn't care. All she cared about was the giant hulk of a man.

"We have to go," Sam whispered into Cole's ear. "They're going to kills us."

After a moment, when Cole hadn't responded or returned the embrace as Sam would have expected, she released her grip. He continued to sit in silence, not moving, barely breathing it seemed, staring straight ahead.

Sam moved around the end of the table so she could get a better view his face, but Cole didn't acknowledge her. Instead, he stared at the wall ahead of him. His eyes were blank and his pupils dilated. He looked drugged.

"Cole?" Sam asked. A wave of panic rushed through her. The memory of calling out to Jordan in her dream and not getting a response flashed through her mind. Cole Porter was here in the flesh, but his mind was miles and miles away.

"Cole!" This time she screamed. Her voice echoed off the stone walls. Her friend still didn't look at her. He didn't seem to register that she was in the room.

"Have a seat, Samantha," General Soto said.

"What's wrong with you, Cole?" She reached out to her friend and grabbed ahold of his arm. His hand fell off the table and hung limply at his side. He made no intention of placing it back on the table.

"Samantha, did you hear me?" The General's voice was so even-keeled, so level, that it made her want to scream. She still felt his fingers squirming between her legs. "Please sit down. You're making a scene, and I do despise a scene."

"What did you do to him?" Sam asked but didn't let her attention stray from Cole's lifeless face. Her friend took short shallow breaths with long pauses in-between and his chest rose and fell in infinitesimal movements. But he *was* breathing. He stared at the wall with listless, unfocused eyes. His thin lips, barely visible through the bushy, gray beard, were parted, his jaw slack, and Sam detected a hint of drool escaping them.

"Samantha, I must insist—"

"Fuck you," Sam hissed as she continued to examine Cole's face. There was something peculiar about it—other than the obvious lack of emotion. She was missing something.

When the two lived in New Hope, she had known Cole Porter only from afar. She'd never studied the man's face or the endless details that made up his features. The wiry eyebrows and the small scar, no more than a few millimeters in length that ran across his left cheek above his beard. Two emerald green eyes were and his cauliflowered ears. All these minute details she had never noticed. But *something* was different. What was it?

And then she saw it. The subtle difference. A tiny bulge extruded from the back of Cole's head just above the nape of his neck. The wispy strands of gray hair had camouflaged it. She reached up and her fingers slide up the warm flesh of his neck and disappear into the unknown of his mane. She gasped as they ran across the beginning of a surgical scar and then cold metal.

"It is no longer a request, Samantha."

General Soto's tone had grown stern, but the words didn't register. She focused on the device implanted into the back of Cole's head. Her fingers pushed away the matte of gray to get a better look at it. A dime-sized metal box protruded from the back of his scalp.

"What have you done?" she asked as her fingers touched the device.

"That's it," Soto said. He rose from the table with such force that the heavy chair went sailing back. "When I say get in your seat, I mean get in your goddamn seat, bitch!"

Sam hadn't heard the heavy wooden chair crashing to the ground, or the heavy footfalls as he stormed closer, but she recognized the venomous words he spewed. She looked in time to see the General standing right above her. He grabbed a handful of hair and nearly lifted her off her feet. Sam screamed out in pain, but Cole remained motionless.

She tried to scream again, but her head lurched forward and slammed into the wooden table. Sam heard the crunch of her nose breaking against the solid wood and then felt the pain that accompanied the bone-chilling sound. Her lips busted as they smashed into table, followed by her teeth crashing against them. White stars appeared and the illustrious room grew faded and distorted. The General screamed obscenities as he dragged her across the room but she didn't fight it. She focused on not losing consciousness. The world had become distant as the stars multiplied and engulfed her field of vision.

She shook her head, and the stars faded. She moved across the room but not under her own accord. A moment later, Soto lifted her from the ground and sat her down hard into the chair. The lower half of her crashed into the heavy wood and rockets of pain shot through her lower torso. The stars reappeared.

"There, that's better." He rested his palm on the back of her head and stroked her hair. "I do apologize, my darling, but you must learn your place here."

"Learn my place," Sam repeated. The white orbs faded, and she touched her busted lips. Bright crimson covered her fingertips when she withdrew her hand.

General Soto snapped his fingers and one of the guards came to him. "Miguel, find out what's taking the chef so goddamn long." The guard nodded and disappeared through the door. Sam heard the muffled click of the door being unlocked and a clack as it snapped shut.

"Now, let's talk about where you two came from," the General said. He spoke as if he hadn't just broken her face. "You two are the first outsiders that Lost Angel has seen since I was a boy. Your coveralls said New Hope but my staff couldn't find that anywhere on the map. Where is that, Samantha?"

"Learn my place," Sam said. Her voice was distant and her thoughts far away from the conversation Soto was attempting to have. Her mind swirled around the three-bedroom apartment in the burning city. But the city wasn't burning in this memory. This was before the infection. Before the quarantines.

Thick, lime-green wall-to-wall carpet and a small RCA television-set in the quaint living room. The balcony full of potted plants and the view of the bustling city that surrounded them. Sam's old apartment. Her family's apartment. A young girl with brown hair pulled into pigtails sat in the center of the room.

"Samantha?" the General asked from far away.

Sam didn't respond. The image of the girl fixed in her mind. She looked so familiar. The pigtails and the icy blue eyes. It was the girl she hadn't seen in an eternity.

Rebecca.

The name echoed between her ears. Rebecca Young. Sam stared as the small girl played with a baby doll and hummed a lullaby. And then the girl with the pigtails and blue eyes, the girl she loved so very much, looked up at her and smiled back.

Far away, the General said, "Leo, go get Doc. I think I broke her." Laughter followed the request, first General Soto's and then Leo's. It faded and Soto added, "And if you see the chef, Miguel is worthless today, tell that useless bitch she has two minutes to bring us our food or I'll cut her from ear to ear."

Leo's laugh cutting out. "Yes, General."

The *click* of the lock opening.

The *clack* of it closing.

It all seemed so distant though, Sam was unable to pull herself from her memories. Or perhaps she didn't want to. She was unwilling to break her stare, mesmerized with the image of the girl. With the memory of Rebecca.

"Play with me, Sam," Rebecca's said. Her voice echoed throughout the living room.

"Why are you here?" Sam asked.

The girl grinned. "I live here, silly goose."

Sam frowned. "No. This was before you."

Rebecca smiled at her and then laughed. "You *are* a silly goose indeed." She held up her baby doll and Sam took it. "Now, will you play with me?"

Sam nodded, and the child's face lit up with a brilliant smile.

"Will you play midnight runners with me?" Rebecca asked.

Sam's jaw fell open and the trace of a smile fled from her face. This beautiful memory, this long-lost recollection, this hallucination, was now engulfing her. Sam was no longer sitting at the dining room table but rather standing in the living room. She had taken her heels off without realizing it and buried her bare feet in the shag lime-green carpet.

"What did you say, baby?" Sam said. The words dropped to her knees. Rebecca stood and took a step closer. She wrapped her small, thin arms around Sam's neck and Sam took a deep breath and squeezed her back. It was Rebecca's familiar scent and tears swelled in Sam's eyes. She squeezed tighter.

Rebecca put her lips to Sam's ear and whispered, "Play midnight runners with me." Then she pulled away and stretched her tiny arm outward. She pointed toward the corner of the small living room.

Sam slowly moved her head, following the little girl's arm, and sitting in the breakfast nook of the apartment was Cole, who stared back at her blankly.

"Midnight runners," Rebecca said.

"Midnight runners," Sam repeated in a whisper.

"I'm sorry, dear. What was that?" Soto asked. "I couldn't understand your mumblings."

The question brought Sam back to the present moment. Rebecca, the living room, the apartment, it all disappeared, and she sat in the dining hall once more. A pounding headache returned. Her lips were swollen and throbbing. Her nose crooked and out of place.

Someone had placed a plate of food in front of her. There was food everywhere. Silver platters filled with vegetables and fruits filled the length of the table. More platters with roasted turkeys and chickens.

The intoxicating aroma of the food pulled Sam even further from the memory—Rebecca's face almost forgotten now. When was the last time she had eaten real food? Weeks? Years? Decades? Centuries?

She looked down the table to Cole, who remained motionless, and then back to the plate in front of her. Steam rose from the plate. To the left of the plate were two forks, one slightly bigger than the other, and to the right two spoons and a knife. All the utensils were gold and shiny, the light from the crystal chandelier gleaming in their reflection. Sam couldn't see a single spot or imperfection on any of them.

She looked to her left and General Soto was staring at her, his eyes focused and his brow furrowed. His jet-black mustache and the lips underneath curled upward in the hideous smile.

Behind the General, Miguel had returned but not Leo. He stood at parade rest, the automatic rifle slung over his shoulder, the muzzle pointed skyward toward the door. Leo hadn't returned yet, or so she assumed because the doctor was nowhere in sight.

"What were you saying, my dear?"

Sam shook her head and tried to knock loose the cobwebs. She didn't remember what she said. She didn't remember the food being brought in or Miguel returning from his chore. But she did remember that they needed to be getting on their way. She remembered that somewhere east of here was a town called Concordia, and she had questions for the people that live there. She remembered her friend sitting at the end of the table. Immobilized and drugged and stuffed into a tuxedo. She remembered that they didn't belong in this city. And she remembered the reprehensible feeling of the General's hand between her legs.

"My dear, you look pale."

Sam didn't answer him.

"I can see that you haven't learned your les—"

"What happened to Cole?"

The General shifted in his seat as Sam turned toward him. The words came rushing back to her: *midnight runners.*

"My darling, I haven't done anything to your friend."

"What's the midnight runner project?" Sam asked.

Time slowed to a stop as General Soto's eyes grew wide and his mouth fell open. The guard by the door tensed—his feet pulling together and his back straightening. In one fluid motion, he had gone from at-rest to attention and now his finger was wrapping around the trigger of the weapon. It all unfolded in slow-motion. All magnified to the *nth* degree. Something had happened when the General slammed her head into the table. Something had jarred loose or perhaps, snapped back into place. Something inside her had changed.

Sam leaned down and removed the high heel from her foot. The General began to shout some order at the guard, this also happened in slow-motion, his voice coming out slow and deep at half speed. His command turned into a high-pitched scream halfway through, as Sam leaned toward him and drove the spike of the heel into the bulging eye of the General. Everything in slow-motion. Everything amplified. She heard the gruesome squish of the eyeball exploding as the heel punctured it.

The guard raised his weapon but Sam didn't hesitate long enough to allow him to get a beat on her. Instead, she pushed out of her chair. The heavy seat topped over and flew back into the wall. She pulled up on the base of the shoe and dug the heel the slightest bit deeper into the General's orbital socket—which was now flooded with blood and a white gelatinous matter. She twisted the shoe, and the angle caused Soto to cry out again, this one more ghastly than the first, and he stood at once, blocking the path of the gunman. As Sam twisted and turned the shoe, the General moved as she wanted, like a giant marionette connected to a horrific string.

"You're my puppet now," she breathed.

The General screamed.

Sam kicked off the other heel and pulled the General in closer. He wrapped his hands around her wrist in an effort to prevent the spike from digging any further into his head. She worried that his struggling would cause the heel to slip farther into the socket and puncture his brain, and she didn't want that, not yet. She needed him.

"Put your fucking arms down," Sam commanded.

The General did as she instructed and removed his hands from her wrist. The awkward angle of his neck and head caused blood to spill in waves onto the stone floor of the dining room. It reminded her of the way Alex looked in the hallway as she was drug around by President Gates. She took joy in another twist of the shoe. Soto shrieked and turned his back toward her allowing Sam to grab ahold of his sidearm.

The gun was a Desert Eagle, titanium gold, with tiger stripes, a carbon-steel barrel and a black-oxide finish. The magazine inside held eight .44 caliber bullets, and judging by the weight of the gun, four pounds and 12.8 ounces, it was fully loaded. A genuine gas-operated, rotating bolt with a single-action trigger. She didn't know how, but she knew all of this a millisecond after pulling it from the General's holster.

She didn't waste time pulling the slide back. This wasn't the movies, and she wasn't looking to strike fear and intimidation into her foes. She was looking to kill.

She pulled the trigger and the top of Miguel's head exploded. A mist of blood and brain splattered the wall behind. He stumbled back a step and looked at her with wide, unbelieving eyes. His pupils dilated to their fullest and then disappeared under an ocean of blood that poured from the gaping hole in the top of his head. A second later, he collapsed and his service rifle clattered against the hard floor.

"You have a choice, General." Her teeth clenched together but her voice remained steady. "You can tell me what's wrong with my friend, or I can give a slight tug and shish-kabob brain."

"There's a device in my pocket," the General said. His voice trembled and his teeth chattered. "It controls the signal to his brain. There's three buttons. The top button will bring his brain in and out of rest. But you must only press that button."

Sam placed the firearm on the table, stuck her hand deep into his pocket and removed the device. It was a silver square with three red buttons running vertical down the length of it, encased by a thin glass cover. A white letter was imprinted over each button, reading: A, B, and C.

"What do the other two buttons do?" Sam asked.

"There's no time to explain," the General said. As if the words were a cue, the second they exited his lips, the wooden door of the dining room burst open.

The room slowed again as first the white-haired man known as Doc stumbled through. Leo accompanied by two other guards, each armed with assault rifles, followed. Outside in the hallway, lights were flashing. An alarm was sounding. Sam saw it all. She could see the surgical staples lining the jaw of the first guard. She could see the flecks of gold in the brown irises of the second. Her two eyes became many as she simultaneously watched Doc clasp his hands over his ears and flee into the corner and the third guard lifting the sights of the rifle.

In one fluid moment, Sam dropped the remote onto the table and exchanged it for the pistol. She fired three shots because three was all she needed and each bullet flew to its target.

The first bullet lodged into the lead guard's chest. It hit center mass and his olive uniform shirt turned bright red. His eyes widened and then he crumpled to the floor. She thought of Jordan.

The second bullet caught Leo in the chin, and to her horror, the entirety of his lower jaw exploded. The man's fragmented tongue wagged loosely from unseen tendons, and then a moment later, he collapsed into a heap.

The last round hummed through the air. The golden slug pierced the man's skull, right between the eyes, and another spray of blood and gray matter coated the entryway of the dining room. The guard went down like a heavy sack of flour and the room went still.

"How did they know to come?" Sam asked. "Why have the alarms sounded?"

"The cameras," the General said. "We're always watching."

Sam released the grip she had on the shoe and the Soto breathed a sigh of relief. He started to turn around and she pressed the hot barrel of the gun to the back of his neck. He stopped turning and straightened. She switched the gun to her left hand expecting the weight of it to be awkward—her left had always been inferior to her right—but it wasn't. It felt as natural as her dominate hand, and somewhere deep inside of her, she knew it could deal just as much death and damage.

The room was quiet now. Not complete silence though. Sam's senses were too far attuned for there to be complete silence. She heard the alarm's muffled wail behind the thick wooden doors of the dining room and the doctor sniveling in the corner. She smelled ammonia and heard the trickling of liquid hitting stone. The inside of the General's pant leg was dark and wet and a small puddle collected underneath him. Sam took a step back.

"Don't move," Sam said.

"Okay."

She couldn't see his face but could tell that he was crying. "You're pathetic."

"Pl-please don't shoot me."

Sam picked the remote control up with her free hand and thumbed the red button marked *A*. "If I press this button and my friend doesn't snap out of it then you'll taste gunmetal right before I blow your spine out of the back of your neck."

"Wait!" General Soto shouted. The shoe shuddered as it hung from the busted socket. "Hit the middle button."

Sam didn't hesitate. She didn't have to. She heard the fear in the man's voice and she knew he had taken the threat seriously. She mashed the middle button and waited. Cole was everything that she had left in the world. If he didn't wake up then she didn't see much of a point to continue. She wouldn't go on witho—

"Miss Sam?"

Cole's voice brought the desperate thoughts to a screeching halt and Sam's eyes shot open. She spun to see the big man staring back at her. A fragile smile toyed at his lips, but she could tell that he was too scared or too confused to let it shine through.

"Cole," Sam said and ran over to her friend.

The mammoth man had just enough time to stand before Sam threw her arms around his neck and showered him with kisses on his forehead and cheeks. He wrapped his arms around her waist and lifted her high in the air, and for that one moment, all was right in the world again.

"Sam!" Cole shouted.

She turned. The General had taken off in a sprint toward the door. Calmly, she lifted the pistol from the table and discharged a single round. Her aim was lower than at the guards. She wasn't aiming to kill. Only to maim. Her shot connected and grazed the General's knee. Soto screamed in agony. His momentum carried him forward, and he slid to a stop next to the doctor who had crept from his corner toward the door.

"You going somewhere, Doc?" Sam asked, as she redirected her aim.

He shook his head from side to side and Sam lowered the pistol.

"What happened to me, Sam?" Cole asked. He looked her up and down and then touched her cheek. Her nose throbbed when he did.

"What happened to you?"

"There's no time to explain," Sam said. She handed him the remote control who took it without question. "Put it in your pocket and don't hit any buttons on it."

Cole nodded and shoved it into the hip pocket of the tuxedo pants.

"Can you walk?" she asked. She worried there would be side effects of the device.

Cole bent his knees, performed a couple of comic mini-squats and then nodded again.

"Good. Grab a rifle from one of the guards by the door," Sam instructed as she walked toward the door.

Soto lay in the fetal position on the floor surrounded by an ocean of blood. Some belonged to the General but most to the fallen guards. She walked over to him and then grabbed the shoe.

"This is going to hurt," Sam said.

"Wait—"

His plea erupted into a scream as Sam plucked the spiked heel from his eye. There was no eye though. Only a mangled, gooey socket remained. The remnants of his eyeball, still connected by the optic nerve, stuck momentarily to the point of the heel and then plopped in a blob against his cheek. Blood trickled from the wound and even more gushed from the hole in his leg.

"Can you patch him up?" Sam asked. "I don't need him bleeding out on the way."

Doc looked around at the bodies, paused on the gaping hole in the General's face, and then back to Sam. His opaque cheeks flushed green and he said, "I'll do my best."

"Don't do your best," Sam said. "Just a patch. He's not a long-term asset if you catch my drift."

"Screw you," Soto said.

Cole stepped past her, lifted a rifle from one of the fallen guards and then walked back toward the General. He grabbed the man by the collar of his uniform and lifted him mercilessly to his feet. Soto cried out in pain.

"I don't even think he needs a patch," Cole said. He pushed Soto so that all of his weight rested on the wounded leg and the General cried harder.

"I think you're right," Sam said.

"Who-who are you people?" Soto asked through blubbery tears.

"My name is Samantha Albright…" Sam answered. Her voice was cold and flat. The blow she had taken to the head *had* jarred something loose. A memory. A vague idea of who she really was and what she was designed for. Everything was still foggy, but she could see the outline of a bigger picture trapped somewhere in her brain.

"My name is Samantha Albright and I'm here to save the world."

7

The placards ascended from 471 to 481 and then finally reached 491. Sam paused for a moment outside of the garish doorway and rested the length of the cold steel barrel against her forehead. The blow to the table had thrown her senses into overdrive—all performing on some higher plane—and they hadn't returned to normal. Now, with her eyes closed, she listened for approaching footsteps of Soto's men but heard nothing.

"Where is everyone?" Sam asked. She thumbed the magazine-release button and let the empty clip fall to the floor. She pulled a full clip from the General's belt clip and slid it into the slot.

"Fortifying their positions," Soto answered. His voice was cold. "Preparing to kill you."

The only opposition they had encountered since leaving the dining room was an ambush by a handful of guards. Sam dispatched them with the same pinpoint accuracy as the first ones. It was as if possessed by some ancient gunslinger. Each time she pulled the trigger of the pistol, she felt the same cold malevolence, the same contemptuous disregard, for the sanctity of the soldiers' lives. Soto's troops protected and enforced the same sick, twisted morals of the bunker that the General had been so proud of. Each of her victims was one less predator feeding off the innocence of the children that ran this place. Now, she knelt outside of the biggest predator's homestead. And she was thirsty for blood.

She listed for a few more seconds. Nothing. "Open the door," Sam said.

Soto looked at her with his one sad puppy dog eye. His other eye— the mushy globule resting on the General's cheek—was still being supported by the thin, red cables of the optic nerve slightly visible through the caked and dried blood. When the General's good eye moved in her direction, Sam detected the slightest of twitches through the remaining mush, and fought the urge to vomit.

"That's not going to happen," Soto said.

"You heard the lady," Cole said and shoved Soto into the wall. The back of his head slammed hard against the gold placard and the General's knees buckled. Cole pressed him against the wall to keep him upright.

"I can't," Soto hissed. "The doors go on lockdown if the alarm is triggered. They can only be opened from the inside or once someone silences the alarms."

The answer was maddening. Sam pushed Cole aside, spun Soto so that his back was facing her and delivered a swift kick to the inside of his good knee. The General cried out as his knees slammed against the floor.

She grabbed a handful of Soto's still perfectly styled hair and yanked back. He tried to scream out, but Cole shoved a white cloth into his mouth. Sam looked to Doc, who was now missing a sleeve from his lab coat, and then to Cole, who offered a coy smile and subtle shrug. She almost allowed herself to return the smile, the long-forgotten facial expression flirting with the corners of her mouth, but forced it away. Instead, she refocused her attention on Soto, and yanked his head back even further, causing him to let out a muffled shriek.

Sam put her lips to Soto's ear, remembering how vulnerable she had felt when the situation was reversed, and whispered, "Seems like that information would have been helpful when I said that we were going to free Alexandria." Sam pressed the steel barrel of the pistol against his throat and nodded to Cole. The big man pulled the sleeve of the coat out of the man's mouth.

"I'm sorry," Soto's words weren't shaky as expected. Instead, they came out filled with venom, "but who the fuck is Alexandria?"

Sam's blood ran ice cold. She let go of Soto's black hair and grabbed the greasy ball hanging against his cheek and pulled. It sounded like a bandage being ripped too quickly from the skin and the slimy organ detached with an unexpected ease.

Soto screamed, but Cole was quick on the trigger and slammed the piece of cloth back into his mouth. The General collapsed to the floor, frantically pressing his hands against the gory, hollow orifice, and wept hard muffled sobs. Sam stared at the repulsive *thing* in her hand and then tossed it down the hallway. She wiped the gook from her hand onto the black dress and spun toward Doc.

The white-haired doctor looked incredulously back at Sam. He held both of his hands up in the air, despite the fact that she hadn't lifted her gun. His eyes were impossibly wide. His mouth stupidly agape.

"I'm sorry," he cried.

"You will be if this doesn't work." Sam said.

She grabbed him by the collar, dragged him to where Soto was standing only moments ago and pressed him against the stone wall. The doctor was even taller than Soto, but possessed none of the arrogance or clout. Sam pressed the barrel of the gun against the doctor's chest. "How are your acting chops?"

The doctor tried to answer, but his words came out garbled and indistinguishable. Sam chalked this up to fear and lowered the gun. She asked again.

"Can...you...act?" She paused between each word, giving the frightened man time to process the question. "Or do you want to end up like this guy?" Sam motioned toward the General.

Doc looked down at Soto and then back to her. "I can act."

"Let's hope so," Sam said and knocked on the door. "For your sake."

Sam pushed Doc in front of the peephole. He stumbled forward, caught his balance and righted himself. General Soto moaned and Cole delivered a swift kick to the man's kidney.

"Shut it, pal."

Soto let out a stifled yelp and resigned to sobbing.

Sam knocked on the door again. This time louder and with urgency. Her super-attuned senses detected movement behind the door and she heard a muffled voice. Sam nodded to Cole who raised his weapon toward the door.

Silence.

She was about to knock again when a feeble old voice spoke, "Who is it?" It belonged to President Gates and hearing it made Sam's blood boil with hatred. She nodded to the doctor who looked back at her dumbstruck.

"Answer him," Sam whispered.

"It's Reyes, my liege. Dr. Reyes." His voice was shaky and frightened and it disgusted Sam to hear the man address the heinous, vile, sorry excuse for a man on the opposite side of the door with such nobility.

"I heard the alarms, Doc," Gates said. "Is everything okay?"

Sam nodded at the doctor.

"Yes sir. Everything is fine."

"But I need you to open the door," Sam whispered.

"I need you to open the door," the doctor repeated.

There was a long pause followed by a very suspicious, "Why?"

"Tell him that you think Alex has been aiding us," Sam said, her voice barely audible. "Tell him that Soto sent you to bring her back with you."

"That would never happen," Doc said.

"Just say it!" Sam demanded, her jaw clenched so tight that she feared it would never open again.

"Dr. Reyes?" Gates asked.

"The girl," Doc said nervously, "General Soto would like to speak with her. He believes she has been aiding and abetting our guests. The outsiders attempted to escape when we were in the dining hall. That's the reason for the alarms, and the reason I am here now."

"And what happened to them?" Gates asked. Sam heard the concern through the doorway.

"Subdued," Doc said. He hadn't looked at Sam for an answer. She thought she detected the slightest bit of confidence as he continued. "We subdued both of them. The men took down the girl but the big one put up an awful fight. That's where the guards are now..." he paused, and then added, "dealing with the behemoth. I'll give you more details, but first please open the door, Jim."

There was another long pause and then the latch unlocked and the doorknob turned.

"I told Soto it was a bad idea to bring them here," Gates sputtered as he opened the door. The old man still wore nothing but the hideous gold chain and the skimpy pair of briefs. "I told that fool they'd be nothing but trouble. Especially that bit—"

President Gates didn't finish his sentence. As he exited out of the doorway, he caught his first glimpse of Sam and Cole standing beside the door. The old man attempted to retreat, but Sam quickly snatched the gold chain along with a handful of chest hair.

She raised the Desert Eagle until it was eye-level with Gates, "Hey there, stud. Mind if we come in?"

"Fuck me," Gates managed. He turned back to the bedroom with enough force that the clasp on the gold chain snapped. The President took off in a sprint into the depths of his lair, leaving Sam standing in the hallway with a handful of gold and gray.

"Dammit," she said and threw the medallion to the floor. She pushed past Doc and sprinted into Gates' chambers, quick on his heels.

As she entered the foyer, her adrenaline spiked again, sending her alien senses into uncharted waters. She could smell ancient oils used to create the paintings hanging on the wall. She smelled the musty, old newspapers framed in their glass cases. She felt every imperfection, each cracked and chipped tile of the finely polished black and white checkered floor underneath her bare feet. Her body and mind merged and ran seamlessly on all cylinders.

The old man disappeared through an adjacent doorway and she pursued him like a lion stalking a gazelle through some African grassland. But she wasn't tracking a helpless gazelle. She was hunting a predator. A sexual deviant. She was trailing a child molester and a rapist. A bastard to the core.

And that was fine, because she was a predator too.

She was a finely tuned machine. A killing machine. And when she caught up to Gates, she would rip his heart out of his chest and feed it to him. Because that's what she had been *designed* to do. Her blood turned cold as the word "designed" repeated through her brain. She forced it away and continued the chase.

Sam sprinted into the next room and her heart lurched. Alex was splayed across the bed, her arms and legs bound to the four posts with heavy chains. Her face was bloody and bruised and she lay motionless.

"Alex!" Sam screamed. She ran over to the helpless girl, temporarily giving up her pursuit.

Thankfully, upon closer inspection, the girl on the bed was moving. Her chest rose and fell so slightly that even a coroner might overlook it. The only other indication of life was the girl's eyelids which fluttered when Sam had screamed.

Sam's heart broke a million times over as she rounded the bed and got her first full look at Alex. The girl's face had been bashed in. Both her nose and her lips were busted and gushing blood. Both of her eyes were swollen like a boxer's at the end of a 15 round war. Despite all the perverted surgeries, Sam thought Alex had been pretty. Now, her face was unrecognizable as human. She dropped the pistol onto the mattress and grabbed ahold of the chain wrapped around her leg.

"You're going to be okay," she whispered as she frantically tore at the metal knot. The girl let out an inaudible moan and the remaining fragments of Sam's heart fractured into even tinier shards. "I'm going to get you out of here, I promise."

A single tear emerged in the corner of her swollen eye and rolled down her cheek.

"Cole!" Sam shouted. "Bring Doc in here."

She finished unraveling the first knot when the girl moaned again. This one filled with fear and panic. Sam grabbed the gun from the bed and spun in the direction she had been chasing President Gates.

Sam took a deep breath, and the moment froze.

She saw Gates running at her, hands extended above his head, clutching a long-handled ax so tightly that his orange knuckles had turned stark white. The ax, an antique battle ax from the 15th century, had a four-foot oak handle and a broad, steel blade. Sam didn't know how she knew this, but the information came pouring into her just like it had when she grabbed the General's gun.

More data streamed in. The exact weight and length. The circumference of the blade. Probable manufactures. It flooded into her instantaneously as if a receiver was buried deep in her brain. She blocked out the data-stream.

The details about the weapon that President Gates was holding over his head didn't matter, because this wasn't a disarm-and-pacify situation. This was a murder with ill-intent and cause extreme amounts of damage while doing so situation.

Sam aimed and fired two shots. The report of the gun was deafening, but the high-pitched scream of President Gates was even worse. The two slugs found their mark and disappeared into his groin. Crimson flooded from the seat of his underwear and his face twisted into a knot of anguish and disbelief. His eyes rolled back into his head and he took a staggered step forward. Then he bellowed a guttural moan and crumpled the ground.

The General bounded into the room and nearly fell to the floor. The imbalance caused by the shove of the giant behind him. Sam barely paid him any attention and instead refocused her attention to the chains wrapped around the girl's bruised wrist. Cole and Doc ran into the room a second later, Cole's rifle was drawn and the Doc's eyes were saucer wide.

"Oh, dear god," Soto cried out. "What have you done?" He dropped to his knees and stared at Gates.

"No!" Sam screamed. She crossed the room, blind with rage. "Don't you dare feel bad for this piece of shit." She waived the Desert Eagle at the fallen pedophile. Gates moaned as he convulsed on the floor and held a feeble bloodied hand above his face to shield himself from the oncoming blast.

"You should feel sorry for the child that's tied to the bed. You should feel sorry for the children you abuse here. Your daughters and your sons. You've turned them all into slaves."

She turned the pistol around in her hand, so she was gripping the metal barrel, and whipped Soto in the back of the head. He dropped to the ground and his face slammed into the puddle of blood originating from Gates' lap.

Sam returned to the bed. Cole had already freed one of Alex's legs and was working on the chain wrapped around her left arm. Sam worked on untangling the chain around her right and fought back the tears forming in her eyes. She managed to undo the knot after a few seconds.

Doc knelt on the bed and shined a penlight into one of Alex's swollen eyes and then the other. He placed the miniature flashlight in the breast pocket of his lab coat and extracted a pair of latex gloves from one of the lower pockets. He pulled them on and gently touched Alex's face, first under her cheeks and then around her jaw.

"Well?" Sam asked.

"Hard to know for sure," Doc said as he continued the examination. "Her right cheek bone is fractured and I'm fairly confident her nose is broken. Probable concussion." He slid his hand down the girl's torso and examined her chest and ribs. "I'll need some things from my medical bag to be certain or better yet we should get her to the medical unit."

"No," Alex whispered. "No surgery."

Sam's heart skipped a beat at the girl's voice and she grabbed Alex's hand. "You're going to be okay, sweetheart. Just stay with us." Alex didn't answer.

"Where's your doctor's bag?" Cole asked.

"There are several," Doc said. "My primary bag is in the office, but I have emergency kits spread throughout the facility."

Sam nodded, but her eyes stayed fixed on Alex's battered and bruised face. When she finally broke her gaze, she turned to Cole. He had also been staring at the girl. His face was flustered and red, and his bloodshot eyes were glassy. A trail of tears ran from each eye and disappeared into the depths of his bushy beard.

"Don't no one deserve nothin' like this, Miss Sam."

"No," Sam said quietly. "No one does."

Sam rummaged through the wardrobe next to the bed and found a sheet. She moved Doc aside and covered Alex's naked body. She whispered in her ear, "You're going to be okay."

"We need to find her clothes," Cole said.

Sam nodded but didn't immediately leave Alex's side. This girl had come to her when Sam was at her weakest and tried to help her escape. Sam wouldn't leave her now—when the girl was at her weakest. She deserved better.

Sam continued to stare at the girl's broken face, as Cole and Doc went to find her clothes. As much as she wanted start working on an escape plan, she couldn't push past the hatred she felt for the two men behind her. Sam thought of how large the bunker was, of how long this had been going on and how many girls had been made sex slaves of these disgusting men. Instead of an exit strategy, a white hot anger flooded her senses. She picked up the pistol and held it in her hand. There was more work to be done, and that work started now.

Sam spun on her heel. Soto's face was half smeared with blood and was slowly crawling toward his fallen comrade. Soto was the least of her worries. Sam would use him until he was useless to her.

She marched across the room and once again lifted the gun. This time Gates didn't lift his hand in fear. His skin had grown a sallow shade of white. His chest rose and fell at a breakneck speed matching each shallow breath.

"I hope there is a hell," Sam said coldly, "and I hope you rot in it for eternity."

Sam unloaded the remainder of the magazine into the vile man's face. Six shots in all. By the time the last shot was fired, his face was nothing more than a bloody wad of hamburger meat, completely devoid of any recognizable facial features. She continued to pull the trigger well after the sixth round had lodged into the dead man's face.

Cole put a gentle hand on her arm, forcing her to lower the weapon. Unwelcomed tears were streaming down her face as her heart broke over and over for the girl on the bed. And for all the children in Lost Angel. And for Rebecca. And for Jordan. She turned to her friend and buried her face in his chest.

"Don't you cry, Miss Sam," Cole whispered. "That was a bad, bad man. You did good by that girl."

Sam cried silently, and the tears abated soon after they started. She was growing cold on the inside. It was her training kicking in. What training? A blurred memory surfaced and vanished before she could grab hold of it.

"I found the girl's clothes," Cole said. His words brought her back.

Sam pulled away and let out a weak laugh as she saw the wet imprint of her face on the big man's white dress shirt. "Sorry." It was all she could manage.

"Don't you apologize to me, Miss Sam," Cole said and squeezed her shoulder. "Ain't no need for it."

"Okay." She wiped the remnants of her tears away with her bare arm.

"Doc found some pants and boots that might fit ya. Only found one top though. Figured we'd give it to the girl."

"Where's her clothes?"

"Torn to shreds."

Sam screamed and buried her foot into the General's bloated gut. Cole grabbed her before she could kick him again and carried her back to the bed. It took her a minute to calm herself.

"Thank you," Sam whispered.

Sam went to the bed and together with Cole and Doc they dressed her in Gates' long T-shirt over the girl's head. It hung down to her knees. The underwear had been ripped off of her as well as the rest of her clothes.

They placed her back on the bed and Sam pulled on the pair of khaki cargo pants. They were three sizes too big for her. She cringed at the thought of wearing the dead man's pants, but the repulsion quickly passed as the comfort of wearing something other than the skimpy dress took over. She unwrapped one of the chains from around the bed post and wrapped it twice around her waist, tied it in a crude knot and pulled the length of the dress over it. The pants were still loose but she would have to manage.

She wiped the blood from the bottom of her feet onto the bed sheet and slipped into the boots. They were only a size larger than her New Hope-issued tennis shoes. She tucked the excess fabric from the cargo pants into them and tied them as tightly as she could.

"How many bullets do you have left?" Sam asked Cole.

The firefight in-between the dining hall and the President's suite had been over quickly. Sam dealt the three fatal shots, but Cole had sprayed a wave of bullets of his own.

Cole pulled the clip from his rifle. "Ten in this mag." He snapped it back into place. "Plus a full mag in my pocket. You?"

"I'm empty," Sam said and motioned to the Desert Eagle on the floor.

"You wanna backtrack and pull a gun off one of those ingrates we left in the hall?"

Sam shook her head. She walked past Gates' body and picked the battle ax off of the floor. The oak handle was covered in blood. She stepped over to General Soto and wiped it on the back of his pressed shirt.

"No," Sam said. "This will do just fine."

Cole looked at her with an odd curiosity in his eye. "There's something different about you, Miss Sam."

Sam only nodded. There wasn't time to tell him about what she had seen in the dining hall or the terabytes of data sporadically downloading into her mind.

"Can you manage her?" Sam said and motioned toward Alex.

"Carried tool bags twice her size back in New Hope," Cole grinned.

The General groaned and lifted his head from the crimson puddle. Half of his face was coated in blood and dripped off him as he stared wide-eyed at what was left of Gates.

"What about him?" Cole asked and pointed to Soto.

"Kill the son of a bitch."

"Wait!" Soto screamed out. He shot up to his one good knee and held his hands up as if he planned on surrendering. "Please don't kill me. I can help you get out of here."

"I think we're capable of doing that on our own," Sam said. "We've got Doc to guide us out of here." She looked apprehensively at the doctor who gave a quick nod and looked back to the floor.

Cole raised the rifle and aimed it at Soto.

"There's more," the General screamed and squeezed his eyelids shut in the process. A fresh trickle of blood slammed out from the hollow eye socket when he did but Sam felt no sympathy for the man.

"More what?" Sam asked.

"The President's room," Soto cried. Fat crocodile tears rolled from his good eye and trailed down his bloody cheek.

"We're in the President's room," Sam said.

"Not this one," he spoke quickly. "The one in the mines. Close to the common area I showed you."

"So? Why would we care about some room down there?" Cole asked.

An awful smile emerged on his face—the wicked, horrible trademark smile—and Soto opened his eyes. "There's a computer down there. A secret computer. Only the President and myself, well, only I know about it."

"What's on it?" Sam asked.

"That I don't know, but—"

This time, Sam lifted her weapon. She reared the ax far behind her head and readied it for Soto's execution. She had every intention of splitting the man's stupid skull in half and ending his miserable excuse of a life. But right before she started her downswing—

"All it says is Concordia."

8

The group didn't encounter any guards on their way from Gates' Presidential Suite to the entrance of the mines. The great halls were empty and much to Sam and Cole's displeasure, General Soto couldn't— or wouldn't—provide any reasonable explanation for it.

"Maybe they've all left," Soto said. He chuckled and Sam kicked him swiftly in his bad leg.

They hadn't left. Invisible warning signs burned hot in her guts. Somewhere in the complex, a trap was waiting for them. She half-expected it to be wherever Soto was leading them, while the other half of her was terrified that it would be sprung as the group tried to exit Lost Angel. Either way, they were low on ammo and had only Soto as a bargaining chip…or a shield if it boiled down to it.

They continued to plunge deeper into the dark abyss. Soto led the way and Sam followed right behind him with her hand on his shoulder. Doc walked beside her and Cole brought up the rear. He carried Alex in his giant arms. Her broken body barely moved as she struggled with each breath.

"How much further?" Sam asked as they passed the mess hall. She couldn't see the door through the darkness but recognized the break in the lighting. Her voice echoed off the cavern walls and her arms erupted in gooseflesh.

"Not much," Soto said. "Near the bottom of the hill."

As they descended further into the mines, the pathway canted at a steep angle. By the time General Soto said 'Not much further' for the third time, the majority of her weight was on her heels to keep her balance.

Her other senses adjusted and compensated for her lack of vision. She heard each footstep of the General's hard-soled shoe followed by the other foot sliding along the rock floor. She heard water rush through unseen pipes running above their heads. Somewhere far off in the distance, she heard the soft thrumming of the generators.

She also grew alarmingly aware of the sudden drop in temperature and she thought of all the unfortunate souls that worked down here in the pitch-black cold. The child slaves. The true *Lost Angels*.

"Where are they?" Sam asked, taking a cue from Soto and dropping her voice to a barely audible whisper.

"I told you," Soto said. "They've probably left."

"Not the soldiers," Sam said. "The workers. Where are the children?"

"Still working. You don't think they'd up and stop production because of a couple alarms, do you? What kind of operation do you think we run here?"

Sam gave him a shove with the handle of the ax and the General stumbled forward. "The word enslavement comes to mind. What are you going to do after I free all the children? How will your precious Lost Angel survive?"

Soto didn't answer. Instead, he slowed his pace and placed his hand on the side of the cavern wall. Sam lifted the blade of the ax from her shoulder and her grip tightened around the wooden handle. It felt slick in her hands, the weight of it less than ideal, but she had no doubt that she could do what was necessary when the time came.

"I asked you a question," Sam said. She angled the steel blade of the ax and pressed it against the man's neck.

"We're here," Soto said.

Sam noticed the break in the string of lights and lifted the blade from Soto's neck. She placed her hand on the wall and felt where the jagged rocks became smooth, cold metal. She let her fingertips slide down the frame until they touched the steel handle. She tried to turn the handle, but it held firm.

"It's locked," Soto said.

Sam sneered at him. "I can tell. Open it."

Soto's hand darted for the utility belt around his waist. Sam let go of the door and gripped the handle of the ax with two hands. The General froze.

"Easy," he said. "Just getting the key. It's in my pocket. Don't cut my head off."

"I'm not making any promises."

"Well aren't you a ray of sunshi—"

Sam slammed the handle into the General's mouth. The blow sent him reeling back. And then the tears returned, and he started to sob.

"Stop crying and open the damn door," Sam said. "No one here feels sorry for you."

Soto wiped his cheeks on his sleeve and then pulled the key from his hip pocket. The clack of the lock sliding open boomed through the silent cavern and Sam's heart jumped into her throat. A hideous squeak followed and Sam held her breath. The room beyond the doorway was somehow darker than the pitch-black cavern.

Soto flipped an unseen switch and light burst forth from the room. Sam shielded her eyes and for a the briefest of moments she felt absolutely defenseless. If the General was going to try to escape then this would be his moment to do so. Instead, Soto stepped into the room and Sam followed without hesitation.

Sam stared in awe as her eyes adjusted to the bright fluorescent overheads. Giant monitors covered the entirety of the walls surrounding them. Every square inch from floor to ceiling. The screens were blank and their black frames were shiny, and at the bottom-center of each frame was a silver logo. A large C surrounding a tiny silver skyline of a city. It caused her stomach to twist into a violent knot.

Concordia.

Sam jumped and her attention was torn away from the logo as the metal door slammed shut behind her. She spun on her heel. Cole looked at her wide-eyed and then apologized. He placed Alex in an empty chair by the door and Doc grabbed the penlight from his pocket and began to reexamine her.

The interior of the room consisted solely of two large wooden desks that mirrored each other. They sat in the center of the room, one facing the doorway where they stood, the other facing the largest of all the monitors which encompassed the entirety of the rear wall.

"These monitors…" Sam said. Her voice trailed off.

"These monitors are how we protect our citizens," the General said, finishing her sentence. "Our watchful eyes in the sky. This is…was the President's private monitoring station."

"Turn them on," Sam whispered.

"I don't think—"

"Do it," Sam commanded.

Soto limped to the center of the room. He made a dreadful whimper with each step. He took a seat at the leather chair in-between the two desks and rolled up to the computer facing them. A moment later, he began typing on an unseen keyboard.

The entire computer unit was hidden from view. As Sam approached the desk, her battle ax still at the ready, she saw an embedded piece of glass in the center of the desk. Underneath the glass a flat-screen monitor angled up at the General. Soto typed commands furiously into the keyboard, his one eye scanning back and forth with each keystroke. Sam wondered if giving him free-reign to the computers had been a good idea but then the screens surrounding the room turned on simultaneously.

"Holy shit," Cole said. He pivoted and ran his fingers through his damp gray hair. "Pardon my language, Miss Sam."

"You're excused," Sam said as she gaped at the screens.

The images displayed around the room shed light on what Soto's 'watchful eyes' truly meant. On one wall, the screens were filled with dozens of rooms resembling lesser versions of the President's chambers. A section of screens monitored the gaudily decorated hallways and another on various rooms throughout the complex. Sam saw the hospital rooms and the dining hall. She cringed at the sight of a handful of screens focused on operating rooms.

She turned to the opposite wall and gasped as she got her first look at the children. The screens were tinted night-vision green, and each displayed heartbreaking scene after heartbreaking scene. Dozens of children littered each screen working furiously as they tunneled through the mines. Dirty children. Skeletal children. Hundreds of them in total. Hundreds of *lost angels.*

"You're monsters," Sam whispered.

Soto didn't answer her.

She walked down the length of the wall as she scanned through the screens. Midway down, her eyes fixed on two monitors. Neither possessed the green tint. One was fixed on a dozen men sitting around a long conference table.

The other displayed a room full of young girls ranging from 13 to 30. Most of their faces had been horribly transfigured by plastic surgery. Sam's skin crawled at the sight of them. Not out of disgust for the girls but rather at the men who did this to them.

The monitor above showed a bird's eye view of two stone structures; perfectly square in shape, with a pathway running in-between them. A fleet of soldiers surrounded the two buildings. Sam guessed one structure housed the girls, and the other contained the royalty. The rapists. The enslavers.

"Where is this?" Sam asked.

The General snorted and continued typing.

"You better answer the lady," Cole said.

"Those are the safe houses. They're in the heart of the mine," Doc said. "Not too far from where we are now. The pathway outside leads to a large opening within the cavern and the two buildings are there."

"Silence," Soto hissed.

Doc seemed to consider this for a moment and then continued, "The royalty are in the building on the left and the girls in the other. There's a supply bag in the room with the royalty. It's full of supplies. We keep it there for situations such as this one. In case of an intruder or a breach. In case they're trapped down there for a long time."

"I said silence," Soto snarled. "Why are you aiding them?"

"Because they're right," Doc said. He turned back to Alex. "We are monsters."

"You're a traitor," Soto seethed.

"Perhaps," Doc said. He lifted Alex's eyelid and flashed the penlight at the pupil. "A traitor to a city that's turned its back on its citizens. A traitor to traitorous men. Rather poetic, no?"

"It doesn't matter," the General said. He waived a dismissive hand toward the doctor and leaned back in the desk chair. "They're all in lockdown and you're ill-equipped to breach the safe houses. The city of Lost Angel will survive just like it so many times before. Even if you were to save a handful of workers, the men in that room will continue to repopulate this city. But that is a big if, isn't it?"

"You think we'll fail?" Sam asked. She couldn't believe the General's smugness after everything that had happened. "Do you honestly think you're prepared enough for—?"

"Prepared enough for you?" Soto roared with laughter and Sam felt the reproachful ire bubble in stomach. "We've lived through worse than you. Our people survived the fallout. We survived for a thousand years in this bunker. You don't think we'd let a couple of outsiders derail us, did you?" He flashed a spine-chilling smile and resumed typing.

"What are you doing?" Sam asked.

"I've taken a calculated risk bringing you here," the General said. He looked up at her. "While there *is* a computer in this room that says Concordia, the true reason I brought you here was to ensure you couldn't cause any more damage." He smiled again and then resumed typing.

"Stop what you're doing," Sam said and gripped the handle of the ax so tight her knuckles turned white.

"I don't think so," Soto said.

The room slowed and Sam's vision focused. Her heartbeat pounded between her ears and her muscles tensed. Every imperfection of the wooden ax handle amplified in her hands and she could feel every notch and groove. Sam took a step toward him.

Soto looked up and flashed the smile Sam had grown to loathe. Then he lifted a fist straight out ahead of him. He extended his index finger and pointed it to the keyboard.

"What are you doing?" Sam asked.

"I'm initiating the contingency plan."

"Don't move another in—"

Soto dropped his fist and his finger mashed down on the button. "Whoops."

Air hissed from the door and Sam watched in horror as it began opening on its own.

"What's happening?" Cole asked. "Close it back."

Soto ignored him. "Now, if you would focus your attention to the monitor above the door..." he paused and waited for them to look,"...our show is about to begin."

The screen above the door had remained blank, but the General hit another button and it flickered on. The camera was aimed at a steel door, similar to the one in front of them. The door on the monitor also began to open and Sam shrieked as its contents were revealed. A mammoth creature slunk from the doorway and then sprinted away. She only got a glimpse at the elongated face and beady orange eyes, but she recognized it at once. It was the creature from her dreams.

"What the fuck was that?" Sam yelled, not willing to accept what her brain was telling her.

"I think you know, Samantha," Soto said.

"I need your help, Cole." Sam dropped her ax and ran to the door. It was completely open. She shoved it but the heavy metal door didn't budge. Above her, the pneumatic door closer had extended fully. A locking mechanism had dropped into place to prevent it from shutting.

Cole joined her and the two pushed. Even with his added strength, the door refused to move. Cole looked up and began pawing at the device.

"We need you, Doc!" Sam yelled. The doctor was already on his way and he took the free spot between them. He threw his weight against the door, slipped and fell.

Soto burst out in laughter.

"Close the door, goddammit!" Sam screamed.

Soto laughed harder.

"I think I can get it," Cole said as he tore at the metal rod above the door.

Sam's blood turned cold as her heightened sense of hearing detected the thunderous footsteps echoing in the distance. "We have to hurry." She slammed her weight against the door and Doc did the same. She pushed with all her might, but it didn't move an inch.

"Keep working on it," Sam said and spun away from the door. She picked the battle ax off of the ground and marched back to the General.

"You know your weapons will be useless against them," Soto said evenly.

"Yeah, but they're not against you." Sam lifted blade above her head. "Close the door…now!"

"My dear, why do you think I brought you here?" The General leaned back in his chair and cupped both hands behind his head. "This is the end game for you and your little friends. This is assurance that the royalty will be safe. I will die as the honorific leader who sacrificed his life to make sure that the great city of Lost An—"

Sam swung as hard as she could and buried the ax deep into the top of his skull, splitting it straight down the middle. A geyser of blood erupted from the gore and covered Sam in buckets of red. General Soto slumped in the leather desk chair, the two halves of his face hanging from either side of the blade. After a moment, his lifeless body slipped out of the chair, and collapsed onto the concrete floor.

Sam gaped stupidly at the gruesome scene she had created. Where had this killer instinct had come from? Something shrieked outside of the room and she snapped back to the present. It was the same unearthly scream from her nightmare. She knew what was coming for them.

It was a midnight runner.

"How's it coming on the door, boys?" Sam asked. She sat down in the desk chair and turned to the computer.

"This damned lock won't give," Cole said. Veins popped from his head and forearms as he pulled on the rod.

Sam's heart thumped wildly in her chest and she focused on the computer monitor. If the Soto opened the door with the computer then she could shut it. She had to believe that.

The screen was black with a single word displayed in the upper left hand corner:

Override

And beside it:

(Y/N):

A green cursor rhythmically appeared and then disappeared.

The beast shrieked again. It was much closer. Sam's skin turned to gooseflesh and the thin hairs on her arm stood on end. The monitor had cycled to an open doorway and Sam could faintly make out the lower half of a computer desk. Her computer desk.

"Any luck?" Cole asked. It drew her attention back to the computer.

The keyboard was smeared in blood, but she could read a portion of the buttons. She quickly tapped the button marked 'Y', hit the 'Return' button and held her breath.

The word 'Override' disappeared and was replaced by a far more daunting one.

Password:

Sam's heart sank into her stomach. There was no time to guess what could be an infinite number of words, or letter/number combinations. They were doomed.

"Miss Sam?" Cole yelled. "Something's coming."

"Think!" Sam yelled at herself.

David is the key, Jordan whispered from the recesses of her brain.

Her eyes lit up. It was a moment of clarity similar to the one in the dining room after her skull was slammed into the table. A distant memory, one from long ago, flashed through her mind, and this time she grabbed ahold of it. She typed a word and then looked down at the screen. Her heart lurched.

Password: David

"Miss Sam?!"

She let her finger hover for a split-second and then mashed it. The screen filled with green text and then a hiss filled the room. A wave of relief washed over her as the door began to close.

"It's not going fast enough!" Cole screamed.

Sam ran back to the door, lodged herself in the middle and the three of them pushed. The door continued to close at its own speed. A scream ripped through the hallway. Sam stepped back from the door and looked to the monitor. Her heart seized.

There wasn't one beast outside of the door. There were six of them. They stood in a cluster on the other side of the door as it closed as if they were waiting for a cue to enter. The door was a little more than halfway shut, but there was still room for at least one of them to get in.

Sam gasped and took a horrified step back. She signaled for Cole and Doc to stop and they did. She held a finger to her lips and pointed to the monitor. The two men stepped away from the door and looked. Their eyes grew wide and their jaws fell open in unison.

"Christ in a hand basket," Cole said and when he did one of the monsters lunged forward.

"Grab your gun," Sam screamed.

Cole snatched his rifle from the floor and wheeled on the door which was now three-quarters of the way shut. Doc sprinted to Alex who was closest to the door. He grabbed her and carried her towards the rear of the room. Sam turned back to Soto, grabbed the ax handle, and tugged. The blade held firm, lodged deeply between layers of muscle tissue and bone.

Sam pulled again, and the blade pulled free. She spun back to the door and a large scaly arm emerged from the darkness. Sam gasped. The arm was long and muscular and the skin of the beast was orangish-pink. Sharp jagged claws dug into the metal door frame and created a blood-chilling screech as it pulled itself into the doorway. The door vibrated against its arm, still trying to close.

"Whatever happens," Sam said and gripped the ax handle tighter, "I just wanted to say thank you...for everything."

"Miss Sam, with all due respect, we ain't come this far to die here."

Cole lifted the muzzle of the rifle and squeezed the trigger. The sound of gunfire melded with the screams of the beast as round after round lodged into its arm. Instead of retreating, the midnight runner lurched forward and shoved its shoulder through the door.

Sam didn't wait for Cole to reload. She ran toward the door, ax held high over her head, and let out a primal scream. A scream almost as unearthly as the one emitted from the creature behind the door. A scream from deep within her.

"Sam, no!"

But Sam didn't listen. She swung the blade and connected with her target. The sharp edge of the ax plunged into the creature's bicep. Dark red blood exploded from the wound and the midnight runner screamed out. Sam dislodged the blade but didn't give the creature time to withdraw its wounded appendage. She lifted the ax again and when she swung she found the same spot with extreme precision. This time the blow severed the creature's arm, and it fell to the ground. Blood sprayed wildly from the wound, and a second later, the monster disappeared.

The door shut.

There was long moment of silence and then a loud *THUD*.

The noise caused Sam to jump, her heart still thumping in her chest like an ensnared jackrabbit trying to kick its way out.

THUD.

Sam backed away from the door and looked up to the monitor. The creature lifted its good arm slowly and banged against the door. *THUD.* A bloody stump dangled at the other side. The other five stood behind their leader, motionless.

THUD.

THUD.

After a moment, the banging sped up and Sam watched as the rest of them joined in. They slammed their giant fists against the door. She stepped back slowly, still clutching her ax. She was worried the door would give way to the creatures' massive weight and power. In the corner of the room, next to the door, the severed claw was clinched in a fist and it gyrated with each bang on the door.

Ten minutes later, the thudding finally stopped.

"What now?" Cole asked.

Sam looked up at the monitor. The creatures had stepped away from the door, but they were still out there. They huddled together in a tight group as if they were a football team coming up with some sort of trick play to fool their opponents.

"Now, we wait," Sam said and dropped the ax to the floor.

9

The monitors encircling the room continued to cycle. All except one. The wall-sized monitor remained dark. Sam stared at it for a long time and then turned her gaze to the others. Cole had taken on the added responsibility of nursemaid and helped Doc lay Alex's broken body out on the floor. The girl still hadn't moved and Sam wondered if she would be able to leave her if their lives depended on it. Killer elite or not...Sam didn't think so. If push came to shove, she didn't know if she could leave the Doc either. But she wouldn't let him know that.

The Doc went through his routine of shining the penlight into her eyes and checking her pulse. Groan. Repeat. An hour had passed since the door had shut and he reemphasized the pressing matter of getting Alex back to the medical offices numerous times.

Sam ignored each one.

Not because she didn't care. Sam cared about the girl immensely and knew time was of the essence. But no matter how much she cared, Sam didn't have a plan for dealing with the monstrosities on the opposite side of the door. Doc looked up at her and she promptly spun a quarter-turn to her right to avoid his menacing glare.

The monitors on the wall displayed live footage of the children working emphatically on the giant generators. The large metal machines dwarfed them in size, but the children clambered up and down the ladders at breakneck speed. The video feeds cycled through countless sunken faces, bloated bellies and haunted eyes. Slaves of Lost Angel. She would free them all if she had time. But if the creatures outside the door had their way, it might not be an option.

She turned her chair again.

The monitor above the door displayed the group of midnight runners. They remained in their tight huddle. Sam stared at the monsters. They took breath in unison, their hulking bodies rising and falling simultaneously. Two black horns jutted from each giant forehead. They curved out like the horns of a steer and ended in sharpened spikes. Their massive heads pitched and rocked back and forth in rhythmic time with one another.

She turned again.

Screens full of empty rooms and dead bodies.

She rotated in the chair once more, back to her original starting place, and faced the dark screen. The screen that dwarfed all the other screens. Why was this one turned off? What was it hiding?

Sam twirled 180 degrees, and she faced the door. The computer screen had gone blank once more, except for the neon green command prompt. Absently, she let her hands fall to the keyboard and let her fingers gently rest on the faded keys.

She couldn't remember ever using a computer but the positioning of her fingers came natural. The few legible letters on the keyboard were out of order and most were either faded from overuse or still covered in Soto's blood, yet she knew where they all were without looking directly at the device.

The vague feeling of remembrance—muscle memory perhaps—felt strange and the intermittent data that continued to be fed from some unseen encyclopedia in her mind was even stranger.

"Cole," Sam said. She beckoned for her friend to come closer.

The big man brushed a thick strand of purple hair from Alex's face, whispered something to the doctor and then came over to her. "You have a plan, Miss Sam?"

"Not exactly," Sam admitted. "I just wanted to know if anything has changed for you since we've been here."

Cole seemed to contemplate this for a moment and then shook his head. "Naw. Not really. Just a headache I can't seem to shake."

She had forgotten about the device in the back of his head. Chills ran up her spine.

"You care to enlighten us about that, Doc?" Sam asked. "You mind telling my friend why there's some sort of receiver implanted into the back of his skull and a remote control that will wake him from a vegetative state."

Cole's face flushed. "What do you mean?" He rubbed the backside of his head. "What is this?"

Sam ignored him. "Or telling me why I suddenly possess the abilities of a blood-thirsty mercenary?"

"I can answer the questions about your friend," Doc said, "and if you'd like me to postulate a theory about your condition, I can do that as well. But now is not the time."

He looked up from Alex and Sam was almost taken aback by the sad, desperation in his eyes. It seemed he really did mean what he said to the General. That he really did feel like a monster.

"We should be focused on getting out of here as quickly as possible," Doc continued. "This girl needs medical attention and judging by the swelling in your face, so do you."

Sam had forgotten all about her own pain. Her face throbbed dully from the blow to the dining room table. She ran a finger over her busted lip. "What do you suggest?"

The doctor rose from his patient and crossed the room to Sam. She looked up at him and tried her best not to cringe at his deformed face. "My suggestion..." Doc paused, placed a thumb on each side of Sam's nose and then pushed hard.

SNAP.

Sam screamed out as the cartilage was forced back into place. Bright stars filled her vision, and she fought the urge to vomit. The feeling passed after a moment and a sense of relief washed over her.

"My suggestion is we find a way out of here." The doctor examined her face a moment longer and then went back to Alex without another word.

"What were you talking about, Miss Sam?" Cole whispered once Doc was out of earshot. "About me being a vegetable?"

"You know the device I gave you?"

Cole fished the small remote control from his pocket.

"When I found you," Sam said and gently it from his hand, "you were in some sort of catatonic state. I pushed the one in the middle and you just sort of snapped out of it."

Cole thought about this for a long moment and then asked, "What do you think that means?"

"Why don't you ask him?" Sam asked and pointed toward Doc.

Cole nodded and returned to Alex and Doc. After a moment, she heard them whispering amongst each other. Angry whispers. Sam shoved the remote into her pocket and tried to think.

She pushed the murmurings from her mind and focused all of her energy on her fingers. Doc was right. They needed to get out of this room. They needed a plan. One that didn't involve fighting their way through the midnight runners. All she needed was a little help.

Sam. As if on cue, Jordan's voice filled her mind. She couldn't see him but knew he was there—standing beside her. His presence comforted her.

"I'm here," Sam said aloud.

"What's that, Miss Sam?" Cole asked.

She waved a dismissive hand at him. Cole shrugged and resumed his talk with the doctor, his giant hand clasped around Doc's shoulder and the doctor's deformed eyes wide. She closed her eyes and prayed the connection hadn't been broken.

What are you waiting for, Sam? You know what you have to do. The mission is waiting on you. Concordia is waiting on you.

Sam's eyes opened as Jordan's words echoed through her. She typed a word onto the keyboard and the she looked at the screen.

CONCORDIA

The word had become the bane of her existence. It was the reason Jordan had been taken from her. And also the reason she kept breathing. It was her motivation to not give up and let the beasts outside have their dinner. She had to justify Jordan's death. She had to make sure his sacrifice wasn't in vain.

Her right index finger hesitated over the 'Return' button and she held her breath.

"Everything alright, Miss Sam?" Cole asked

Sam didn't answer. Instead, she mashed the button.

Another loud hiss of air filled the room and Sam jumped to her feet. Her breath caught in her lungs and her eyes darted toward the heavy steel door. A second later, Cole appeared at her side with his rifle cocked and aimed. But the door didn't move, and after a moment, Sam managed a breath.

The hissing wasn't coming from the door but rather from behind them. She turned slowly to see the top of the other desk opening. A large square in the center of the desk appeared first. The wood panel lowered and then split down the middle. The two panels retracted inside of the desk and then the hissing paused. When it resumed, an ancient computer monitor emerged from the newly formed hole and rose from the belly of the desk. At the same time, a panel on the front of the desk slid open, and a keyboard popped out. Once the computer had fully emerged, the hissing stopped and silence filled the room. Sam sat down hard in the chair and was face to face with the mysterious monitor.

This computer was much older than the one behind her. Its drab gray color was coated in a thick layer of dust and the screen was curved and thick. On the bottom right hand corner of the monitor was a square button, and beside it, the word: MicroApple.

Sam hit the button and the screen flickered on.

The screen rolled through lines of foreign text and numbers. When they stopped, a chill ran up Sam's spine as she read what was on the screen.

A sentence lined the top of the monitor. Sam's skin erupted in gooseflesh as she read the words aloud, "Concordia Remote Terminal 36."

"Did you say, what I think you did?" Cole asked.

"Concordia," was all that Sam could manage.

Underneath this was another sentence that made even less sense. Sam gulped hard and read this one aloud as well, "Copyright 2032 by the MicroApple Corporation."

"2032?" Cole asked.

"The year the virus was released," Sam said.

Judging by the state of the monitor, 2032 had been many, many years ago. Her hands once again rested on the keyboard and she mashed the 'Return' key. The words on the screen disappeared and were replaced by another password prompt. Sam hesitated and then typed in David's name. She held her breath and hit return.

PASSWORD INCORRECT

Sam thought for another moment and then typed Concordia onto the screen. She pressed return again and again the monitor returned:

PASSWORD INCORRECT

She typed a succession of words now, hitting return after each one. First, she tried: 'Lost Angel', and then: 'New Hope.' She tried: 'Infected' and 'Halfways.' She tried the names of each of the two leaders of Lost Angel: 'Soto' and then 'Gates.' Each time the screen returned a simple:

PASSWORD INCORRECT

"Damn it," Sam muttered after the umpteenth attempt.

Cole had joined her beside the monitor but stood silently, not offering any thoughts of his own. She looked up to him, and he shrugged. Sam was on her own. Once again, she closed her eyes and waited for Jordan. After what seemed like an eternity, he finally answered her.

You know what the password is, Jordan said.

"Not this time," Sam answered. "I don't."

Yes, you do.

"But it can't be," Sam said as two words fluttered through her brain. She swallowed hard, and a chill ran up her spine.

Why? Jordan asked.

"Because it just can't."

Why?

"Because it's fucking impossible!" Sam screamed.

Her heart beat furiously inside of her chest and tears stung at her eyes. She forced herself to take a deep breath and then another. The two words that had fluttered through her mind only a few moments before reappeared.

Try it.

"No."

David is the key...and YOU are the light.

"Jordan, I can't...this is crazy."

Try it. For me.

Sam sighed. Jordan knew she wouldn't be able to not type them in now. He knew she would never disgrace the memory of him by refusing his request...even if his request was nothing more than a figment of her imagination. Even if his request was her own.

Sam let her fingers fall back to the keys and when she opened her eyes tears fell out of them. Slowly, her fingers typed the two words as saltwater streamed down her cheeks. By the time she finished, she was sobbing. She hadn't noticed Cole's big hand resting on her shoulder. She looked up at the screen and read the two words:

SAMANTHA ALBRIGHT

She took a breath, wiped her eyes and hit the return key.

PASSWORD ACCEPTED

The sight of it made her want to vomit but the words quickly disappeared. They were replaced by a single word:

CONNECTING

The word was followed by a succession of dots that continued to replicate. First, only a few and then as the seconds ticked by, they filled a quarter of the screen. And then half. By the time they reached the three-quarter mark, Sam's nerves had quelled. And then the monitor on the opposite side of the room flickered on.

The screen didn't immediately illuminate. Instead, the darkness only lightened a bit and stayed that way for a long moment. Somewhere, either being pumped in through the speakers above them, or perhaps on the built-in ones of the monitor...it sounded like a phone was ringing.

Finally, after what seemed like an eternity, the screen exploded with color. On the screen was a man, half naked and covered by the sheets of his bed, the light being emitted from a bedside lamp. He wore a very tired expression on his face. His bleary eyes were bloodshot and his gray hair was disheveled.

The man's eyes were not fully open when he began speaking. "This better be good, Gates. It's fucking Sunday for Christ sakes." His voice was gruff, but much to Sam's dismay, it contained a familiarity that sent chills up her spine.

"Gates is dead," Sam said.

The man's eyes shot open wide, and he stared back at them with an intense fear. The man looked as if he wanted to speak, as if he needed to speak, but couldn't. Sam took this as a cue to continue.

"Gates is dead and so is Soto." She motioned to the floor, not sure if the man could see the General's corpse lying in a pool of blood and feces.

"It can't be," the man on the screen whispered, "it's far too soon." He snatched something off screen, and a moment later, he was speaking rapidly, "We've got a code red at facility 36. I repeat, a code red at 36. Yes, I'm sure." The man looked back at the screen, his face gray, and then added, "I'm looking right at her, sir." The screen went black.

"What do you think that was all about?" Cole asked.

Sam shrugged. Whatever it had been, the man on the screen had been expecting Sam to call, just not so soon. And judging by his reaction, it wasn't some stranger's face that had him all riled up. No. This man knew Sam…and somehow she knew the man.

The monitor beeped and Sam turned her attention to it. The screen now read:

SELF-DESTRUCTION SEQUENCE ACTIVATED

"That's not good, Miss Sam."

"No, Cole," Sam said, "That is not good at all."

There was no countdown timer accompanying the words, so Sam had no way of telling how long they had. Nor did she have any idea what would happen when the unseen timer reached zero. It was possible the computer would fry itself from the inside. It was also possible that the entire underground city of Lost Angel would implode. Either way, she planned on being gone.

Sam plucked Cole's rifle from the floor, pressed the butt of the gun to her shoulder and fixed her aim on the door. They would have to shoot their way out and then back to the upper levels. The odds were far from good, but something from deep inside of Sam assuaged her nerves. Her mind knew what needed to be done.

Sam looked to the monitor above the door. She waited as it cycled through countless views of abandoned hallways before landing on the camera pointed on the outside of their door. She blinked twice to make sure that her eyes weren't deceiving her. The midnight runners were gone. A cold ball of steel formed in Sam's guts.

"You see that, Cole?" Sam asked and nodded to the monitor.

"Those monsters are gone."

"Why?"

"Don't make no sense," Cole said. He knelt down beside the girl and lifted her up with ease. Gently, he swung her body over his shoulder. The girl moaned and then muttered something inaudible.

"What'd she say?" Sam asked.

Alex repeated her words, Doc listening intently beside her. He turned to them and said, "She said we have to get her brother. That Sam promised we would."

Sam's heart sank into her stomach. She had made a promise and now faced with uncertainty she had to make a choice. Her mind flashed to Jordan and to Rebecca, the only family she had since being relocated to New Hope.

Sam looked back to the words on the monitor and then to the screen displaying the empty hallway. They didn't have time to wait while she thought of all the pros and cons of a rescue mission. They would have to seize the opportunity, regardless if the beasts were hiding just out of view of the camera. They would have to go now…deeper into the mines.

10

The craggy passageway was empty just as the monitor had depicted. Sam led the foursome out of the late President's office, the rifle raised and pressed against her shoulder. Cole followed close behind, now cradling Alex's crumpled body as a groom would carry his new bride over the threshold on their wedding night. The doctor brought up the rear and Sam wondered if it was fear or an actual desire to help that drove him to continue. She hoped for the latter as they plunged deeper into the darkness.

They moved silently down the near pitch-black corridor. After a few minutes, the slope of the pathway leveled and then spilled out into a monstrous cave. Jagged stalactites hung ominously from the cavern's ceiling nearly 50 feet above them and moonlight poured in from a large opening in the center of the ceiling. It bathed the two stone buildings in the heart of the massive chamber in soft white light.

The buildings were 200 square feet in area and ten feet tall, each with a flattened roof and a wooden door built into the front. A small pathway, barely large enough for a man to walk through, was nestled in-between the edifices. Surrounding the two structures were soldiers, each armed with an assault rifle.

The buildings cast dark shadows over the cavern floor and Sam could barely make out their outlines. She counted a dozen in total but estimated there was at least one of two hidden in the darkness. The room was dead silent except for the soft drone of the generators humming from the depths below.

Sam turned back to the group and silently pointed two fingers at her eyes and then pointed to a spot further along the cavern wall. A hundred yards along the wall, barely visible, was a cropping of stalagmites, just large enough for them to hide behind. Cole and Doc nodded. Without any further cues, Sam turned and slithered out into the darkness toward the barrier.

Sam's skin turned to gooseflesh as she hugged the cool cavern walls. The pants provided some comfort but the sleeveless top of the dress was paper-thin. She longed to be back in the dirty, bleach-spotted coveralls.

"You hear something?"

Sam froze at the sound of the guard's voice. It was only a whisper, but she heard it in stereo. Cole, on the other hand, hadn't and nearly barreled her over. Sam motioned for them to hunker down.

"Nah," another guard said. "Those creepy-crawlers got your panties in a bunch, Xavier?"

An eruption of laughter spread through the group of soldiers.

"Those creepy-crawlers are no joke, man."

Another wave of laughter.

Sam motioned for the group to continue.

When they arrived at the outcropping, Cole gently put the girl down on the rocky ground. The doctor did his penlight routine and Sam got into position so she could see building's entryway. After a moment, Cole joined her.

"You think they saw us?" he whispered.

"If they did, I think we'd be dead."

"You gotta plan?"

There was a long pause as Sam contemplated this. The 16 bullets in the clip of the rifle would be enough if every one of her shots were dead on. The four extra bullets even provided some wiggle room. But if there were more soldiers hiding around the rear of the buildings or if the darkness affected her accuracy, then they would be sitting ducks. The plan to shoot it out wasn't a viable option.

"No," she said.

Sam's eyes darted around the room, but there was nothing to indicate another plan would be any more plausible.

Jordan's voice filled her mind once more, *Midnight runners.*

Sam sighed.

"The enemy of my enemy is my friend," she whispered.

"What does that mean?"

She didn't answer him. The answers would come soon enough. But she couldn't chance telling him that she was about to risk their lives on a hunch from her dead boyfriend. Time was already running out. The self-destruction sequence had been activated. She would have to act fast.

Without a word, she lifted the rifle, took aim at one of the thinner overhanging stalactites, and squeezed the trigger. The sound of the gunfire was deafening. The blast echoed off the canyon walls causing Cole to quickly throw his giant hands over his ears. He looked to her, his eyes wide and filled with shock.

The bullet hit its target, separating the rocky spike at its midpoint. It rocketed toward the ground and a handful of soldiers dove out of the way as it collided into the hard floor of the cave and exploded in a dust cloud of debris.

"As long as they didn't see the muzzle blast, I think we'll be okay," Sam whispered.

To her horror, Cole responded in a yell, "What'dya say?"

Sam's eyes grew as wide as Cole's had at the shock of the gunshot, and then Cole's grew even larger at the realization of his mistake. Through the rocky barrier, Sam saw the guards turn toward them and a moment later a cacophony of gunfire exploded through the caverns.

Sam and Cole both threw their hands over their ears and slid down as far as possible as bullets slammed into the rock wall behind them. The doctor used his body as a shield and draped himself over Alex.

Wave after wave of bullets lodged into the rock wall and each time Sam's heart skipped a beat. Death was close now. She could feel its icy touch on her skin. In only a few moments, she would be reunited with Jordan. Her mission failed but her heartache over. Shards of rock exploded above and debris rained down on top of them. Cole pulled her close to him and then covered her head with his giant arms.

After what seemed like an eternity, the gunfire died off. Sam managed to quell the fear coursing through her body and broke free of Cole's grasp. She raised her head slightly until she could see through the rocks. From her position, she heard muffled screaming, could see the soldiers reloading, some already drawing aim on them again. She dropped back down again, preparing for the next wave of gunfire when suddenly the unearthly screams of the midnight runners ripped through the cavern. Not just one but all of them. And they were close.

Sam drew a finger to her lips and Cole nodded his head feverishly. The doctor rolled off of Alex and much to Sam's dismay, the girl's beautiful purple eyes were wide-open and filled with terror. The sight sent Sam's anxiety into overdrive. She tried to steady her breathing but instead her breaths came more quickly, each one more shallow than the last. Her heartbeat doubled and then seemed to treble to the point of pain, as hot blood was forced through her arteries. Her palms became clammy. Her pupils constricted to the size of pinheads, causing the world to grow dark and blurry. And then again she heard the disharmony of screams and she knew that the monsters had arrived.

Terrified shouts from the soldiers melded with the shrieks of the midnight runners and created a ghoulish opera. They lasted only a moment before a fusillade of bullets ripped through the air ending the macabre ensemble and Sam covered her ears once more.

And then there were more screams. Different kinds of screams. Screams from the soldiers. Bone-chilling, blood-curdling screams. Sam squeezed her eyes shut and waited for the horrible nightmare to be over with. She had bet on the wrong team and now she prayed the midnight runners would kill them quickly once they were done with the soldiers.

The screaming finally desisted, and for a long moment, there was nothing but silence. Sam's entire body trembled and her heart jack-hammered in her chest as she awaited the midnight runners to ascend their tiny barrier and finish the job. The doctor was on his hands and knees, his head bowed underneath his chest, in what Sam could only think of as a crude prayer position. Alex's eyes had closed and again she was lying motionless. Cole, his face stricken with worry, placed a giant, calloused hand over one of hers.

A gunshot broke the silence and then a man screamed out. This scream, however, was not filled with terror or pain but rather victory. It was fused with a sick laughter and Sam couldn't tell which was worse. It was a familiar voice despite of this. It belonged to Eric.

"Take that you motherfuckers!"

Another gunshot.

"You bastards aren't going to take me out! No sir. Not today. Not ever!"

Two more gunshots.

"I run this bunker, bitch."

More gunshots.

More profanity.

Sam took a deep breath and braved raising her head so she could see. From her vantage point, she saw the heaps of bodies and blood strewn across the cavern floor. Mixed in with the human bodies were those of the midnight runners. The massive creatures were twice the size of any man, but their corpses were lying as motionless as the soldiers.

In the center of the aftermath was Eric. His face was bathed in moonlight and Sam shuddered at the sight of him. Blood dripped from a dark goatee, his face as mutilated as the doctor's, but twisted in a sinister sneer. He walked through the crowd of bodies, the muzzle of his gun sweeping back and forth between the hulks spread out on the floor. He paused at one, fired another shot, the creature's body seized and jerked and then went still. He laughed manically and then he continued his sweep.

Sam lifted the barrel of her rifle, rested the stock in-between two narrow rocks and set her sights on the man. She wanted to take advantage of the moment and put a quick end to this victory party before he remembered his original target. This act of cold-blooded aggression might offend Cole or Doc, but Sam didn't feel any remorse. She knew this soldier was as guilty as all the others and she needed to put him down like the rabid dog that he was.

She wrapped her finger around the trigger but paused right before squeezing. Looming over the man, balanced like some sort of majestic bird on the stoop of the building, sat one of the creatures. Its wide jaw was open and the razor-sharp teeth were dripping wet with blood. Its muscular hind legs perched eloquently on the edge of the roof, gripping the stone with ease. Sharp claws on one giant hand hung in midair over the victor below. Only a bloody stump remained of where the other hand should have been.

Sam contemplated shooting the creature from its perch and then dealing with the man below fairly, but she never got the chance. The creature jumped down noiselessly and landed on the lone survivor from the group. The man collapsed under the weight of the beast and Sam watched in horror as it wrapped the massive claw around the man's throat and promptly detached Eric's head from his torso.

"Good god," the doctor whispered.

She felt the knot in her stomach tighten as the beast lifted the severed head of the man into the sky. It stared at it for only a moment and then shoved it into its mouth. The creature chewed once, the blood-curdling crunch of bone grinded against the razor-sharp teeth of the beast, and then it swallowed. The midnight runner lifted its head into the sky and howled. Sam seized the unexpected opportunity.

She hopped up from her position, took aim and unloaded the clip. The midnight runner spun toward her when she popped up, but its eyes went wide as the first of the slugs lodged into its chest. Sam kept the trigger squeezed tight and counted as each of the 15 rounds found its target. Each one buried into the chest and abdomen of the beast.

The last round disappeared into the creature's chest and Sam watched as its eyes went cold. It took two steps forward, stumbled and then collapsed into a heap.

Sam stood still, her heart echoing between her ears, her stomach clinched so tight that she could puke, terrified that the beast would rise back up or that another would emerge from the shadows to finish the job, but nothing happened. When Cole placed a hand on her shoulders, she screamed before resigning to a flurry of quick jabs to the big man's chest.

Ten minutes after Sam had killed the midnight runner, she swung the door open to the building. The long conference table had been abandoned. Cowered behind it, on the opposite side of the room, were the royalty—huddled together and trembling. There was one soldier who had been assigned to wait inside with them, but he didn't attempt to raise his weapon. Sam pointed her rifle in his direction and motioned for him to drop his rifle which he did without question.

"Evenin', fellas," Sam said, her voice almost whimsical.

The men didn't answer her, nor did any of them rise from the floor. Some had drug their leather chairs to form a makeshift wall for what Sam could only guess was protection. A few peaked out from behind, but didn't dare make eye contact with her.

"Doc, get your bag," Sam said. She was unwilling to waste any time on the animals residing in the room. They were all dead men walking in her opinion.

The doctor squeezed past her and entered the room. He went to the far corner without making eye contact with any of the dignitaries, grabbed a large leather bag from the seat of a chair and returned to her.

"I'll be with the girl if you need me," Doc said. He looked back to the men and then added, "I pray that you won't."

Sam nodded, and the doctor exited the structure.

"Wh-what do you want from us?" a white-haired man stuttered from behind a tall leather-backed chair.

"I want you to stop asking questions before I put a bullet through your brain, Chief," Sam said. She surveyed the room to make sure she had their undivided attention and then continued, "Now, there's nothing else I'd love to do than unload this clip on you sick, old perverts and blow every one of your dicks clean off." She watched as the old men squirmed. "Your families might have kept this city alive for hundreds of years, but all you've managed to do is to turn your own children into slaves. It's a perversion so corrupt and evil that even your ancestors would be rolling in their graves. You should be ashamed of yourselves."

Silence.

"I hope you all rot in hell."

She exited back into the cave where the girls from the adjacent building had been waiting. A few were armed with the rifles and revolvers from the fallen soldiers. Sam scanned the crowd, her eyes landing on a blonde-haired girl toward the back of the crowd.

"Do you know Alex?"

The girl nodded.

"Do you know her brother?"

"Yes."

"Bring him here," Sam said. "Cole will go with you in case you run into any resistance." She half-expected some sort of pushback to the request, the girl undoubtedly knowing what she was about to miss, but instead the blonde-haired girl nodded and took off toward the rear of the building. Sam watched as she and Cole disappeared down a corridor in the back of the cave.

She looked back to the group and eyed the girls. All of them had been modified in some way or another. Augmented breasts were coupled with liposuction and glute implants. Facelifts. Nose jobs. Cheek implants. They were all dressed in slutty clothes and all wore the same emotionless expression on their plastic faces. But beyond that, just beneath the layer of modifications, Sam could see the same burning hatred in all of their eyes. Her eyes landed back to the center of the group and then silently she gave a nod.

A dark-haired girl with bright orange streaks and a nose four times removed from its original state entered first. Her rifle, plucked from the clutches of one of the slaughtered, held high in the air, bloodlust in her eyes. A split-second later the rest of the girls followed and then the interior of the building was ablaze with gunfire, protests and screams.

11

"We'll need to get her back to my office," Doc said and plucked a syringe from inside the leather medical bag. He shuffled through the rest of the contents and extracted a small brown vial. He inserted the needle into the rubber stopper at the top of the vial and pulled the plunger. The syringe filled with a clear liquid.

"What is that?"

"A muscle relaxer," the doctor said. He inserted the needle into Alex's forearm and pushed down on the plunger. "She has a possible concussion, but I'll need to run some more tests back at my office."

"We're not going back to your office," Sam said. "We're getting her brother and we're getting the hell out of here."

"But I need—"

"You saw the same computer screen that I did, Doc. The self-destruction sequence has been activated. We're living on borrowed time."

"Well, that's precisely my point," Doc interjected. "If nothing has happened so far, then who's to say anything will? You know as well as I do the computer was ancient. From a probability standpoint, don't you think it's safe to assume whatever was supposed to happen, can't or won't at this point?"

"I'm not assuming anything, Doc."

The doctor shook his head. "Is it possible to at least stop by my office to get some additional supplies? If we're going to be braving the elements then we'll need to be prepared."

"Who said anything about *we*?"

Doc stiffened.

"You're the one responsible for all the modifications, aren't you?" Sam asked. "These surgeries and *enhancements*. The girls have you to blame."

"I was doing what I was told," the doctor said, his voice barely above a whisper.

"The same as the soldiers who stood idly by and let the royalty rape their children?" Sam seethed. "Because weren't they just doing what they were told?"

The doctor stood and took a step toward Sam. "I've never approved of what those men do to the children nor do I approve of the surgeries or the experimentation. Why do you think my face is like this? Do you think I enjoyed performing the surgeries so much that I elected to deform myself? Or could it be that I've used my body as a testing ground to ensure that I don't do any additional harm to my patients?"

"Here's a third option," Sam said and took a step toward Doc, not backing down. "Don't do the procedures. Stand up and fight."

"You're assuming even a small minority would be willing to revolt with me. If I would have stopped performing their procedures or never performed them in the first place then I would be no better off than one of those monstrosities." The doctor pointed in the direction of the carnage that lay outside of the buildings.

"What does that mea—?"

A severe shout came from the tunnel leading to the mine. Sam raised her rifle and then lowered it as Cole emerged from the darkness. A teenage boy was on his heels and he shouted again as he reached the opening.

"Alexandria!"

The moonlight gleamed in the boy's hollow eyes and his gaunt face was racked with fear. Tattered rags wrapped loosely around his groin and feet. "Where is she?" he called.

Cole pointed in their direction. The boy tried to sprint but slipped and fell to the ground. Cole helped him to his feet, and the boy limped the rest of the way. Blood oozed from the scrape on his bony knee.

Behind Cole and the boy, Sam watched as the blonde-haired girl, tasked with finding Alex's brother, surfaced. She was followed by a countless number of children. They all wore the same confused smile on their face. The girl leading the way called out and the other teenage girls, the royalty's sex slaves, emerged from the building. Squeals of joy erupted as brothers and sister found each other. And then the girls led the children out of the cave and back toward the up-top.

Alex's brother dropped to his knees at his sister's side. The boy's eyes filled with tears and then he wrapped his emaciated arms around her. He sobbed as he pulled Alexandria into his chest.

"She's going to be okay," Sam said. She put a hand on the boy's shoulder and squeezed.

"Where is he?" the boy whispered.

"He's dead."

There was a long moment of silence before the boy spoke again. "Good."

The boy released Alex and laid her back on the ground. Then he stood and faced Sam and Doc.

"What's your name?" Sam asked.

"Nick."

"You've met Cole," Sam said. "My name is Sam."

The boy wrapped his arms around Sam's neck. It was an unexpected hug but welcomed and Sam returned the gesture. After a moment, he pulled away.

"So what happens now?" Nick asked.

Sam didn't answer. Instead, a siren ripped through the cave. It was louder than anything she had ever heard. She dropped the rifle to the ground and covered her ears. Cole and Doc also covered their ears. Nick fell back to his knees and wrapped his hands around Alex's head.

"What is that?" Sam shouted.

There was an earth shattering crack as a giant stalactite broke away from the ceiling. It smashed into the building's roof, the one where the girls had been held, and disappeared inside. A thick cloud of stone and debris ejected from the hole and from the door.

A split-second later another of the spiked pillars broke away and then another. The self-destruction timer on the mysterious computer in Gates' office had hit zero. The mines were collapsing.

"We have to go!" Sam screamed. She snatched the rifle from the ground with one hand and grabbed Doc by the collar with the other. Cole gathered Alex into his arms and the five of them were took off toward the tunnel.

Emergency lights that had been hidden by the darkness now illuminated the large corridor, flashing in melodic strobes. Others pushed past them as they made their way up the cramped pathway. Girls carrying assault rifles led children covered in soot past them, most running at full speed with bare feet. Behind, the sound of the cave collapsing was deafening.

"Pick up the pace, Doc!" Sam yelled.

"I'm going as fast as I can!" Doc shouted back. He turned his head to look back and lost his footing. His head slammed hard into the ground. Cole and Nick slowed, but Sam screamed at them to continue. Nick tried to protest, but Cole grabbed the boy by the shoulder and pushed him up the pathway.

"On your feet, Doc." Sam jammed a hand under his armpit and pulled. The doctor tried to get his feet under him, stumbled and then fell back to the ground. Sam saw a thick stream of blood emerging from the doctor's white hair.

"Go on. Get out of here while you can."

"I'm not leaving you," Sam said and pulled at his arms. He didn't budge.

"You have to get—"

A large rock broke from the ceiling and slammed into Doc's back. He screamed in agony. Sam pushed the miniature boulder off of him and made another attempt to help him to his feet, the path leading back to the mines collapsing before her eyes.

"Take this," the doctor said and slid the leather bag to Sam. "The answers you seek can be found within."

"I'm not leaving you."

"I can't move my legs. Leave me."

Sam grabbed the bag from the floor and hesitated. She had no reason to feel any sort of sympathy for the man. He was as guilty as the rest of them whether he was willing to admit it or not. But she did feel something.

"Thank you," she said.

"Your friend will become one of them."

"What does that mean?" Sam asked.

But the doctor never got a chance to answer. More of the tunnel wall gave way and collapsed around him. A moment later, he was buried in a mound of rubble. His hand was the only thing left visible; extended as if he were reaching for help.

"We have to go, Sam!" Cole shouted from somewhere in the darkness.

Sam didn't need to be told twice and sprinted as fast as she could. She ran until her veins felt like they were filled with acid. Until her lungs burned with each breath. She ran until she felt like she couldn't go any farther. Until every muscle screamed for her to stop. And then she ran faster.

The four of them reached the mouth of the caverns and then climbed the steel staircase. Sam let Cole lead the way and watched in amazement as he carried not only his weight but the deadweight of Alex up the tight flight of stairs at a breakneck pace. They reached the top and exited into the gaudy hallways.

"Do you know the way?" Sam asked to Nick.

Much to Sam's dismay, Nick shook his head no.

Sam wasn't sure if the destruction of the bunker would stop at the mines or if it would extend to the royal apartments. The ground shook violently, and she wasn't willing to find out. She turned left and led the group down the hallway.

They turned another corner and Sam saw a group of kids up ahead of them. She could only assume that one of the girls was leading them to the exit. Sam yelled to hurry, and they picked up the pace.

The labyrinth of hallways seemed to continue forever, and the building shook more and more. Sam was losing hope but then noticed the decorations of the hallway becoming sparser and then they disappeared altogether. The gold and green marble floor changed to smooth concrete and Sam barely noticed that they were traveling up stairs. Her adrenaline peaked and everything seemed to fade into some dreamlike state. She saw daylight up ahead and smiled. They had escaped. She had kept her promise.

Sam reached the top of the stairs and burst into the outside world. The early morning sun felt glorious against her skin and she took a deep breath of the hot, desert air. And then her eyes adjusted and she stopped in her tracks at the foot of the steps. The muffled dreamlike state disappeared, and the screams came through in stereo.

There was blood everywhere. An older lady screamed at a group of children to keep running as a midnight runner lifted her into the air. It was Greta. The woman emitted a short scream and then the beast ripped her head from her body.

"No!" Sam screamed.

The beast shoved Greta's head into its jaw and tossed the woman's lifeless body to the ground where a heap of headless bodies littered the desert floor. The midnight runner chewed once and swallowed. Sam screamed again, and the creature turned toward her, its hulking body glistening with crimson.

This midnight runner was different than the ones in the caves. It bore a resemblance to them, but it was bigger, and even more muscular. The horns atop its head were pointed forward instead of outward and its skin was a murderous shade of red.

Sam lifted her gun but before she could squeeze the trigger, the midnight runner sprung a foot to the right and then leapt at her. Everything went blurry as the gun was violently ripped from her hands. A second later, she flew through the air. She had just enough time to put her hands up before crashing head first into the hot, desert sand.

There was a moment of pitch-black and then somewhere there was screaming. Sam forced herself to open her eyes. The blinding sun burned her retinas, and she realized she was on her back facing up at an angry sun. She managed to turn her head and saw the beast on top of Cole. It pinned Cole's massive arms with ease. It opened its enormous mouth revealing two rows of razor-sharp teeth.

Sam screamed but her voice seemed distorted and muffled. From her vantage point, she could see the fear in her friend's eyes and could see him screaming for help. She had failed him. Sam choked back tears as she watched helplessly.

Use the remote, Jordan whispered.

She pawed desperately at the pockets of the khaki cargo pants and cried aloud as her fingers touched the metal casing of the device in her pocket. She extracted it and flipped open the protective glass cover. At the very least, her friend wouldn't have to feel the pain of his death. That was one thing she could provide him.

"Goodbye, Cole."

She mashed the center button and Cole's eyes closed immediately. Sam took a breath of relief and then screamed as the creature lowered its head, slamming it into Cole's face. She waited for the creature to lift its head and reveal a half-eaten face but the midnight runner lay motionless.

Sam looked around, searching for an answer. Huddled by the door leading back to the bunker were Nick and Alex, who was now awake, but neither of them had any sort of weapon. Sam rolled over to her stomach, despite the pain raging inside of her. She eyed the horizon and saw groups of the children, those that had been lucky enough to escape the collapsing mine and then the midnight runner. None of them had weapons either. None of them had caused the beast to stop.

"What the hell?" Sam said.

The remote.

Jordan's words.

She stared at the device in her hand and then to Cole. She forced herself to her feet and walked towards her friend. A slow, deep panic bubbled in her stomach. She was terrified of what she was going to find as she approached the beast.

You know what you'll find.

She did know. The realization washed over her that when she had woken Cole up in the dining room, she had also awoken the monstrosity that lie atop him now. Sam reached the two of them and her heart sank as she saw the small metal device embedded in the back of the creature's skull.

"No," she said in disbelief.

Adrenaline flooded her veins, and she pulled the hulking beast—450 pounds of solid muscle—off of Cole with ease. Her friend was breathing and looked unscathed aside for a handful of scratches and scrapes. She held her breath and rolled Cole to his stomach. Slowly, she lifted a portion of his hair to expose the silver device that she had felt in the dining room. It was a mirror image of the one that was embedded into the beast.

"No!" she screamed.

Red lights flashed in Sam's eyes as she screamed out. She was drunk with rage and anger. Her eyes scanned the sandy surface until they locked on a jagged rock the size of a softball. She picked up the stone and smiled as it burned her palms. The pain felt good. It felt real. She hoped it would wake her up from this horrible nightmare. But this nightmare was as real as the pain.

She stumbled back to the midnight runner and dropped to her knees. The creature's chest raised and lowered rhythmically as its lungs filled with air. She looked to Cole who was breathing in and out in the same rhythm as the beast.

Sam choked back tears and lifted the sharp stone in the air, high above her head. She swung it down with a primal scream and buried it deep into the creature's neck. Dark red blood poured from the puncture wound. She pulled out the stone and lifted it again. Her arms trembled fiercely and she let out another scream. She swung again and crimson splattered onto the hot, yellow sand each time she did. She lifted the stone over and over, each time digging it deeper and deeper into the creature's neck. Each time screaming inaudible profanities and cursing whatever god would take away everything that she loved.

Over and over.

Faster and deeper.

She had swung the rock until every muscle burned within her arms and chest. Until there were no more tears to cry. Until she was coated with the blood of the midnight runner and its head severed from its body.

She sat in the sand for a long time and silently sobbed and stared at the creature's blood soaking into the sand. Alex remained slumped by the doorway of the bunker, Nick tending after her. From time to time, the ground would shake violently as echoes of the underground city collapsed underneath them. Sam wasn't worried about the ground beneath caving in. She wasn't worried about anything anymore.

After a long time, Sam hit the middle button on the remote again and Cole stirred from the catatonic state. He woke confused and gawked at the grim landscape stretched out around them. The bodies and blood. It made her sick to her stomach.

"What happened, Miss Sam?"

"Nothing," Sam said. Her words were cold and reproachful. "You passed out. That's all."

"Are you okay?"

"Yes." She didn't look at him.

"Are you sure?"

"Yes."

"I reckon a thank you is in order."

"For what?"

"Saving my life."

Tears stung at her eyes. She hadn't saved anyone. They had all died or soon would die. She shook her head but didn't say anything. After a few minutes, he retreated to the doors of the bunker where Alex and Nick were resting.

She stared into the distance as the sun beat down on them. A few minutes later, Nick joined her. He took a seat next to her but didn't speak at first. He picked at the leaves of a brittlebush.

"You should come over in the shade," he said after a long time.

"I'll be fine," Sam whispered.

There was another long moment of silence as Sam eyed the horizon. A great road stretched out in front of them, the blacktop faded and crumbled. Sam could only guess where it would lead. There were no maps in the binder or the bag. She would have to rely on Cole to lead them to Concordia. She assumed Holden had told him the way. Assumed they were heading in the right direction when the truck had flipped. And she assumed the worst about what would become of him. The thought brought a fresh round of tears to her eyes.

"What now?" Nick asked.

Sam pointed to a blue and red metal sign sticking up near the road. The paint was faded, and the sign was cracked down the middle but the number on it was still legible. It read 'EAST' and underneath '15' although the words were extremely faded.

"We head east. That's what."

"How far?"

"I don't know."

"And your friend?" Nick asked.

Sam looked over at Cole. Alex had laid her head in his lap and he stroked the young girl's hair. The other giant hand rubbed the back of his head and his face twisted into puzzlement. As if he could sense Sam was watching, he looked up at her, and she turned back to the sign. She made one last assumption. Nick had put two and two together. He knew what would happen to her friend. And that scared her most of all.

Finally, Sam whispered, "When it happens, I will deal with it."

Nick nodded. Sam eyed the boy and met the cold-tempered stare in his hollowed eyes. She knew what the nod meant. It was an understanding. It meant that when the time came, if she didn't take care of things, he would.

If Nick were as adept as she thought he was, then he could see the same cold stare in her eyes. Her stare that echoed his. *When the time comes, I'll kill him myself.* They stared at each other for a moment longer and then Nick retreated back to the bunker entrance where the tiniest bit of shade could be found.

Sam held her spot, baking in the hot heat of the sun and continued to plot out their next move. They would stop in the city on the sign and gather whatever supplies they could scavenge, kill whatever monstrosities lie in wait, and then continue to the bastard city.

She knew that one if not most of them would die along the way to Concordia...but not her. She would keep going until things were right in the world again. Until she had saved it. Because that's what she had been *designed* to do. After a long time, when her shoulders started to turn pink and she could no longer bare the heat, she decided to join the group.

They decided to wait until sunset before moving out. They scavenged the dead bodies and pieced together clothing for Alex and Nick. They would look for more clothes along the way.

The temperatures grew bearable and the bright red blood had baked into the sand and turned it black. The sun idled on the horizon casting the last rays of orange and yellows across the skyline. The four of them took their first steps forward. The escaped children of Lost Angel had fled shortly after Sam had killed the beast, or maybe during, she didn't know...she didn't care. All she knew was there were only four of them now.

They had no food and a limited amount of ammo, but Sam had a purpose. She would carry on until she reached Concordia and then she would claim vengeance for Jordan's death. For Rebecca's death. She would get retribution for the citizens of New Hope and those of Lost Angel. And when Cole Porter turned into one of the midnight runners and she had to take his life, she would get revenge for that as well. The sign under the interstate marker was a green one. The white letters barely legible, but Sam could still read it.

Las Vegas – 266.

It would take at least a week to walk there...perhaps longer. Maybe months to make it to Concordia. But she would persevere. There were questions that had to be answered and more importantly retributions that needed to be paid. And in-between this forsaken place and their goal was a world full of the infected. A world full of halfways waiting to bring them down.

PART THREE: CONCORDIA

1

Steel skeletons stretched from the desert floor and kissed the dawn sky. Piles of rubble and mortar lay at their feet like shed skin. Las Vegas was nothing more than a forgotten graveyard nestled in the wastelands of a godforsaken world. Sam glassed the city gates from afar, counting the halfways near the entrance. There was at least a dozen. Maybe more. The government had walled up the city in the same way as New Hope, but the gates hadn't held.

The remnants of the city provided a sense of relief for Sam. It shot a giant hole in the General's millennial theory and she guessed that Holden's assessment of 300 years was closer to the truth. Although the thought of three centuries passing without her knowledge didn't give her the warm fuzzies.

She focused the lens on the rotting corpses as they trundled near the pyramid's entrance. A man in a frayed business suit hobbled across the boardwalk with his neck canted at a 90-degree angle. He stumbled past a woman wearing a pink show costume as she gyrated her hips in his directions. A dozen others seemed to be following similar ritualistic routines from their old lives.

Sam shifted her weight, and the scaffolding groaned underneath her. She had perched herself on the edge of a billboard, fifty feet in the air. The metal creaked again, and she inched back from the edge. The wind picked up, and she grabbed the railing. The entire sign swayed, and her heart climbed into her throat. Coming up here wasn't the brightest idea, but it had been necessary. She shoved the telescope into her pocket and made her way back to the service ladder. Carefully, she climbed down the rungs where Cole was waiting.

"What'cha think?" he asked as she reached the ground.

Sam shook her head.

"We gots to do something, Miss Sam. Those kids are gonna die soon if we don't get 'em some real food. Hell, we all will."

"I know," she whispered.

She looked to the west and her eyes fell upon the two refugees from Lost Angel. Nick and Alex, two skeleton-thin effigies of their former selves, huddled together in the middle of the sand-swept road. They hunkered against the concrete divider and Nick suppressed a harsh cough with the crook of his arm. Blood spattered the sleeve of his shirt and Sam looked away.

He was dying. They all were.

It had taken them a little over two weeks to walk to Las Vegas. They had been fortunate with the water supply and had filled their jugs on three separate occasions. But food had been limited to a few handfuls of mesquite beans and banana yucca fruit. They'd need protein if they expected to make it across country. Sam's stomach rumbled, and she looked back to the city.

"We can't risk it. One of those halfways gets a whiff of us and they'll swarm faster than we can run away. There aren't enough bullets to fight off a horde and I couldn't swing a weapon if my life depended on it. Hell, I can barely carry this bag anymore."

Cole nodded.

"How much water do we have left?" Sam asked.

Cole examined the two gallon jugs hanging around his neck. "A day's worth," he said. "A day and a half if we cut back."

"We can't afford to cut back."

"Then a day's worth."

They found the jugs in a junkyard outside Lost Angel. They spent a full day scavenging for supplies and ended with an ancient metal pot, a Bic lighter, half a binocular, some string, a couple rusted knives and a duffle bag. Cole had tied the jugs together with the length of string and worn them around his neck without complaint.

They lucked out for the first dozen miles of their trip and hiked through the foothills of a lush mountain range. Sam had spotted a stagnant pond from the road and they had made camp for the evening. They emptied the canvas duffel bag, filled it with rocks and dirt and they filtered the water through it. Then they gathered some limbs from the brush, lit a fire and boiled the water. Sam made everyone drink as much as they could stomach before leaving and then they filled the jugs to the brim.

When they had reached the desert, their luck had run out. They had resorted to extreme rationing over the last week and the inside of Sam's mouth felt like sandpaper. She let Cole's words resonate in her mind.

"How much more can we cut back?" Sam asked after a long moment.

Cole didn't answer.

"What about ammo?"

"Got a full clip in my sack. Three rounds left in the rifle."

"Next time we make camp, I want you to switch clips. We need to hold on to those three rounds, just in case."

"In case of what?" Cole asked.

"You know what," Sam answered. "One of us gets bit and turns..." Sam hesitated trying to keep the image of Nick or Alex as a halfway far away from her mind's eye. "If push comes to shove, do you think you can bash one of their brains in?"

"Naw," Cole said. "Don't reckon I could. But I don't reckon I could shoot 'em neither."

"Let's hope it never comes to that," Sam said.

Sam returned the makeshift telescope to the pant-leg of her cargos and ran her bandaged hand through her thick matted hair. It was dry and gritty and she had contemplated hacking it off with one of the knives about 12 times a day since leaving Lost Angel. She would give anything for a shower.

"Where's Concordia from here?"

"If I remember the maps Deckard showed me," Cole said and looked at the sun hanging low in the hazy sky, "should be due east. Little ways to the North. Middle of the country."

"If you remember?"

"Been a long time," Cole said. "Been over a month since we left New Hope. Even longer since he showed me. But I suppose I still remember them pretty good."

Sam sighed. "We passed another big roadway a couple miles back. Looked like it was heading east. I say we head that way."

"Okay," Cole said and scratched his bushy beard. "What about food?"

"We'll keep scavenging. Maybe once we get out of the desert we can hunt."

"Desert's a big place. We're gonna need food before—"

"What do you suggest?" Sam interrupted. "I'm doing my best here."

Cole looked to the ground. "I know ya are. It's just—"

"It's just what?"

"I'm worried about the boy. He didn't have a lot of meat on his bones to start. He's not doing good."

Sam turned back to Nick. His face was gray and sunken and blood stained his lips. "I know," she said.

They started back toward Alex and Nick but Cole stopped her before they got within earshot. "Miss Sam?"

"Yeah?"

"You've been looking in that book of yours every night," Cole said. "The one you found in Doc's bag."

"Yeah," Sam said. She looked away, afraid to meet his gaze, and out toward the sky. The sun stagnated just below the horizon, not yet ready to stretch out and brighten the day. Instead, the eastern skyline was pink with large purple clouds hanging low in the air. To the west, the darkness kept its stranglehold on the forthcoming morning.

"You ain't found anything that talks about what this thing is they put in my head, have you?" Cole wrung his hands together and frowned. "Or how to take it out? Or what the other two buttons do on the remote—"

"No," Sam interrupted. She looked at him and prayed he couldn't see through her lies. His face twisted in disappointment and Sam looked away again. It hurt to lie to him. "I promise," she continued, "if I find something, you'll be the first to know."

Cole ran a giant hand through his hair and rubbed the back of his scalp. After a long moment, he said, "Okay, Miss Sam."

They resumed walking until they reached Nick and Alex. As they neared, the children clambered to their feet, an unwarranted optimism coating each of their faces. A pang of guilt shot through Sam's heart.

"Any luck?" Alex asked.

Sam shook her head. "City's crawling with halfways."

"Goddammit," Nick said. He started to say something else but broke into another coughing fit. Sam cringed as more red spittle flew from his lips. The episodes were getting worse. It wouldn't be much longer.

Alex tried to speak but her words caught and instead she burst into silent sobs and collapsed back to the asphalt. The small-framed girl had already lost ten pounds and Sam wondered how much more she could stand to lose. Tears streaked down her soiled cheeks and Nick knelt down and wrapped a stick-thin arm around her.

"So what do we do?" Nick asked.

"Concordia is east of here," Sam said. "We head that way and pray for water. Pray for food."

"No offense," Nick said, "but I stopped praying a long time ago. What if we go around the city and try to sneak in through a rear entrance."

Sam shook her head. "We'll scavenge anything and everything on the way, but we need to keep heading toward Concordia. It's the best course of action."

"How do you know that?" the boy asked. "How do you even know

Concordia is real?"

"It's real," Sam affirmed.

"And so what if it is," Nick sputtered. "What's the point if we all die trying to get there?"

Sam didn't answer.

Nick kissed his sister atop of her head and then coughed again, this time into his hands. When the coughing subsided, he wiped his palms onto the legs of his jeans leaving two faint trails of blood behind.

"We need to keep moving," Sam said. She lifted the doctor's handbag from the broken pavement. "It'll be noon in a few hours. If it's as hot as it was yesterday then we'll need to set up camp and wait until nightfall to resume travel." Neither Nick nor Alex protested. Instead, they gathered the rest of the gear they had pieced together throughout the trip and turned back in the direction they had come.

A half-mile from the entrance to the city they passed a broken-down slot machine slumbering on its back in the center of the road. The words and paint were faded to the point of transparency from decades, or perhaps centuries, of living under the cruel desert sun. Sam felt as faded and far removed from reality as the broken-down machine.

The group slowed as they passed the charred frame a vehicle. A skeleton slouched against the car door and stared back at her from the driver's seat. There was another in the passenger seat and two smaller ones in the rear. Sam wanted to feel sorry for them but she couldn't. They had been lucky the ones.

Cole grabbed her by the arm and Sam nearly screamed aloud.

"What?" Sam whispered.

"Halfway," Cole whispered back.

She signaled for Nick and Alex to stop and then eyed the stretch of road ahead. Standing next to the concrete divider, 200 yards away, was a person. Sam pulled the telescope from her pocket and looked through it.

"It's a woman—" Sam said, and then corrected herself, "was a woman." The decayed flesh was a sickly gray color and pocked with open sores that oozed black pus. The woman looked down between her knees and then back to the horizon.

"Is it alone?" Cole asked.

She glassed the area but saw no one else.

"Looks that way." She dropped the looking glass into her pocket and unsheathed the chef's knife from her waistband. "It wasn't here when we passed the first time. We'll need to be on the lookout for others."

The knife's stainless steel blade had rusted from years of being exposed to the environment and the tip was dull, but it was a quiet alternative to the rifle. She could sever the halfway's spinal cord without drawing attention from others in the area.

"You want me to handle it?" Cole asked.

Sam shook her head. "No. Stay with the children."

"You want the gun?"

"No," Sam said. She grasped the handle of the knife and started toward the creature.

She measured each step and moved silently across the broken blacktop using the cars as cover. The halfway continued to stare at the ground as she moved within striking distance. She raised the knife above her head and prepared to jab it into the back of the dead woman's neck. And then she saw what had captured the halfway's attention. Lying in-between the decomposing legs of the woman was an infant—a rotten, leathery cord tethering the child to its mother.

Sam gasped and fell backward. She stumbled over a piece of debris and dropped the knife. The halfway looked up at her and screamed, and Sam had to cover her mouth to stifle a whimper. The woman's glassy eyes darted back and forth from the child to Sam. It yelled something inaudible and then took a step toward her. Sam grabbed blindly for the knife afraid to take her eyes from the dead woman. The halfway took another step closer, but the umbilical cord pulled taught. It had caught on a piece of rebar jutting from the divider. The dead woman screamed once more at Sam and then returned to the child.

Sam picked herself up from the pavement and took a tentative step forward. She couldn't take her watery eyes off of the child. It too was crying. Its skin was the same ashen color as its mother and pocked with the same infectious sores and gaping wounds of exposed muscle and tissue. The dead woman growled and shrieked as Sam took another step closer, but it didn't leave the child's side.

"Good god," Cole whispered.

Sam's heart leapt into her throat. She wheeled around to see he had left the children and was now standing by her side.

"Sorry," he said. "Didn't mean to scare ya."

"It's okay," Sam said and pressed away the tears that had formed in the corner of her eyes with her palms.

"You think they've been here this whole time?" Cole asked.

"No," Sam said.

"Where'd they come from then?"

Sam said nothing. Instead, she wiped the tears from her eyes, but the effort was futile. The tears continued to fall and soon Cole wrapped her in his arms and she sobbed heavily into his chest.

"It's not right," she said between tearful breaths.

"No, Miss Sam." Cole squeezed her tightly. "No it's not."

He held her until Sam stopped crying. She pulled away and wiped her eyes. Something had happened to her brain in the General's dining hall. Something unexplainable. She had transformed into some sort of killing machine, and after they left the bunker, the skills seemed to carry over to survival. But she wasn't prepared for this.

"You sure you don't want me to handle this?" Cole asked.

"I'm sure," Sam said and swallowed hard.

"We could leave them here," Cole offered.

"No," Sam said. "We can't."

Cole nodded.

She took a step forward and picked the knife off the cement but that was as far as she could make herself go. The dead woman looked up at her and then back to the child, but it didn't advance again. Instead, the corpse knelt down beside the infant and put a rotten hand atop it.

Cole put a hand on Sam's shoulder and whispered for her to look away. Sam did as he asked and looked back toward Las Vegas. A gunshot ripped through the air and the woman collapsed onto the blacktop with a thud. Frantic screams from the child cause Sam's skin to turn to gooseflesh...another gunshot...silence.

2

The sun broke from its slumber and clambered through the sky as the foursome journeyed back toward the intersection. An hour after sunrise, Sam had already broken into a sweat. It would be unbearable by midday. She glanced back toward the children who hobbled behind. An uneasiness overtook her when she saw how gray Nick looked.

"Let's take five," Sam said as she waited for Nick and Alex to catch up. "Hydrate and rest your legs." The refugees from Lost Angel half sat/half collapsed onto the blacktop. Nick broke into another coughing fit, spewing the asphalt with crimson.

"This ain't good," Cole said.

"You and Alex take a few sips and give him the rest," Sam said. "Make him drink."

"What about you?"

"I'm fine."

"The hell you are," Cole scoffed. He pulled the water jugs from around his neck and forced one of the bottles into her hands. "At least take a swallow."

Sam lifted the dirty plastic to her lips and took the tiniest of sips. She sloshed the warm gritty water around in her mouth for a few seconds before swallowing. It was one of the greatest things she had ever tasted. Her body yearned for more, but she handed the jug back to Cole.

"Thank you," she whispered.

Cole nodded and walked over to the children. Sam removed the binocular from her pants and searched the horizon for any sign of life. She listened as Nick protested and then gave in to Cole's wishes.

When the jugs were empty, the group set out again. They moved even slower than before through the sweltering temperatures and down the sand-strewn highway. They slid past the scorched shells of ash and bone until they reached a massive fork in the road.

"This is it," Cole said as they approached a metal overhang. Pieces of a smashed, faded green sign covered the ground below the broken metal scaffolding. "We can go east here until we get around the city. Then we head north and catch back up with I-15."

The intersection was three miles from the city gates but it had taken the withered and battered group almost two and a half hours to reach it. They shambled down the off-ramp and started east on the low road.

The sun's brutal rays hammered them as they continued to march forward. Sam's mouth felt like sandpaper and she regretted letting Nick drink the rest of the water. Then she caught a glimpse of him in the corner of her eye. His blood-red lips shone in the sunlight and the bright color of them made his skin look impossibly paler. She made the right decision.

"What's that?" Alex said and pointed toward the horizon.

A large metal object had appeared on the skyline. The sun gleamed off it creating bright orbs of reflective light. Whatever it was, it didn't belong in the middle of the road. Sam removed the telescope from her pocket and eyed the distant object.

"What is it?" Alex asked.

"A plane," Sam said. She glassed over the mangled fuselage. The debris covered the width of the road. "What's left of a plane, anyway." She handed the glass-piece to Cole who surveyed the object.

"Looks military," Cole said.

"C-7 Galaxy cargo plane. There's an airbase on the opposite side of the city," Sam said.

"How do you know?"

Sam shrugged. The flood of information had ebbed since the dining room incident but it was still there. "Same way I know how to harvest mesquite pods. Same way I know how to filter water or shoot a gun."

"The data stream?"

"Yeah."

Cole handed the telescope back to Sam and rubbed the back of his neck. "You think we should head back. Find another way around the city?"

"No," Sam said and studied the area again. "Nothing seems to be moving. Let's check it out. We can camp there if it's safe. It's getting too hot to be out here."

It took half an hour to reach the wreckage. When they neared, Sam and Cole readied their weapons and the children stood back at a safe distance. The center of the fuselage angled upward and had split into two halves. The front of the mangled plane was beyond recognition, but the rear remained largely intact.

"How do ya want to do this?" Cole asked.

Sam pointed her knife toward the rear of the plane and started to speak, but a loud scratching noise from inside the plane interrupted her.

"Get back," she hissed, spinning on her heel to face the teens. They were already retreating. The sound of claws screeching against metal blasted through the air again and Sam whirred back to the plane. The noise stopped, but her heartbeat continued to race.

"Go back?" Cole whispered after a long moment.

Sam focused all of her attention on the plane. The rest of her senses seemed to fade away. She heard Cole's steady breaths in stereo. Nick anxiously tapped his foot and Alexandria whispered prayers to whatever god she thought might save them. And then she heard the scratching again. Sam's mind flashed on the long claws of the midnight runners scratching against the rock floor of Lost Angel. The rational part of her brain took over as she concentrated on the sound.

"Rats," Sam said. "It sounds like rats. It's just amplified because there's nothing else out here."

Cole took a deep breath and took a step forward. Sam grabbed his arm.

"If it's not rats," Sam whispered. "If it's something bigger, you let me deal with it. You go back and get Nick and Alex out of here."

"Miss Sam, I don't think..." Cole's voice faded, and he frowned. "If something were to happen, do you really want me watching over them? I don't know nothing about caring for any kids."

Sam's blood turned cold. She stared at him for a long moment and sighed. "I trust you, Cole. If something happens you get them to a safe place..." she paused and looked into his eyes. "Promise me."

"I'll do the best I can—"

"Promise me you won't hurt them."

Cole gave her a long searching look. "Why would I hurt them?"

"Promise me," Sam said.

Cole's eyes darted to the ground as if he was embarrassed, but nodded his confirmation. There wasn't time to dwell on the moment. Another screech burst from the plane and Sam unsheathed her knife. "Let's go."

Sam's heartbeat quickened as they crept through the field of debris. The cargo bay door was missing, and they entered through the large opening. Sam gripped the chef's knife in her hand and then let out a low whistle. Nothing inside moved.

She took a tentative step inside and found two large steel crates against the interior wall of the plane. At one time they were ratcheted against the wall with cargo straps but the fabric of the straps had deteriorated, leaving two buckles lying on the floor next to the cases.

On the opposite side of the plane two Humvees slouched against the wall lined up behind one another. The harnesses holding the trucks in place had held firm, leaving the vehicles in relatively good condition. The tires were flat and the synthetic rubber had started to deteriorate, but other than that Sam couldn't see any discernible damage. If only they still had gas, she thought. Sam inched forward and the metal grating creaked under her weight.

Something flashed in the corner of her eye and Sam screamed as something bolted from under the rear vehicle and ran toward her. She cocked the knife back, and just as she released, she caught a true glimpse of the animal. She made a last second adjustment to the blade's trajectory, and it struck a bare spot on the floor. Sparks flew as metal collided with metal and the knife clanked across the grated floor. The creature yelped, changed direction and ducked behind one of the crates. Cole emerged at her side, his finger on the trigger and the barrel of the gun aimed in the creature's direction.

"Wait," Sam said. Her heart slammed against her chest and she struggled to catch a full breath in the sweltering heat. There had been something familiar about the animal. She took another step forward. The sound of claws grinding against metal filled the fuselage but this time the image of the midnight runner didn't flash. Something else did. Something unbelievable. She took another step and the creature's head came into view.

Sam gasped.

The small dog cowered against the metal crate, its big ears pressed against the top of its head. It was scrawny, and its brown and black fur was matted together in thick clumps. It made eye contact with Sam and gave a low whine and then its tail beat against the steel floor of the plane.

"Well I'll be," Cole said as he stepped closer. "You think it's infected?"

Sam shook her head. "RIZ-4 only affected humans."

"What is it?"

"Terrier if I had to guess." She took a step closer and extended a tentative hand. "I think I used to have one...before."

The terrier lowered its head and wagged its tail harder. From the corner of her eye, Sam saw something else move and jumped back. The dog's ears shot up, and it hopped to its feet. A rat, almost as big as the dog, emerged from the shadows and scurried past them. The dog chased it from the plane, and a second later, Sam heard Alex squeal and Nick shouting something indistinguishable.

"Go check on them," Sam said.

Cole bounded out of the cargo door leaving Sam alone. The fuselage canted 30 degrees into the air and she climbed its length, slowly but steadily, using the Humvees for support. When she reached the open air separating the two halves, she looked out and saw the children. They huddled together where she had left them. Just beyond, Cole was chasing the dog, which was chasing the rat.

She bent forward and looked over the edge into the mangled shaft. There was nothing of interest. She gave another low whistle and listened. No movement. No sound. She half-walked, half-slid back down to the bay door. The plane felt solid and even though it was hot inside, there was enough airflow from the broken windows and cargo opening to serve as a tolerable camp for the afternoon.

A few minutes later, all four of them were standing inside the plane. The rat terrier had escaped with the rat and Cole's face was beet red and he breathed heavy, short pants. Chasing after the dog had expended a lot more energy than it was worth. He would need to rehydrate. Sam looked at Nick and Alex. They would also need to drink soon. She would have to scout while the rest of the group rested or wait and hope to come across some tonight.

"Try to get some rest," Sam said to the group. "I'll take first watch. We'll move again at sundown. Any halfways join the party and you know the drill." When no one spoke she said, "And what's the drill?"

"Hide and let you and Cole take care of them," Alex sighed as she lay down next to the tire of the Humvee. Nick sat down beside her and Sam's heart broke at the sight of him.

"And then what?" Cole asked.

"Wait until we get the all clear," Alex said through a yawn. "If we don't get the all clear after ten minutes then we turn around and go west until we hit the ocean or until we find someone that can help us." Alex situated a thin arm under her head and a moment later was snoring.

"I can take care of us," Nick said through gritted teeth. He had said little since they had reached the intersection. His eyes were glassy and his skin even grayer before. "You don't have to worry."

"I'm not worried," Sam said.

Nick lay down beside his sister, and a moment later, he was asleep. Dark sweat stains were prevalent underneath his arms and through the back of his shirt.

Sam found both of the crates in the rear cargo hold locked. Maybe they could bust them open. Maybe not. She walked to the bay door and stared out into the wasteland. Cole appeared at her side a moment later.

"You want me to take first watch?" Cole asked. "You look tired."

"No," she said. "Get some rest. I'll look for water."

"When are you going to rest?"

"Later?"

"Miss Sam—"

"I said later."

There was a long moment of silence before Cole spoke again. "Are we okay, Miss Sam?"

"What do you mean?"

"Seems like things are different since Lost Angel. I've seen you lookin' at me. It's different from how it used to be, ain't it?"

"Yes," Sam said as tears stung at the corners of her eyes.

"The reason you don't sleep is 'cause you think you're gonna wake up and I'm gonna be changed. Changed into one of those things from Lost Angel."

"A midnight runner," Sam whispered.

There was a long pause and then Cole asked, "Is that what this thing in the back of my head does? Turn me into one of those monsters?"

She didn't answer him. Sam would have cried if she could but she was too thirsty. The thought of Cole as a midnight runner stung just as bad though, tears or not.

"Shoot me then." Cole said. "Go ahead and get it over with."

"No."

"Why?"

Sam stayed quiet.

"You think you can fix me?"

"Maybe," she said. But she didn't believe it. The truth was she didn't have the heart to kill him. He had saved her in New Hope; twice. She owed him more than a bullet in the brain. That was the real reason.

"Keep lookin' through that book of yours, Miss Sam. If I start feelin' any different then I'll take of the problem myself."

She nodded and then watched Cole walk back up the ramp. He lay down on the opposite side of the plane from the kids and buried his head in the crook of his massive arm and wept. Sam pulled the kitchen knife from the waistline of the cargo pants and tightened and loosened her hand around the grip as she continued to watch him. It would be over before he knew what was happening. The thought made her heart ache even more. She turned and stepped out from the shadow of the plane.

The sun beat down on her as she walked the perimeter of the makeshift camp. Her face, arms and shoulders had tanned exponentially since the start of their journey and Sam feared that if the temperatures didn't stagnate soon that she'd develop skin cancer. Sam chuckled at the thought of dying of something like cancer after surviving the RIZ-4 virus.

She encircled the wreckage twice and decided that she would have to wait until it cooled off before looking for the water. She returned to the cargo bay, pulled the doctor's journal from the medical bag and took a seat against the wall. Cole had joined in the snoring and the three of them created a tiresome orchestra making Sam long to be back in her bed in New Hope. Back in the city with her love.

She tried to imagine Jordan's face and drew a blank. Terrified that her memories of him were fading into the blank slate of her mind, she shook her head and opened the journal. She flipped through several dog-eared pages until she reached one entitled:

Midnight Runner Project

For the next two hours, she read. There was no new information in the journal. She had read it cover to cover within the first few days of their trip. Every break, each time they set up camp, Sam had buried her nose in the book hoping for some new understanding of the metal device in Cole's skull.

The book was full of scientific jargon but she had gleaned a few things. First, was the procedure was irreversible and Cole Porter, her friend and savior, would mutate into a midnight runner. Second, the metal piece embedded into Cole's skull controlled the communication between neurons and could be operated using the remote control. But there was also an internal device manipulating serotonin, somatotropin and testosterone levels. And finally, after the incubation phase, his brain would produce a new hormone called terratrophin. The terratrophin would meld with the somatotropin and cause his bones to elongate and his muscles to grow at a rapid rate. It would cause his limbic system to completely take over the rational evolved part of his brain, leaving him in a ravenous, murderous state.

What Sam had yet to learn, was what the other two buttons on the remote did and why the General had tried to get her to push the top button instead of the middle. The doctor had listed the device's specifications in the book, but the technical notes concerning how it operated might have well been written in Chinese. However, Sam read it over and over, every night longing for some understanding. Today, just like all the others, there was none.

Frustrated, she put the book back in the bag and put her face in her hands. Beads of sweat ran from her forehead and down her cheeks. Her tongue felt like sandpaper as she licked her cracked and dry lips. She needed water. She needed rest.

"What do I need to do, Jordan?" Sam whispered. "How do I get us out of here?"

There was no answer. Jordan hadn't said a word since telling her to use the remote on Cole. He hadn't visited her dreams either. Maybe that's why she had stopped sleeping. She had lost Jordan in real life. Losing him in her dreams was too much to handle.

Sam concentrated on his face until despair turned into absolute hatred. Concordia was responsible for this. For everything. She was concentrating so hard she almost didn't hear the caw above. At first she thought it was a figment of her imagination, but then she heard it again. She turned her head toward the cargo door, and a moment later another caw filled the air. She scooted to the edge of the plane and looked up to the sky. Her heart lurched. Flying over them was a giant black bird.

She watched in amazement as the crow encircled the dusty highway and then let out a raspy squeal of joy as another one came into view. An overabundance of joy and happiness washed over her. If there were birds, if there was life, then there was some means to support it. Somewhere close to here, there was water.

"The birds," Sam said. Her voice was so dry and scratchy that the words were barely understandable. She tried again. "Cole, the birds."

Cole stirred and then his eyes fluttered open. An odd shade of yellow filled the whites of his eyes, but Sam dismissed it as dehydration. She pointed up to the birds as they flew east, toward the horizon. Cole joined her at the edge of the bay door and together they watched it in silence.

"First the dog and now the birds," Cole said.

"There's water," Sam said and smiled.

A blood-curdling scream ripped through the air and all the joy and elation that Sam felt dissipated in an instant. Sam's head spun toward Alex and her heart dropped. The young girl hunched over her brother and shook his shoulders, but Nick didn't stir.

"Nick, wake up!" Alex shouted as she shook the boy's shoulders.

Sam knelt down on the opposite side of him. The boy's thin, cracked lips were pale shade of blue and his skin was cool to the touch. Sam placed her head to his chest and listened but all she heard was Alex's frantic sobs. "Quiet," Sam said, but Alex continued to bawl.

"Miss Sam?" Cole asked.

"He's not breathing," Sam said and placed her hands over his heart. She pressed down hard and Nick's brittle bones snapped. Alex screamed but Sam pressed down again and again. After five compressions, she tilted his head back and blew two quick breaths. She put her ear to his lips and listened.

Nothing.

She started the compressions again and looked to Alex. The girl's violet eyes were cloudy with tears. "Look at me," Sam said as she pumped her arms. The girl met her stare. "We're not going to lose him. I won't let that happen." Alex nodded, but the tears continued to fall.

"Miss Sam," Cole said again.

Sam filled her lungs and then blew two more quick breaths into Nick's mouth. The boy's chest rose, and she listened. Nothing. She started the compressions again. Her forearms burned and sweat poured from her brow.

"Miss Sam," Cole said gravely, "the boy's been bleeding."

Sam paused and looked up at Cole. He pointed to the boy's lap. Dark red blood covered the seat of Nick's pants. How long had it been that way? Since they fell asleep? Longer? An icy wave of anxiety washed over her. Sam didn't know. She pushed even harder on his chest and felt two more ribs crack.

"Oh god," Alex said. "Don't leave me, Nick. Please, please don't leave me."

The words made Sam think of Jordan and for the first time since they left Lost Angel she was able to see his face. He sat on one of the metal cases on the opposite side of the plane. His face was grave and a large stain of blood dotted his chest. Sam felt the first tear escape from the side of her face. She took another deep breath, the desert air hot in her lungs, and then blew it into Nick's mouth.

Cole wrapped an arm around Alex and the two wept together. Sam counted off the compressions not ready to give up. And then she looked back to Jordan who somberly shook his head.

"No, goddammit!" Sam screamed. "We're not going to lose him!" She lifted a balled fist into the air and struck Nick above the heart. Alex screamed and Cole wrapped his other hand around her face to block her view. Sam ignored it and swung again, striking him in the same spot. "Don't you leave me."

She struck him again and again.

"Don't you leave me, Jordan." Tears stung at her eyes and her voice shook with anger and a horrible sadness. "You promised that you wouldn't leave. You promised."

She lifted her fist again but Cole caught it on the downswing. "He's gone, Sam."

Sam burst into tears. She looked up and locked eyes with Jordan. He mouthed a silent apology and his blue-gray eyes burned hot inside of her soul. Sam put her head in her hands and sobbed away the little water left inside.

After a long time, Sam stopped crying. She felt numb as she looked upon Nick's sunken face. Alex, who had also stopped crying, rested her head on Nick's chest and whispered something inaudible to him. Sam didn't have to hear the words to know it was goodbye.

"Do you want me to bury him?" Cole asked after a long time.

Alex shook her head. "He looks peaceful here."

"We can put him in one of those crates," Cole said. "That way the animals don't get at him."

As if Cole's words were a cue, the rat terrier clambered in through the bay door. It sniffed wildly at the air, gave a low whine and then trotted over to Alex. He nuzzled up next to her and then plopped down on his haunches.

"Hi," she said. Her voice was weak and tired. The dog yipped and his tail pounded against the floor. Alex scratched its ear, and the tail wagged harder.

The dog panted and barked again. Alex smiled. It was the first time she had smiled in days. Sam knew the question forming in Alex's brain and prepared herself. The girl's brother had just died and now Sam would have to tell her they couldn't keep the dog. She sighed.

"Can we give it some water?" Alex asked.

"We don't have any water," Sam said in a measured tone. She expected pushback or even panic.

Instead, Alex said, "Okay." That was even worse.

Cole broke open the lock of one of the crates with the butt of the rifle. "Nothing," he said.

Sam continued to stare at Alex who had yet to lift her head from her brother's chest. The dog nuzzled its snout against the girl's neck. "We can't keep it, either," Sam said abruptly. "We have nothing to give it and we can't even feed ourselves at this point."

"Okay," Alex said. She looked glumly from the dog to her brother. She stopped petting the dog and put her hand in her lap. The dog, not ready for the petting to stop, stretched out and licked her hand. Alex smiled.

"Might not be a bad thing to keep him around," Cole whispered. "Bet he can hunt."

"How much are you willing to bet?" Sam asked. "Our lives?"

"Naw," Cole said. "Don't reckon so."

"What kind of dog is it?" Alex asked.

"Rat terrier," Cole said.

"And it's a boy dog?"

"Yes, ma'am."

"Let's call him Artie."

"Why Artie?"

"He's a rat terrier. R.T. Artie."

Cole laughed. Sam didn't.

"Don't name him," Sam said. "You don't need to get attached to it. He can't stay."

The dog returned to Alex's side, and she stroked his head. "He can have Nick's share of the food and water. That way there's no difference."

"Alex—"

"If Nick were still alive then he'd be getting that share," Alex said. Tears fell from her cheeks. "So what's the difference?"

"The difference is," Sam said, "we didn't have enough water or food when Nick was alive. This way we can at least make it a little further before—"

"No," Alex interrupted. "Either he stays or you leave me here."

Sam hadn't expected this. It was the ultimatum of a child but Alex was just that...a child. Sam shook her head and sighed. There was no point in arguing. If she refused then it was only a matter of time before the girl threw Nick's death in her face.

"Fine," Sam said.

They stayed in the cargo bay for another as the earth cooled off. Cole placed Nick's body in the crate and they all said their goodbyes. Afterward, Sam sat down on the metal grating and looked up for any sign of the black bird. There was no trace of it.

It was still hot, but Sam gathered the doctor's bag and duffel bag and the four of them rejoined the road. Alex paused as they emerged from the shadow of the plane and said one last goodbye to her brother. Cole said another goodbye as well but Sam didn't speak. She couldn't speak. She had failed him. She had failed Alex. Rebecca and Jordan. And Cole. She had failed everyone. She added Nick's name to the list of retributions to be paid and marched onward.

3

They walked through late afternoon and into the night. The road's deteriorated condition slowed their pace to a crawl. They scaled mountains of rubble that was once superhighways, and slunk past abandoned rotted-out buildings, careful not to bring attention to themselves. They moved slow across the broken bitumen and rested often.

The majority of the road signs still standing were rusted and faded to the point of illegibility, but they reached a small brown sign that looked almost untouched by the weather. Sam's heart leapt into her chest as she read the words.

LAKE MEAD
NAT'L REC AREA
6 MILES

"Do you think it's still there?" Alex said.

Sam racked her brain for everything she could remember about Lake Mead. She remembered little, but what she did remember brought little hope. The data stream seemed to only work when it wanted to. "Hard to say. If the dam busted, there might only be a river. Or there might be nothing at all. I'm not sure."

"I hope it hasn't," Alex said.

They ambled through the night. When the moon reached the midpoint of the sky, they gathered at the side of the road and ate the rest of their honey mesquite pods. Alex offered Artie some of hers but the dog turned its nose up at the green seeds. Sam's stomach rumbled after she finished the last bite of hers and her spirits sank. They were out of food and water now. Lake Mead would have to be there or they would all be dead by the end of the week. They gathered their items and walked until the eastern sky lightened.

The sun broke over the horizon and spilled rays of yellow and gold that gleamed off of the water ahead of them. They all stopped as they reached the end of the road and stared at the giant lake.

"Am I dreaming, Cole?" Sam asked. The words barely escaped her dry throat. They came out raspy and it hurt her to talk.

"No," he said. "You're not dreaming, Miss Sam."

They stood in silent awe for a long time before Alex said, "Race you."

The four took off in a dead sprint, and when they reached the edge, Sam fell to her knees and placed her hands in the water. It was cool and crisp. She knew they should collect the water and sterilize it, but the thirst overcame her. She lifted a handful of water to her mouth and tasted it.

It was the best thing she had ever tasted. She gulped a couple more handfuls and then dropped her head to the water and drank straight from the lake. Beside her, Cole and Alex were doing the same. She drank until her stomach was full.

"What do we do now?" Alex asked.

Sam smiled and slipped the boots and socks from her feet. Blisters covered her feet, and the skin was cracked and raw from the hard miles. She tossed them aside and said, "Now we bathe." She stripped down to her underwear and ran into the lake.

The water was cold and refreshing and perfect. She stayed underneath for a long time, wishing for the moment to last forever. She had died and gone to heaven, or possibly the next best thing. She emerged in time to see Cole, wearing nothing but a pair of briefs, dart into the water. A moment later, Alex jumped in but Artie remained on the shore. The small dog lapped at the water and then trotted further down the shoreline.

They laughed as they swam and splashed each other. Sam dove underneath the water and ran her fingers through her dirty brown hair. She swam deeper into the lake and felt the dirt and sand and blood and tears disappearing in the cool water. Her eyes shot to the shoreline when she came up for air. Artie was barking.

She swam closer to the shore and let her feet fall to the sandy floor. She scanned the horizon and a wave of terror washed over her. Two large clouds of dust had formed to the north and in the distance a foreign rumble. She listened for a moment longer and stared in disbelief at the two dust clouds. The sound registered and Sam took off toward land.

"We have to go," Sam said and sloshed to the shore. She looked back at Cole and Alexandria. They stared back at her with blank expressions. Sam's eyes widened and her finger shot toward the two jeeps speeding toward them and screamed, "Now!"

Chaos ensued as they scrambled to the shore and pawed for their gear. Artie continued to bark as the two trucks sped down the shore road. They were a quarter mile away and coming up fast. Sam pulled on her dress and it clung to her body. She didn't have time for anything else. By the time she grabbed Cole's rifle, the two trucks skidded to a stop. Sam lifted the barrel of the rifle and aimed. The engines revved and cut out.

The truck doors opened in unison and six men climbed out with guns drawn. They wore in military fatigues, and each carried a service revolver on their hip. Sam wondered whose army they belonged to but figured she'd never find out. She would kill them before she found out.

"Drop it," one of the men ordered. He resembled Cole in both height and build; stocky and intimidating. His thick red beard hung to his chest and a giant spider web tattoo stretched over his bald head.

Sam kept the AR firmly in her grasp and the man in her sights. She steadied her breath and placed her finger over the trigger.

"I'd rather there not be any bloodshed if it's all the same," the man with the red beard said. His words oozed with a thick southern drawl.

"I will shoot you," Sam said. "We don't want any trouble. Let us go."

"If I lower my pistol, will you do the same?" the man asked.

"No."

The man smiled. "Well, I'm going to lower it anyway." He let the pistol fall to his side but kept his finger on the trigger. "My men are going to lower theirs too." He nodded and the five other men lowered their weapons. "If you shoot, you'll be doing it in cold blood. Can you live with that?"

"I'll manage," Sam said.

"I reckon that's true." The man with the beard chuckled and holstered his weapon. "Any of you infected?"

Sam shook her head.

"Well, I suppose you need to finish getting dressed and come with us." He spit a brown wad of chewing tobacco on the ground and wiped his mouth with the sleeve of his filed jacket. "Our camp is a little ways up the shore. Got food and medical supplies. Got a couple of doctors that can patch you up."

"And if we don't?" Sam asked.

"If you don't what?" Red Beard asked.

"If we don't come with you?"

"Well," the man raised a hand to his chin and stroked the thick beard, "I reckon you can do as you please. But judging by the way you all look..." the man paused and spit on the ground again, "I don't think you'll last much longer out here. Isn't that right, Albright?"

Sam's heart skipped a beat. "How did you—"

"We can talk back at camp," the man said. "There's a lot to discuss. Ain't that right, Porter?"

"Who are you?" Sam asked.

"Name's Sawyer. Jack Sawyer." He started toward vehicles, took a few steps and turned back, "Don't worry," he chuckled, "it's only going to get a million times weirder." He flashed a smile and then climbed into the jeep.

The men retreated to their vehicles and Sam lowered her weapon. She looked to Cole whose mouth was agape and then to Alex who half-naked and shivering. "Finish putting on your clothes."

"What're we gonna do?" Cole asked, still staring at the jeeps.

"We'll fill our water bottles up and go back the way we came," Sam said. She picked the cargo pants and awkwardly put them on while still holding onto the rifle.

"But they said they have food," Alexandria said.

Sam's stomach grumbled at the concept and she looked over to the jeeps. She could see the man called Sawyer staring back at her through the windshield. She shook her head. "There was food in Lost Angel, wasn't there?" She pulled on her socks. "Didn't mean you wanted to stick around for it."

"They got a doctor, too," Cole said as he shoved a leg into the frayed leg of the tuxedo pants.

"Yeah, I heard that part." She shoved a blistered foot into one of the boots and then the other. The pain made her eyes water.

"Miss Sam—"

"What are you waiting for, Cole? Fill up the water bottles. Alexandria put your shoes on. We need to go."

"Miss Sam," Cole started again, "I think—"

"You think what exactly?" Sam cut him off. "That these men are a bunch of nice guys out for a stroll. That the assault rifles and service pistols they're carrying around are for protection?" Her words were angry and bitter. "Come on, Cole. Use your goddamn head. With food being as scarce as it is and they just up and offer us some? And medical attention? You really think that's what they're trying to do? They know our names. They found us in the middle of nowhere. Why would we go anywhere with them?"

"Sam," Alex whispered, "I'm really hungry."

Sam turned to Alex and lowered her voice. "We're all hungry. All of us. But I'm not going to let your brother have died in vain so the first person we meet up with ends up killing us. Or worse."

Alexandria looked away and tears filled her eyes, but when she spoke again her voice was cold and bitter, "But you'll do him the injustice of letting me starve to death? You'll let me starve like he did because these men might interfere with you getting to Concordia?"

The words hit her like a shotgun blast. Tears stung her eyes, and she looked away from the girl. "What if he's a bad guy?" she whispered. "A bad guy like the President?"

There was a long moment of silence. Finally, Alex said, "I think if he was a bad guy like that then we'd already be in the back of their trucks. They know your name, maybe they're good guys. They didn't shoot and they're not forcing us to go anywhere."

Sam made eye contact with the man named Sawyer. Deep inside his face struck a nerve of familiarity. As familiar as the man in the monitor had in Lost Angel. He nodded to her, and she looked to Cole hoping he would err on the side of caution. But she knew she had the lost battle the moment their eyes met.

"We can't do this alone, Miss Sam." His words were somber but true. "If you want to make it to Concordia then we need to take their help."

Sam winced at the words.

"When we left Lost Angel," Cole continued, "we didn't have nothin'. We pieced together what we could from the scrapyard and we got lucky with findin' water, but we ain't gonna last much longer without food and some medicine. If Nick dying don't prove it then I don't know what else will." He wrapped an arm around Alex's shoulder and squeezed the girl tightly. She buried her head in his chest and sobbed.

"We can't go with them," Sam pleaded. "This is all wrong. Don't you understand? We're in the middle of the desert and these men come out of nowhere and they know our names. We can't go."

"You're free to do what you like, Miss Sam." Cole took a deep breath as if the words hurt to say. "But me and Alex are gonna go to that camp regardless."

A wave of terror washed over her. "You can't leave me."

Cole frowned. "I ain't leavin' you. If you don't go to the camp, you'll be leaving us."

She looked to the road leading back to Las Vegas, back to Lost Angel and to New Hope, and then she looked to the men in the trucks. She could make it alone but at what cost? If she turned her back on them and the men turned out to be evil then whatever happened would be on her.

When she turned back to Cole and Alex, she saw Jordan's ghostly frame lingering behind them. He nodded, as if to confirm Cole's words, and then gave a sorrowful smile. Sam blinked, and he was gone.

"Okay," she whispered. "We go with them."

The threesome gathered their gear and walked to the fleet of vehicles. Alex picked Artie up from the desert floor and he vigorously licked her face. Sam crawled into the empty passenger seat next to Sawyer and Cole, Alex and Artie climbed into the back. Sawyer looked at them and then smiled.

"Glad you decided to join us," he said.

"Didn't have much of a choice," Sam said.

"Well, I'm glad none the same."

Sawyer shifted the tranny into drive and turned the jeep around. "The camp's on the north side of the lake," he said over the roar of the engine. "It'll take us about an hour to get there. Used to be a town called Overton. It got walled up during the infection. After the first couple of us were awakened, we cleared it out. Started rebuilding."

"Awakened?" Sam asked.

"I'll explain that part once we get to camp. I find it's better to hear things on a full stomach."

As the jeep rolled north, a question emerged at the forefront of Sam's thoughts. How did they know where to find us if their camp is an hour away? They had only been at the lake for 15 minutes when the soldiers had shown up. Panic clutched at her heart and she gripped the handle of the knife and slowly pulled it from its sheath. "What were you doing an hour away from your camp?"

The jeep sped up as they reached the remnants of an old service road.

"Had to come pick you up, Albright. Why else would we be burning all this fuel?"

"How do you know our names?" Sam asked and shifted the knife to her other hand. A millisecond later and she poked the tip into Sawyer's abdomen; not hard enough to break skin, but enough to get his attention. The man looked down at the blade and then back to the road. "How'd you know where to find us?"

"How about you holster your weapon and enjoy the ride?" Sawyer said evenly. "You'll be debriefed when we get back to camp. Don't worry your pretty little head about all the details."

Blood-red rage flashed in Sam's eyes and she lifted the knife to Sawyer's throat. "You'll tell me now."

The half-smile Sawyer wore beneath the bushy beard faded but he kept his eyes on the dirt road ahead of them. Suddenly the jeep slowed and a moment later they pulled off the road. The convoy behind them pulled over as well.

"What's going on?" Cole asked from the back.

"Albright seems to have a wild hair up her ass," Sawyer said. The handle of the knife vibrated in her hand with each word he spoke and a bright red trickle of blood emerged from underneath the tip of the blade. He lowered his voice to a whisper. "Holster your weapon, Captain. That's a goddamn order."

"Captain?" Sam asked, taken aback.

"Yes," Sawyer said. "Captain Samantha Michelle Albright. Daughter of Randall and Connie Albright. Sister of Rebecca Albright. Your father was a plumber and died when you were three years old. Your mother was technical engineer for a large healthcare corporation and died during the quarantines. Two hours ago, a blip appeared on our radar. There's a GPS tracking chip inserted in your left frontal cortex. There's one in all of us. That's how we knew you were out there. That's why we're here."

Sam's head spun. "Rebecca?"

"Rebecca wasn't infected," Sawyer said and gently pushed the knife from his throat. "But her situation is a little more complicated."

The image of the little girl from laundry flashed through her mind. Her fingertips gripped against the doorframe as the Ministry's soldiers carried her to her death. The panic in her eyes. "How old?"

"That's complicated too," Sawyer said. "But if I had to guess, I'd say about nine."

"No," Sam said. Tears rushed to her eyes and spilled down her cheeks. "No. Her name was Rebecca Young." Sam remembered how the two of them looked like sisters. How Sam always felt so close to the girl. She dropped the knife to the floor and buried her head in her hands. "No, no, no, no." Her chest heaved and breath quickened. The memory of Rebecca in the old apartment. The memory of her being dragged to her death. Sisters. "No!" she screamed.

4

The jeep sped north up the coastline until the lake disappeared. A steel gate, pieced together from sheets of aluminum, appeared on the horizon and the jeep slowed to a crawl. A makeshift wall of old cars, worn-out appliances, and other junk had been stacked and stretched in either direction. Sawyer honked the horn twice, and the gates rattled open.

"How did you know all that?" Sam asked. It was the first time she had spoken since Sawyer's revelation about Rebecca. Her body was numb. Empty. "I can't remember anything before…"

"Before the fires?" Sawyer asked.

Sam nodded.

"That's how it works for everyone. Trust me, Albright, I can't promise to make things less strange moving forward, but they will become a lot clearer. By the time it's all said and done, it'll be crystal. Just hang in there a bit longer."

"Okay," Sam whispered.

Once the gates opened all the way, Sawyer nosed the jeep inside and parked just within the barrier. Sam marveled at the city inside as she stepped out of the truck. Military-grade tents stretched out on either side of a dirt path; dozens on either side. Men and women, all clad in military fatigues, bustled through the encampment.

"It's unbelievable," Cole said as he climbed out of the back of the jeep.

The other truck pulled into a spot beside them and the gates clattered shut. The half-dozen soldiers climbed from the truck and stared at Sam. Cole helped Alex from the jeep and she set Artie, who had ridden silently in her lap, onto the ground. The dog sat down beside its new owner and scratched at his ear with his hind leg.

Sawyer exited the vehicle last, and started barking orders. "Herd. Sanchez. Front and center." Two men broke away from their squadron.

"I need you two to track down the Dr. Alvarez and Dr. Etter and help them prep the medical tents. Let them know that we've got three in need of an oil change and two that'll need a tune up. Full diagnostics for all three."

"Sir, yes sir," the two said in unison and took off toward the epicenter of the camp. Sam watched as they disappeared between the rows of tents.

"What's an oil change?" Alexandria asked.

"I reckon you three are pretty dehydrated from being out in the Mojave," Sawyer said. "Couple bags of saline should get any toxins flushed out of your system and have you headed back in the right direction."

"And a tune up?" Sam asked.

"We need to awaken your brains," Sawyer said and stroked his beard. "Let you in on what's been going on out here for the last 300 years."

"Sounds good," Sam said.

"Baker," Sawyer continued, "you and Price go tell the chef to get us three extra plates and don't be stingy with the fixin's."

Alex cleared her throat.

"Oh," Sawyer said and smiled down at Artie, "and tell him to make a bowl of chow for the pooch."

Two more men sounded off in unison and then took off into camp.

"That sounds even better," Cole said and smiled.

Sawyer chuckled. "Well, you look like you missed a few meals, Sarge." He clapped Cole on his shoulder and smiled. Cole looked back in stunned amazement. "Hell, last time I saw you, you were about—" Sawyer's words cut out and the grin faded from his lips.

"What's wrong?" Sam asked.

"You three came from the west, didn't you?" Sawyer asked, not taking his eyes off the back of Cole's neck.

"Yes," Sam answered.

Sawyer turned to Alexandria and looked her up and down and then spun back to Cole. His face grayed despite the mid-morning sun beating down on them. "Lost Angel?"

"How'd you know?"

"The girl's as pale as a ghost and Sgt. Porter has a fucking metal box protruding from the back of his skull," Sawyer said. There was a long moment of silence before Sawyer spoke again. "I'm goddamn sorry, Sarge." He sighed and tears welled in his eyes. Acid filled Sam's stomach. "Hell, sorry don't even describe it."

"Got anybody around here who can remove it?" Cole asked.

Sawyer shook his head and a dreadful silence overtook the group. Sam reached over and squeezed Cole's arms but he said nothing. Tears beaded in his eyes and rolled down his cheeks. Alex sobbed and scooped Artie off the ground. She buried her head against his fur.

"How do you know about Lost Angel?" Sam asked after a long moment.

"You're not the first to make it out of that hellhole," Sawyer said. "Come on. Let's get something to eat."

They followed Sawyer to a grouping of picnic tables set up in the middle of the camp. A dozen men and women sat at neighboring benches. They all stood and saluted when Sam walked past them.

"At ease," Sawyer said. The men and women lowered their hands but remained standing. "Eat your damned food for Christ's sake." The group dropped back to the bench but their eyes remained locked on Sam.

"What was that all about?" Sam asked as they passed.

"You'll find out soon enough, Captain."

Sawyer took a seat at the far picnic table where four plates of food waited. Bacon, eggs and an assortment of fruit covered the plate and Sam's stomach rumbled as she caught a whiff of it. A bowl full of eggs and gravy sat on the ground and when Alex put Artie back on the ground, the dog trotted to over to the bowl and chowed down. Sawyer motioned for them to sit down and shoved a strip of bacon into his mouth.

Sam and Cole sat on the opposite side of the bench and Alex joined Sawyer on the other side. Sam stared at the food in disbelief. Her mouth salivated as the growl in her stomach erupted into pangs of hunger.

"Please," Sawyer said and beckoned at them with his bacon. "Eat. I can hear your stomach's from here."

Alex grinned and then dug into her food. Cole and Sam did the same. Sam ate so fast she barely tasted it. She knew it was a mistake, knew that her stomach would reject such a feast if she didn't pace herself, but couldn't help it.

"I guess I should fill you in," Sawyer said and pitched Artie a strip of bacon. The terrier caught it in the air and devoured it in two bites. "You got any burning questions before I start?"

"How do you have all this food?" Alex asked without hesitation.

Sawyer grinned at her. "We run a farm on the back half of the property. Got pigs, chickens and goats. Had a few cows a while back, but a couple stubborn heifers and a bull more interested in rubbing his dick in the dirt and that was that. No more cows. We've got a few crops as well. Corn and potatoes. Okra. Some herbs. We've got a decent irrigation setup and a few guys that were farmers in the old world."

"And you just give these supplies out to strangers," Sam asked.

"You're not strangers, but I get what you're saying. We haven't seen too much in the way of foot traffic around these parts. There are close to 70 soldiers here and there's still too much for us to eat. We store what we can but we only have one working solar generators to power the camp. So in the rare instance that a *stranger* makes it to our world, we like to take care of them."

"How do you know our names?" Sam asked. "And why did you call me Captain Albright?"

Sawyer stopped chewing and looked at her a long time.

"What?" Sam asked.

"What all *do* you know?" Sawyer said and raised an eyebrow.

"Not much," Sam admitted as she shoved a forkful of eggs into her mouth.

Sawyer looked from Sam to Cole. "And you?"

Cole shrugged. "Bits and pieces. There was a man named Holden Dec—"

"Holden Deckard," Sawyer finished. "He was supposed to fill you in about everythi—"

"He's dead," Sam interrupted.

Sawyer sighed. "Damn. Holden was a good man. That's a shame."

A long moment of silence passed as Sawyer stared at his plate.

"I think you should finish what he started," Sam said. "We know about Concordia, and that they've done something to our brains. Altered our memories. And we know about the elite setting off the virus and using us as some messed-up science experiment."

Sawyer nodded. "Well, that's a pretty good overview of it, but it sounds like you're still missing a few key pieces to this puzzle. Where do I start? There's so much to tell you."

"What really happened after the virus was released?"

"Okay," Sawyer said. "The Flowers Corporation released the virus—"

"What?" Sam grabbed ahold of the table as Jordan's words echoed through her mind. *I remember the flowers. They're not what you think. They're bad. Remember them. Remember the Flowers.*

"The Flowers Corporation was a cutting-edge bio-lab before the infection. They're the company that the upper echelon tasked with creating the virus. It's their memory suppression chips whirring in your brains. Their cryotanks. Their experiments.

"The rich folks, the Vondenberg Group, wanted a world all to themselves so they hired the Flowers Corporation to make that happen."

Sawyer paused and tossed another strip of bacon to the dog. Artie woofed it down and then barked happily. "And after the virus wiped everything out, they were tasked with managing the city from a scientific standpoint. Their goal was to create a world where we wouldn't relive the mistakes of the past. They are the nerve center of Concordia."

"They're the ones to blame for all this," Sam said.

"Well, I'd put a fair share of blame on the Vondenberg Group for starting this mess to begin with, but all of this is the Flowers Corp's playground. They're the mad scientists and we're they're monsters. Well, besides for the actual monsters roaming around outside. They created the virus, they made the cryotanks, and they made the new cities. But they made a huge mistake before they stuck us in those ice buckets."

"What mistake?" Cole asked.

"They trained us to be killers."

Sam shook her head. There were too many facts to keep straight and it wading through it all. "Start from the beginning," Sam said.

"They released the virus in 2032. One day we're all walking around sniffing the roses, and the next day, almost everybody's dropped dead. And the day after that, a small portion of those dead people are waking back up as fucking zombies. Un-fucking-believable. It was like we woke up in some George Romero movie."

"Don't curse in front of the ladies," Cole said.

Sawyer looked taken aback for a moment and then chuckled. "It's the end of the world and Sgt. Porter's worried about bad language. Ain't that something. A true gentleman amongst our ranks. Alright. I'll do my best."

He laughed again and then continued, "So now we've got people rising from the grave and Concordia doing their best to firebomb every city from here to Timbuktu to control this undead outbreak. Meanwhile, they discover another unexpected result yielded from the virus."

"Us," Sam whispered.

"You're goddamn right," Sawyer said and took a drink of water. "They send in quarantine teams to all these cities and find handfuls of survivors in each one. So they gather us up and take us to Concordia to run lab work on us. Turns out the virus has the reverse effect on us. Sharpens our senses. Strengthens our muscles and our immune systems."

Memories of Sam holding the General's Desert Eagle and killing his soldiers with such ease and willingness flashed in her brain.

"At first," Sawyer continued, "they trained us. The infected threatened Concordia's security, and we were viewed as a solution. And for five years, they developed an army to fight this horde that's now taken over every city that's left standing."

"And I'm a captain in this army?" Sam asked.

"To say the least," Sawyer said and smiled. "Anyway, while they trained us, the Flowers Corp developed an anti-virus from our blood. Not a cure but the equivalent to the flu shot. Something that would help protect the Concordians from catching the disease, but something that would have to be tweaked as the virus kept evolving, and that's what prompted the freezing. All of a sudden we became too valuable to send out and battle with these deadheads. So they dumped the majority of us into ice tanks and kept a few warm bodies for the sole purpose of blood harvesting. When one person died, another was unfrozen, and so on and so forth until the Flowers Corp decided that we could serve two functions at once.

"A dozen or so locations around the U.S. were picked, and they constructed the new cities. Miniature versions of Concordia. When construction was complete, they started waking us up, inserting these fucking chips so we couldn't remember anything and then dropping us off in the cities. Data harvesting took precedent over blood. Each city contains a different set of variables. And they measure how we react to certain things. What happens if we force them to breed or refuse to let them? What happens if we take away this or give them that?"

"We're lab rats," Sam said. Sawyer had confirmed what Holden had told them. They were one big science experience. Their pain and suffering helped Concordia thrive. White hot rage coursed through Sam's blood.

"Yep," Sawyer agreed and pitched another piece of pork to Artie. The dog caught it and wagged his tail. "We're all little white mice trying to navigate some sick, twisted board game."

"How do you know all this?" Sam asked.

"I was an electrician in a town called Devil's Pass. It's about 400 miles north of here. One day, me and a buddy of mine were working on restoring this old generator when something went wrong. Zapped the ever-loving snot out of both of us. But it fried the chip in our brains, too. All our memories came flooding back. We both remembered everything. We were the first to be awakened. We escaped and headed south. Found an old unmarked army base in the desert. Deep underground. That's where we found the jeeps and the tents. Found all sorts of stuff there. Medical supplies. Weapons. We think Flowers used it as a remote operating facility because we found a device that acts as an EMP. It can short-circuit the chip in your brain. And more importantly, we found a GPS unit that detects when a chip is in range. That's how we knew you two were coming. So we took the EMP and the GPS and started recruiting. Found this town and set up shop. Been here for three years. Found four other cities within a hundred-mile radius. We never made it to—"

"New Hope," Sam finished.

"Well isn't that fitting," Sawyer said.

"So what happens now?" Sam asked.

"Now we give you your memories back," Sawyer said. "We'll hook you up to the machine and fry the chip."

"And I'll remember everything?"

"Good and bad." Sawyer sighed and then looked grimly to Cole. "We won't be able to use it on you, Sarge."

Cole said nothing.

"That device they implanted into the back of your head," Sawyer said, "like I said, it's not the first time we've seen it. We've had a few run-ins with those shitheels in L.A. before. We zapped a recruit that had a similar device in his head. Dropped dead before we could turn the machine off. As much as you'd like your memories back, I'm sure you're not quite ready to kick the bucket for them."

"No," Cole whispered. Sam reached out and grabbed his hand, but Cole didn't return her grasp.

"Didn't think so," Sawyer said and then turned to Alex. "The doctors can fix you up though, pretty lady." He offered the girl a smile. "I'm willing to bet they can take some of that plastic out of you and if you want, I can shave that purple shit out of your hair. You didn't register on our GPS unit, so I'm willing to bet you were born in that hellhole."

Alex offered a tiny smile, nodded and then bowed her head, tears dripping from her eyes.

"Her brother," Sam whispered, "We lost him along the way."

"Damned sorry to hear it," Sawyer said.

There was a long pause as Sawyer drank the rest of his mug. When he finished, he offered them a big grin. "There's a lot to get done here," he said, "but we'll find a place for all three of you, and over the next few years, we'll continue—"

"Next few years?" Sam asked incredulously. "We need to go now."

"Can't," Sawyer said. "We're dealing with the smartest, most evil motherfuckers this world has ever known and they live behind a hundred-foot concrete wall. We can't just go headstrong into battle. It'd be a bloodbath. We can disable the GPS chip, give you back your memories and the three of you can live a normal life here while we scout out other cities."

"I don't want a normal life," Sam said.

"Oh," Sawyer said, "you're one of those, huh?"

"What does that mean?" Sam asked.

"Seen your kind before," Sawyer said. "Patched them up and sent them out to face the big, bad city. They come in here like we don't know what we're doing. Like we're running some 2-bit operation and fly out of here on the same bullshit notion. All of them running by that live or die attitude. Like they're the only ones that can bring down Concordia. I've got news for you, Captain, you ain't the first and more than likely won't be the last. You go and you will fail."

"They killed my..." Sam's words trailed off.

"Hell, they killed a lot of people. They killed the whole fucking world. Try to grasp that concept. The world was dying, so they killed off almost every single person living on it. Mothers, fathers, children, all of them."

"This is different," Sam said. "This is—"

"Personal?" Sawyer interrupted. "Preaching to the choir. They got both my parents and four of my brothers." He shook his head and his face flushed. "But we'll patch you up. Hell, we'll load you up with supplies and point you in the right direction. I've got some gnarly hunting supplies that are going to waste. But I'll tell you this, Captain Albright...you walk out of here by yourself, and you will die in vain."

"She won't be alone," Cole said.

"No offense, Sarge," Sawyer said, "But you're a ticking time-bomb. One of these days, you're going to change into one of those overgrown demon fucks and you'll end up ripping this poor girl to shreds."

Cole looked at Sam, but she didn't break her eyes with Sawyer. Sawyer looked from Cole to Sam and then back to Cole.

"Shit. She didn't tell you. Well, bad news, you're going to become a giant creature that's as mindless and bloodthirsty as those damned zombies out there, except you'll be a hundred times stronger and have a pretty nasty temper to boot."

"That will never happen," Cole said.

"Seen it happen," Sawyer said. "One killed 12 of my men before we could bring it down. You two don't have the slightest fucking idea of the state of shit you're in, do you?"

"I'll be there too," Alex said.

Sawyer took a deep breath and seemed to relax. "No offense, little lady, but you look a bit on the banged up side. We're gonna patch you up, but one of those damned infected cats gets its hands on you, or the big guy shows you what's really on the inside, and it's going to be lights out for you too."

"So you're saying there's no point—" Samantha tried, but Sawyer interrupted again.

"I'm saying that you're better off settling down here for a while. We have beds. We have food and doctors. You can have a decent life here while we make the necessary preparations. And then we can all take on these assholes together."

"We're not staying," Sam said.

"Well, for all our sakes, I hope you gettin' your memory back will change your mind," Sawyer said. "But if not, it's your funeral. In the meantime, we'll patch up you all up. Your girl will need a few days to heal up good enough to be road-ready. Are you going to wait around that long at least?"

"Two days," Sam said. "You check her out. Get her back to good. And we'll be on our way."

Sam had a funny feeling in her guts. Too much information had been given. She was having a hard time processing it all. It confirmed everything that Holden had said and confirmed some of her biggest fears. But waiting around for years to launch an attack on Concordia would be unbearable.

"There's an empty tent toward the back of the lot," Sawyer said. "You and Cole can stay there. We'll get started fixing Alex—"

This time, it was Sam that interrupted. "No. I stay with her."

Sawyer grinned. "Well, no offense, Albright, but unless you're a goddamn doctor then I suggest you get some rest and get your mind right. You'll be more in our way than anything else. Now, I've fed you, I've given you a place to rest your head before your suicide mission, and I've offered to give you supplies. Plus, I've filled you in on all the fuzzy little details. Now you can choose to appreciate those things or choose not to, I could give a shit less. I think I've earned the slightest bit of trust."

"No offense to you, Sawyer, but it takes a lot to earn my trust. Just because you randomly showed up in the desert and happen to know my name doesn't earn shit. I stay with the girl. She'll be in eyesight at all times."

Sawyer rolled his eyes and then nodded. He looked at Alex and said, "I'd at least like to go ahead and get some saline pumping. Do you think you can trust us for five minutes while you two finish your breakfasts?"

Sam nodded and Alex stood up from her seat.

"Finish eating and then come find us at the medical tents. Straight back and on the left. They're marked with white crosses. You get lost and someone will point you in the right direction."

"Okay," Sam said.

Sawyer nodded and he and Alex started off toward the center of the encampment. Artie followed at their heels. Sam had offended him and perhaps turned an ally into an enemy. She was sure that he had told them the truth about the Flowers Corporation, but she still didn't trust him.

Sam and Cole finished their meals in silence but didn't leave the table when they were done. They stared at each other for a long time, an awkward tension between them. Finally, Cole spoke, "You should have killed me."

A chill ran down Sam's spine but his words weren't unexpected. "What?"

"Back at the plane. You should have killed me. Why didn't you?"

"Because I need you," she said.

"No you don't. You don't need anyone, Miss Sam. I've seen you in battle. I've seen the way you handle yourself. You don't need me. The truth is you *can't* kill me."

Sam put her elbows on the table and rested her head in her hands. Her head was pounding, and she felt nauseous. "Maybe."

"Why?"

"I don't know."

There was a long pause. Finally, Cole said, "I'll turn into one of those things. I'll hurt you. I'll hurt her."

Sam raised her head and looked at him through blurry eyes. "You won't."

"How do you know?" Cole asked.

"Because I won't let you."

Cole opened his mouth to say something else but was interrupted by shouting from somewhere inside the camp. Sam's heart dropped and the two of them sprung from the table and ran toward Alex.

They sprinted toward the center of the camp until they came across a large crowd of soldiers that had gathered outside one of the tents marked with a white medical cross. The group was all talking amongst themselves and didn't notice Sam and Cole.

"What's going on?" Sam said as she pushed through the crowd.

Another one of Alex's blood-curdling screams shot out from behind the canvas flap and Cole barreled over several of the soldiers. Sam followed close on his heels. She unsheathed her knife, ready for whatever was waiting for them on the opposite side of the tent.

They made it to the front of the crowd and entered the tent. Alex was standing on the opposite side of the room. She was holding a pistol and waving it around erratically at anyone who came within a few feet of her. Sawyer stood in the back corner of the room motionless, his side holster empty.

"Alex," Sam said. "What are you—?"

"I'm pregnant," she said, her voice shaking. Tears streamed down her face and the gun trembled in her hand.

"What?" Sam asked.

"I'm pregnant!" she sobbed. She aimed the barrel of the gun toward her stomach as if to emphasize what she was saying. "I'm pregnant with the President's baby." She took a deep breath and then screamed again. "There's a fucking monster growing inside of me! I have to get it out."

Sam grasped the reality of the situation, laid the knife on the floor and took a small step toward Alex. "They can take care of it," she said trying to keep her tone as even as possible. "They'll make it go away and everything will be okay."

"Like the doctor in Lost Angel took care of Cole?"

Sam didn't say anything. She held her breath as Alex processed the dozens of emotions that were swirling through her brain.

"It should have been me that died," Alex said.

"No," Sam said. "I promise you, we'll get through this together. Everything will be okay."

"No it won't," Alex said through tears. "Nothing will ever be okay again. Nick is dead. He's fucking dead!"

Sam took another step forward, but Alex raised the gun. It was enormous in her small hand. She aimed it at Sam and placed her finger on the trigger. "We should have never left Lost Angel. You should have never come back for me. This is your fault. This is all your fault. If it wasn't for you, none of this would have happened."

"Alex…" Sam searched for the words that would make her put down the pistol, but nothing sounded right. Finally, she said, "I'm sorry."

"I am too," Alex said, and then she placed the barrel of the gun against her temple and pulled the trigger.

5

"This isn't going to end well," Jordan said.

Sam opened her eyes. The nightmare had returned, and she stood face to face with the horrific memory of her past. She stood in the field staring out over the inferno. A breeze picked up carrying an odor of burnt flesh and decay from the burning city beyond. Behind her, the Ferris wheel rocked back and forth, letting out ominous squeaks each time.

"Why?" Sam asked. The shattered remnants of her heart dug into her chest. "Why does it have to be like this?"

"Because David wants it that way," Jordan answered.

"David?"

She turned and saw the boy from her past standing near the Ferris wheel. His naked flesh seemed to be peeling from his body and his eyes were milky-white orbs. The boy didn't move, didn't breathe, or make a sound.

"This is all his work," Jordan said. "This whole world is all his creation."

"What do you mean?"

David's body jerked and his head snapped backwards, his neck cracking in a bone-chilling fashion. The boy fell to his hands and knees and crawled a few steps toward them. Sam gasped and took a step back, but Jordan grabbed her hand and squeezed.

"Don't be afraid," Jordan said. "He can't hurt you here."

"Why does he want to hurt me at all?" Sam asked.

"Because he can. Because he's one of them."

"One of whom?"

"One of the bad people."

The words were juvenile and unlike something Jordan would say. She turned to see not Jordan Riggs holding her arm, but Rebecca. Blood filled the small girl's eyes and a stream of crimson dripped from her nose.

Sam pulled away and took an awkward step back. She fell into the high grass and the girl grew in front of her eyes. Her blonde hair turned a shade of lavender and her skull cracked open where the bullet had exited. Blood poured from her head and Alex took a step closer. In her peripheral vision, David was moving closer as well; his head canted all the way back so that his skull touched his upper back. He crawled toward her in short jerky motions and let out a high-pitched squeal.

Alex lowered herself on top of Sam, straddling her hips. Sam's heart raced in her chest as her outstretched arms searched for anything to defend herself, but found nothing. A moment later, she felt David clutching her hand, and she screamed.

"Sam," Alex said, but the word came out in a gurgle and blood poured from the girl's mouth. "You did this. You promised it would be okay."

"No," Sam said as she tried.

"You promised!"

Sam opened her eyes as she woke up into a world of darkness. She sat up and put her arms out in front of her in case the nightmare carried over into reality and Alex or David was in arm's reach. They weren't. She was alone.

Tears streamed down her cheeks as she fought to gain some semblance of familiarity, but the world was pitch-black. She put her head in her hands and sobbed until someone unzipped her tent flap. Moonlight spilled into the tent and a large hulking beast emerged in the entrance. Sam slammed her eyelids shut and dug her fingernails into her thigh. She was convinced she was still dreaming.

"You alright, Miss Sam?"

It wasn't a monster. It was Cole. She exhaled and opened her eyes. She wiped her cheeks off with the back of her hand and stymied a sniffle. "I'm okay," she whispered. Her eyes struggled to adjust to the lack of light, but she could make out Cole's face through the darkness. The big man looked as if he had aged ten years. "What happened?" she managed.

"You took it hard," Cole said. "The doctors' had to drug you before you killed somebody. Nothin' bad, just somethin' to make you sleep."

Sam didn't remember losing it. The image of Alex standing in front of her flashed through her brain. Then the aftermath of the trigger-pull. But nothing after that. Sam tried to clear her mind but couldn't. "How?"

"What?"

"How did she have Sawyer's gun?"

"Asked the same question after everything was over," Cole said. "Sawyer said she must have lifted it off of him when they were walking to the medical tent."

Sam shook her head. It didn't make sense. "You believe him?"

"No, but I don't know why he'd lie. And it's not like he pulled the trigger."

Sam thought about this for a moment and then asked, "What if she wasn't pregnant?"

"But why?" Cole asked dropping his voice to a whisper so low that Sam had to strain to hear him. "Why would they go to all the trouble to get us back here? Why would Sawyer go on for so long about what's really going on outside? Just to trick some little girl into killin' herself? It don't make sense."

The image of the blood-soaked canvas tent filled Sam's brain. She remembered running to Alex and putting a hand in the girl's warm, wet hair. She forced the image out of her mind and thought. "What if that's how they were going to get us to stay?" she said after a moment. "Tell her she was pregnant, expecting us to stay with her."

Cole stroked his beard. "What about the gun? Why would she have pulled it off of him before they got to the tents?"

Sam shook her head. "I don't think Alex has ever even held a gun. How would she get it out of Sawyer's holster without him knowing?"

"Then when?"

"I don't know…" Sam's voice trailed off as an even darker thought crossed her mind. What if the plan was to just get them to stay long enough? What if someone was coming for them? "How long have been out?"

"Day and a half."

"Cole, we need to get out of this place. Now."

They had stripped off Sam's clothes; the remnants of the little black dress and President Gates' cargo pants. The moonlight revealed that they had replaced the tattered rags with a pair of sweats. She was barefoot and tiny pebbles cut into her already blistered feet as the duo slunk back to Cole's tent next door. She would need to get shoes before they left. A wave of panic washed over her. "Cole, do you still have the supplies?"

"Some," he said as lifted the flap of the neighboring tent.

Sam stood in the darkness as Cole fumbled around for a long moment. There was a loud click, and a flame cut through the pitch-black. Cole held a glass lantern, but Sam wasn't focused on him. All of her attention was drawn to the man with the red beard sitting in the corner of Cole's tent.

"You two goin' somewhere?" Sawyer asked.

Without thinking, Sam lunged toward him but the man moved with same speed and skill as her. He sidestepped her and then delivered a rear kick to Sam's knee. She crashed into the ground, hitting her head on the metal folding chair that Sawyer had been sitting in.

"I'm not here to stop you—" Sawyer tried to say, but Cole punched him square in the jaw. Sawyer stumbled and his bloody lips gleamed in the lamplight.

Sam was back on her feet in an instant with the collapsed steel chair in hand. She swung as hard as she could, but Sawyer blocked the brunt of the blow with his forearm. In one swift motion, Sawyer flicked a left jab that connected with Sam's nose while simultaneously snatching the chair away with his other hand. The blow rocked Sam, but she managed to keep her feet.

"I'm trying to help you two," Sawyer said, but the scowl on his face said otherwise.

Cole wrapped his massive arms around the soldier in a reverse bear hug. The chair fell to the floor as Sawyer struggled to break free. Sam lunged forward and snatched the pistol from the holster on the man's waistband. In one smooth motion, she flipped off the safety and pressed the barrel underneath Sawyer's chin. The man stopped struggling at once.

"Tell me how a little girl unholstered your gun without you knowing," Sam said.

"You're no little girl," Sawyer answered.

Blood rushed into Sam's face and she slammed her knee into Sawyer's groin. The man groaned, but Cole kept him upright. "You know who I'm talking about. How the fuck did Alex get your gun?"

Sawyer was about to speak when Sam detected a flutter of movement coming from the tent's entrance. She removed the barrel of the gun from Sawyer's face and aimed it at the tent.

"No," Sawyer barked. "Stand down. Whoever is outside, stand down."

Sam's finger tightened over the trigger.

"Please," Sawyer pleaded. "Don't do it. The girl didn't lift the gun off my person. I was an idiot. I set it down and went out for a smoke. I hate carrying it. I'm sorry. I'm so sorry."

"Shut up," Sam said as she tried to process what he said. Outside the tent, she could hear voices whispering. It was only a matter of time before the whole camp was gathered out there.

"We're on the same side," Sawyer said. "What happened to the girl was an unfortunate accident, and I take full responsibility for—" At this,

Sam shoved the pistol back against his throat. Sawyer's eyes widened, but he continued. "I understand if you want to leave. We'll give you as many supplies as you can carry. All I'm asking for is that you don't hurt my men."

A long moment of silence passed before Sam spoke again. "Was she really pregnant?"

"Yes."

"And your doctors can verify this? They can show me proof if I ask for it?"

"Yes."

Sam removed the gun from Sawyer's throat and nodded to Cole, who released him. "We're leaving tonight. I want two weeks' worth of supplies, fresh food for the next few days, and whatever you have that will last beyond that. And as much water as you can give us."

Sawyer nodded.

"I want a change of clothes, socks and shoes. I need weapons and survival gear. And I need one of your trucks with a full tank of gas."

Sawyer scoffed at this and the gun barrel shot straight back to his throat.

"You will do everything I say, give me everything I ask for, or when Cole and I leave this place, we'll be leaving a city full of bodies. I will kill every single one of you myself if I have to." She feathered the trigger with her finger. "Do you believe me?"

"Yes."

"Where's Alex?" Sam asked. Sawyer shifted uncomfortably and Sam buried the barrel of the gun even deeper into his flesh. "Where is she?"

"The medical team did an autopsy of her body," Sawyer said. "We buried her a few hours ago. Sgt. Porter was there. He'll attest that we gave her a proper burial."

The words caught in her throat and tears stung at her eyes, but Sam wouldn't cry in front Sawyer or anyone else. She was done crying. "Is that true, Cole?"

"Yes, Miss Sam."

Sam relaxed her arm. "You'll take me to her burial site while the rest of your team preps our gear. And then you'll accompany us to the gate where we will drive out of here. Do you understand?"

Sawyer nodded. His tough exterior had melted into a mixture of sorrow and fear.

"And you understand what will happen if you or anyone of your team doesn't comply?"

Sawyer nodded again.

"Then lead the way."

6

She wanted to cry but didn't. There was no gravestone or even a marker. Just a mound of loose dirt in the back corner of the campsite. It was surrounded by a dozen other graves. A dozen more needless deaths in Concordia's little game. Sam buried her fingers into the cool dirt and wondered when it would all stop. With Cole's death? With hers? Ever? She hadn't started this war, but would she be the one to end it? Or would she end up in her own unmarked grave somewhere along the way. The questions ran through her mind as she kneaded the earth between her fingers.

Cole stood somberly behind her, and to his left, Sawyer said what sounded like a hushed prayer. Their host had ordered the doctor's lab results to be brought to them immediately, as well as firing off a bevy of other commands, as they departed for the gravesite. In her peripherals, she could see the two doctors approaching them from the distance. Sam whispered a goodbye to the teenage refuge and stood.

"Captain," Sawyer said and cleared his throat, "this is Dr. Etter and Dr. Alvarez. They were the ones that examined Alex."

Sam turned and faced the two men. One of them was a tall, heavy-set man with curly gray hair. He held a piece of paper in between his long pale fingers. Sawyer identified him as Dr. Etter. The other, a squat frog-faced man, sported a long black ponytail and wrung his hands nervously.

"Tell me what happened." Sam said as she pulled Sawyer's pistol from the waistband of her sweats. She wrapped her finger around the trigger, but kept it aimed at the ground. "And if you skip any details, you'll be dead before you hit the ground."

The shorter doctor spoke, "We hooked the girl—"

"Alex," Sam interrupted and raised the pistol in his direction. "Show some respect."

"S-s-sorry," the short doctor stammered. He wiped his brow with his sleeve and continued. "W-W-We tried...we tried..."

"We hooked Alex up to a saline drip," the taller doctor said, taking over the conversation, "and drew a few vials of her blood to test for traces of the RIZ-4 virus. Results came back normal except..."

"Except what?"

"Except she had an elevated hCG level of approximately 150,000; a level you would expect to see in a woman during the end of her first trimester." The tall doctor extended the printout to Sam, but she didn't take it. After a moment, the doctor lowered the paper and continued. "We asked Alex about her sexual history, and after hearing about her encounters in Lost Angel determined that a vaginal examination was necessary. The exam confirmed our diagnosis, and we informed her about the pregnancy."

"And then?" Sam asked as she lowered the pistol, dreading to hear the rest.

"And then the patient—" the short doctor began.

Sam covered the short distance between them with two quick steps and swung. The barrel of the pistol smashed into Dr. Alvarez's face, opening a deep gash above his eye. He stumbled backward and as he did Sam swung again. This time the metal connected with the top of his scalp and the doctor crashed into the ground. "Her name is Alex!" Sam screamed. "Do you fucking understand?"

The doctor made no indication that he did or did not understand, and instead twitched on the ground. Sam was vaguely aware of Sawyer approaching from her rear and spun on him, aiming the sight of the Beretta right between his eyes. He stopped in his tracks and held both of his hands up in surrender.

"We are not enemies," Sawyer said.

"We are today," Sam answered.

Two men emerged in the distance, but Sam kept the pistol aimed at Sawyer. They approached quickly at first but slowed when they realized the severity of the situation. One of them called out, "We've got a jeep gassed and loaded, Captain."

Sam cringed at the title. She wasn't sure of Sawyer's rank but she was sure that the soldier had been talking to her. What if they really were on her side? What if they could have helped her beyond the supplies? It didn't matter now. "Cole, are you ready to head east?"

"Yes," Cole said. But the tone in his voice said otherwise.

"Then let's go."

Sawyer led the group back to the front of the encampment as the moon dipped lower in the sky. It would be sunrise soon. Sam never took her aim off of his backside, and kept her senses attuned in case someone jumped out from the shadows to stop them. No one did though, and they made it safely back to the front of the walled city where the jeep and a small cluster of soldiers waited for them. A small mountain of canvas towered above the rear of the jeep, and Sam's heart ached.

"Keys are in the ignition," one of the men said as they approached, "and the tank is full."

"Thank you, Baker," Sawyer said dismissively.

They paused at the rear of the vehicle and Sam lowered her pistol for the first time since leaving the gravesite. There was a long awkward silence that was finally broken by the city gates rattling open.

"It doesn't have to be this way," Sawyer said. "I can still wake you up. Fry the chip in your brain. You would stay if you could see the big picture."

"No, I wouldn't," Sam whispered and then turned toward the jeep. She took a couple steps before Sawyer spoke again.

"We can't do this without you, Albright." Desperation filled Sawyer's voice "You go out there and get yourself killed…then we're all doomed. Every single person outside their walls is counting on you."

Sam stopped, but didn't turn back. "I can't help you."

She opened the passenger side door and heard a bark. Artie bolted out of the darkness of the camp, sprinted past the soldiers that had gathered around the vehicle and then hopped into the front seat. Sam had forgotten about Artie, but as she stared into the dog's dark eyes, all she could think about was how hard Alex had fallen for the little pup. She nudged it over, climbed into the jeep, and then shut the door. In the rearview mirror, Cole shook Sawyer's hand and words were exchanged. A moment later, the driver's side door opened and Cole climbed in.

"Dual tank," Cole said as he turned the key. "We've got a good chance to make it through Utah if the roads aren't too bad." The engine sputtered once and then roared to life.

"Do you want to stay?" Sam asked.

Cole grabbed ahold of the shifter but paused. "Yes."

Pain shot through Sam's heart and she struggled to find the right words to convince him not to stay. She didn't want to do this by herself. She needed him more than she had ever said. Cole spoke again before she had time to think of an argument to make him stay.

"But I reckon I need to see the end of all this," Cole said and shifted the jeep into drive.

Sam let out a sigh of relief. She didn't know whether to feel guilty or happy as she slouched down in the jeep's seat. Cole pressed on the accelerator and nosed the jeep out of the complex. Sam watched as

Sawyer and his soldiers turned to small blurs in the rearview and then disappeared into the darkness.

7

They drove for almost nine hours before the engine sputtered to a stop. Sam had dozed on and off for the first few hours of the voyage, but each time the nightmares of the burning city had grabbed ahold of her mind. Finally, she invited Artie to ride up front with her. It had curled up in her lap, but now its head was cocked as the vehicle coasted down the road.

They slowed to a stop before Cole shifted into park. They stared ahead silently for a long time. A mountainous landscape lined the horizon, blocking their path to the eastern side of the country. Artie's tail thumped against Sam's leg and he sniffed wildly at the cool air.

"Do you know where we are?" Sam asked.

Cole stroked his beard and looked upon the world. "Colorado. That's the Rockies in front of us."

"How many miles are we from Concordia?"

"A thousand if I had to guess."

She cringed at the answer and opened the passenger door. The thought of a two-month hike was nauseating. Artie jumped down and relieved himself on a nearby tree.

"Should we try to find some gas around here?" Cole asked. "This was a main highway once. Should be a service station around here somewhere."

Sam walked to the rear of the vehicle and unzipped one of the bags. It contained two pairs of military fatigues, five pairs of knit socks, a pair of leather boots, two hatchets, an old road map, and a first-aid kit. Sam shook her head at the sight of the gear. Sawyer had really been on their side. Why else would he have sent such precious resources with them?

"Miss Sam?"

"No," Sam said, moving onto the next bag.

"There's gotta be something in between here and Concordia. How else would the blood trucks make it back and forth?"

The next bag contained nothing but boxes of MRE's. Dozens of them just like the ones from New Hope that she and Jordan had shared. She remembered how stale the crackers were and how they couldn't figure out how to cook the enchiladas. The thought brought a smile to her face and an emptiness to her soul.

"Looked like there was a town about a half-mile back. I can check it out if you'd like."

"Be quick," Sam said. "We can't afford to waste any time. If you don't find anything then if we come across one in the next few days, we'll turn around. Right now, we need to divvy this gear up into two bags and figure out how we're going to carry it all." She opened the third bag and her heart leapt. Inside were an Atchisson Assault Shotgun, two MAC-10 submachine guns, two Glock 19's, and a dozen boxes of ammo. "Because we are not leaving this behind."

Cole scouted the nearby city while Sam prepped the gear. In total, there were five bags. The fourth bag was packed with more clothes, these much bigger in size and obviously meant for Cole, and the last bag contained a half-dozen canteens, all full of water, a metal spile, an awl, a rubber mallet, and a cloth rag wrapped around something. Sam took the object from the sack and unraveled it. The remote control was inside and a chill ran up Sam's spine.

Cole returned a couple hours later with two rusted shopping carts and an empty plastic jug. The carts' bodies were a hardened plastic and made to withstand a lot of weight. A wide smile found Sam's face as she checked them out. "These are perfect, Cole."

"I checked a couple of stations around town, but tanks were all dry."

"Figures." Sam shrugged as she tested out one of the carts. The wheels wobbled and groaned, but when she heaved one of the heavy bags into it, it held the weight with ease.

Cole grabbed the empty jug from his cart and then got down on the ground. The giant managed to wedge himself under the front of the jeep and Artie hopped around his feet as if he was uncomfortable with the situation. Cole grunted a few times and a moment later he said, "Ha!" When he emerged from the undercarriage, the jug was half full with pitch-black oil. He graciously got to his feet and then knelt by the cart. Cole poured a liberal amount on each of the wheels, on each of the cart, leaving small inky puddles on the faded asphalt.

Sam stripped off her socks and shoes and rubbed an antiseptic on her feet that she found in the first-aid kit. She bandaged them as well as she could and then slipped on a double layer of socks and then the boots. Cole did the same and then they each pulled out a weapon and loaded the bags into the carts.

"Are you ready for this?" Sam asked as she strapped the M-16 across her chest.

Cole nodded and holstered one of the Glocks.

They set off east as the sun climbed down the sky behind them. It was cooler than the desert, but they still made plenty of stops to hydrate. They walked into the night and finally made camp when the moon had reached the apex of the night sky. They had covered close to thirty miles. Sam decided to take the first watch as Cole and Artie curled up beside a small fire. She found the L.A. doctor's journal in one of the bags and read as the wood crackled and smoke bellowed into the heavens.

They traveled like that for days on end. Walking 20 to 30 miles during the day and sleeping by firelight during the night. They hunted each morning after the ration of MREs ran out and caught small game that they could carry with them during the day. They filled their canteens with stream water or would tap sugar maples with the awl and spile. Artie would sometime walk alongside them, but sometimes would beg to ride in the cart. Each night, the small dog would crash down beside the fire and not move again until morning. Each morning they rose, and each day the road stretched out in front of them like a never-ending bad dream.

The infected they encountered along the way, *halfways* Alex called them, *zombies* Sawyer called them, were few in number. They would spot them, normally staggering alone in an open meadow or a small group huddled in the middle of the road. Sam would pick them off one by one with the MSR like she was born with the sniper rifle in her hand.

They walked for days and days; through ghost towns and stretches of nothingness. Sam's hair grew longer as did Cole's beard. Cole grew thinner and thinner as the weather grew colder and the hunting became scarce, but he never complained. There were days when Sam could walk 40 miles without breaking a sweat and some days where she could barely force herself to walk ten.

On the forty-fourth night of their travel, Cole took the first watch, and as he told Sam the tale of the night he knocked out Marcus Gilmore in the 14th round of a title fight, this was the only story he remembered from his past and he told it often, she fell asleep. And for the first time in over a month, she dreamed.

She stood in the center of the city, only it wasn't burning. Jordan stood facing her, a goofy grin on his face. "What are you grinning at?"

"It's almost over," Jordan said and his smile widened. "We'll be together soon."

Sam took a step forward as he enfolded her in his familiar arms. The tears welled in her eyes as his sweet aroma filled her nose. "Do you promise?"

"Yes. Do you promise to do what you need to when the moment presents itself?"

Sam thought about this for a moment and then asked, "What do you mean?"

"When the time comes, are you prepared to do whatever it takes to bring down the Flowers Corporation?"

"Yes."

"Even if it meant making the hardest decision of your life?"

Sam pulled away and offered him a smile. "I've lived without you for so long now. There's nothing that can be harder than that."

Jordan's smile faded. "There will be something."

"What?"

"You'll have to see for yourself."

"See what?" Sam asked.

"I'll show you," Jordan said and extended his hand. Sam took it and the two walked through the epicenter of the city. Through the epicenter of Concordia.

"Why isn't it burning?" Sam asked after a while.

"It isn't that time yet," Jordan said. "Don't you remember?"

"No," Sam said.

"It will come to you," Jordan said, "when the time is right. You'll remember everything. Even the flowers."

The two strolled past skyscrapers that she only remembered painted in flames. Seeing them now, in their normal state, was almost unsettling. They moved deeper into the heart of the city, and the buildings gave way to an open area. A park full of luscious green grass and trees sprawled in front of them.

"I've never seen this part of the city before," Sam said in amazement.

"Sam," Jordan said in a dark tone, "what I have to show you...it's going to upset you."

"Then why are you showing me?" Sam asked.

"Because you need to see it. You need to see it before it's too late. It's the only thing stopping you from reaching the city and you must deal with it before you get there."

"Does it have to do with the fire?" Sam asked.

"When the time is right, you'll remember, you'll remember everything about the fire. That's not why we're here. "

"Then why?" Sam asked.

Jordan looked around and then pointed in the distance toward the park. Sam followed his finger with her eyes and nearly screamed as she saw what he was pointing at. In the distance, bathed in the soft light of the moon and covered from head to toe, was a midnight runner. The creature screamed toward the night sky and as it turned toward them, Sam's heart bottomed out into her stomach. The beast had the body of a midnight runner, but its face was pale and distorted. It was the face of a boy. The face of David.

The monster, not paying them any attention, leaned down and lifted the carcass of a baby deer. It stared at the dead animal for a long time, David's bright blue eyes, the midnight runner's sharp teeth gleaming with moonlight, and then it ripped the head from the animal. It tossed the torso of the deer back down to the ground and then took a bite out of the deer's face. Sam gasped and the monster fixed its gaze on them.

"Do you see it, Sam?" Jordan asked.

"Yes," she said as her heart quickened in her chest. David's face was morphing in front of her eyes.

"Then really see it," Jordan commanded.

As if his words were real, Sam opened her eyes. She stood at the edge of the campsite and fifty yards away, standing at the edge of a stream, Cole Porter was doused in blood. He held a decapitated river rat over his mouth as bright crimson poured from its body.

"Oh my god," Sam whispered.

Cole's head jerked to the sound of her voice and Sam gasped. Cole's eyes were no longer green, but a poisonous yellow. He stared at her blankly before grunting and then lifting his head back to the body of the rat. He squeezed its torso tight and a mound of guts and organs squirted into his mouth. Sam took a step back and Artie padded over next to her. The fur on the back of his neck stood on end and the terrier bared his yellowed fangs.

Sam swallowed hard as she continued to watch the gruesome sight in absolute silence. This was not the man that had saved her from New Hope. This was not her friend. The monster that stood in place of the man she loved like a father, chewed feverishly, swallowed and then screamed at the moon.

"Cole?" Sam asked. The world spun around her and her voice echoed weak between her ears. The giant man turned to her and she watched in disbelief as the yellow eyes faded into his normal shade of green.

"Sam?" Cole asked, his voice trembling. "What's happening to me?"

Sam shook her head as tears streamed down her face. "Nothing, Cole." The tears broke into a sob, but after a moment, she managed to stifle them. "You were just sleep walking, that's all. You just need to get some sleep."

Sam led Cole back to the campsite and he fell fast asleep by the fire. Sam watched as he stirred restlessly in his sleep, her finger hovered over the trigger of the pistol but she couldn't make herself shoot him. The time was coming though. The dreaded time that she had fretted over for days. The time that had been gnawing at her soul like a dog chomping on a piece of meat. The time had come to kill Cole Porter.

8

The first rays of morning spilled over the horizon and Sam and Cole broke out their campsite in silence. Sam washed herself off in the stream, but kept her eyes locked on Cole. The remote control was buried deep in her pants pocket and it pressed against her leg each time she moved. She had fingered the button throughout the night, flipping the glass casing up and down, up and down, but couldn't muster enough courage to press the button.

The little information she had managed to make any sense of in the doctor's journal was about the remote. The middle button would bring any midnight runners in the vicinity in and out of rest. The bottom button would increase hormone production sending the target into a berserker-like state—Sam saw no reason to ever press that one. And the top would cause the midnight runner operation to terminate, ceasing all brain function permanently.

"You're staring at me, Miss Sam," Cole said as he loaded his bag into the cart.

"I'm sorry," Sam whispered.

"It's happening, isn't it?" Cole asked.

"Yes."

"You should just do it then. Before it's too late."

"No," Sam said.

"Why not?"

"Because if there's a way to reverse this then that answer lies within Concordia."

"And if it happens before we get there?"

She looked at him for a long time. "We need to go faster."

They traveled the whole day in silence. Artie walked on the opposite side of Sam and constantly stopped to growl if Cole got to close to him. It got so bad that Sam forced the dog into one of the empty canvas bags and zipped him in. She left enough of a hole for air, but the dog's apprehension towards Cole had slowed them down.

As the sun hovered above the horizon behind them, a glint of sunlight flashed on a piece of the metal on the side of the road, and they slowed to a stop. A road sign, covered with dense weeds and foliage, stood almost unnoticed. The glint of exposed blue metal caught Sam's eye, and she removed one of the hatchets from the canvas bag and hacked at the overgrowth.

Her heart leapt as they discovered the words on the sign were still legible:

"Welcome to Independence, Missouri," Cole said, reading the sign aloud.

"We're close," Sam said, and went back to the cart to get the map. Hope filled up her chest. Maybe there would be time to save her friend. Maybe Jordan had been wrong. Maybe—

"Sam," Cole whispered.

"If the map is accurate, we should have about fifty more miles until we see the walls." Sam carefully unfolded the map and searched for Independence.

"Miss Sam," Cole whispered again.

"That's two days," Sam said. "One if you feel like walking about 16 hours today."

"Sam," Cole said.

This time his words did not come in a whisper and Sam looked up from the map. "What?"

Cole pointed in the direction they had been traveling. His thin face had turned stark white and his arm trembled violently. Sam followed the path of his arm and her stomach turned to jelly. Half a mile away was a horde of halfways. At least a hundred. They had spotted Sam and Cole and were walking in their direction. Correction…running toward them.

"We have to go," Sam said. She shoved the map into one bag and unzipped another. Artie shot out of the bag and hopped onto the ground. He started barking at once. "Grab the bag with the guns and follow me." Cole did as he was commanded and then the three of them raced off of the road and into the thick forest to the south.

Branches ripped and tore at Sam's face and exposed flesh as she sprinted through the thick brush. She grasped ahold of the hatchet tightly as Cole thundered behind her and she caught glimpses of Artie's gray fur in her peripherals. From further behind them, she heard the sound of branches and limbs snapping as the horde closed in on them.

The woods grew less and less dense and Sam pushed through the remaining brush until she was free from the forest. She stopped dead in her tracks. On the other side sat a large field, the grass wild and overgrown, stretching above her waist, and in its center, a giant, rusted Ferris wheel. And beyond the field, lay the scorched city of her nightmares.

"Cole, do you see this?" Sam asked. "Am I dreaming?"

"No," Cole said and grabbed her by the arm. He pulled her through the sea of grass and towards the wheel. Sam couldn't make herself walk any farther. She stared out over the city, at the charred remains of all her memories.

"We have to go, Miss Sam!" Cole screamed. "They're coming."

"This isn't real," Sam said. "I'm dreaming."

"This ain't no dream," Cole said and lifted her by the waist.

He attempted to throw her over his shoulder but Sam screamed. "No!" She flailed until Cole, unable to handle the bag and her squirming, dropped her back to the ground. "This isn't real!" Sam screeched.

"Miss Sam—" Cole started, as the first wave of infected crashed through the tree line. An older man led the pack, his rotting flesh hanging from his skull like pulled pork. A dozen more followed close on his heels. The dead man spotted them, snarled, and then took off in a sprint.

Cole drew his pistol and raised it, but the sight of the creature brought Sam back to reality. She leaned back and heaved the hatchet. It whirred through the air, end over end, until the blade smashed into the old man's skull. Gray and black goop spilled out from behind the blade of the ax and the infected fell to the ground, disappearing beneath the thick grass.

Sam unholstered the Glock and the two of them fired. Wave after wave of gunfire ripped through the air, and clouds of black mist filled the air as the zombies dropped one by one. Headshot after headshot. Another surge of infected emerged at the edge of the forest as the last of the bullets flew from Sam's gun. A heartbeat later, Cole had emptied his clip.

"Fall back to the Ferris wheel," Sam said.

They ran as fast as they could to the midpoint of the field. When they reached the giant rusted wheel, Cole set down the bag, and they each drew a weapon from it. Cole grabbed the AA-12, while Sam took the two Mac-10s.

Sam spun in time to see the horde within a dozen yards and unloaded the guns. A spray of shell casings rocketed through the air as she squeezed the trigger. The first and second line fell and then Cole unloaded on the few that were remaining. He fired once and blew the head of an old lady clean off her shoulders. He fired again and sent another old man flying backward. Sam let out a sigh of relief as the two empty mags fell from her gun. They were going to make it. Everything was going to be o—

One of the stragglers managed to go unseen and get around them. A young woman jumped on Cole's back and sank her broken, rotten teeth his shoulder. Sam struggled to slam a full magazine in when another emerged from the tall grass just a few feet away. It speared Cole and brought all three of them to the ground.

"No," Sam said as panic flooded every sense.

She dropped the guns and pulled the remote from her pocket. In the distance, more halfways were appearing in the tall grass. She heard the sound of flesh being torn from Cole's body and flipped up the glass case. Her finger hesitated over the middle button, ready to end all of her friend's pain and suffering, but instead her finger slid down to bottom button. And she pressed it.

Cole erupted to life and rose to his feet. The young girl had taken a huge chunk of meat out of his shoulder and was about to clamp down again. Cole let out a terrible, spine chilling howl and flung the girl as if she was weightless. Without hesitation, he grabbed the zombie that had speared him by its throat and ripped its head from its body with ease. He spun toward the girl he had thrown down and lunged on top of her. He smashed in the girl's face with one swing of his giant fist. It sounded like eggs shells cracking and Sam watched in horror as the innards of the girl's face poured out onto the ground surrounding her flattened head.

Sam rested her finger against the middle button as Cole jumped to his feet. But he took off toward two more of the infected that lingered by the trees. He sprinted at a subhuman speed and Sam cringed as began to tear them to shreds.

She decided to grab the sniper rifle to pick off any stragglers when she was thrown to the ground. Her instincts took over, and she managed to spin as the halfway vaulted atop her. The remote slipped from her grasp and she jammed a forearm between herself and her attacker. The creature, a man in his late 40's, snapped his rotten teeth at her, as strings of long gray drool cascaded from his mouth. Sam struggled to push him off, but the man dug his heels into her legs. Sam managed a single scream, "Cole!"

A split-second later, the zombie's head was ripped off in front of her eyes and the body flung off of her. She reached out her hand, expecting Cole to pull her up, but instead he crashed down on top of her. His green eyes were bright yellow, and he howled as pushed Sam's arms to the ground.

"Cole, no!" Sam screamed. "It's me! It's Sam."

He opened his jaw and Sam's skin crawled. Cole's teeth all look razor-sharp as he widened his jaw. Tears spilled down Sam's face as he lowered his head towards hers. She had failed. Everything she had done was for naught and now she was going to be murdered at the hands of her own savior.

"I'm sorry, Jordan," she whispered.

There was a loud bark and Artie sprung onto Cole's back. He took his hands off of her arms as he pawed at the dog and Sam seized the opportunity. She reached out and managed to grab the controller and mashed the middle button. Cole collapsed on top of her at once, blowing hot exhales of breath onto her neck. Above, Sam watched as the first glimpses of twilight appeared in the sky.

She managed to push Cole off of her and checked her surroundings. Nothing moved in the field. Artie paced around her feet, his fur still stood high on his neck, growling at Cole who lay motionless. She stood there breathlessly looking at the chaos. The ground was littered with corpses and blood. And one midnight runner, whose chest heaved up and down, in rhythmic breaths. Sam turned toward the charred remnants of the city, dropped to her knees and began to sob.

9

Dark thunderheads gathered on the skyline as the sun faded behind the Ferris wheel. Down in the valley, the city lay dark and quiet. Echoes of ghosts and forgotten memories swirled through the brisk air as dead leaves rustled through the thick grass.

Sam drug Cole's body through the field of blood and propped him against a tree stump so he sat upright facing the city of ash. Artie was nowhere to be seen. Sam imagined he was hunting for food or perhaps patrolling the outer tree line for more of the infected. She didn't know and didn't care. All she cared about was getting to Concordia and making them pay for everything they had taken from her. Rebecca, Jordan, Nick, Alex and now Cole.

She dared a glance at the slumbering giant. His jaw was slack and black blood had dried and crusted in his beard. Deep lines pressed into his cheeks which had started to turn the slightest shade of orange. An image of the midnight runner flashed in Sam's mind and she turned away and screamed into the night air.

"Why?" she screamed out into the silent night air. "Why would you take Cole from me? Why have you taken everybody?" Her shouts were loud, but she wasn't worried about calling attention to herself. She dared another horde to show up. Begged for an outlet to defuse the pain and anguish drowning her soul.

"What the fuck did I ever do to you?" she shouted.

In the distance, a bolt of lightning flickered across the sky.

She cursed God as tears poured from her eyes and spilled down her cheeks. She cursed Concordia and Minister Troy. President Gates and General Soto. David. She cursed them all at the top of her lungs. She yelled until her throat was raw and the tears stopped falling. She felt empty and numb. She felt nothing.

She squatted on a neighboring stump and slowly removed the remote control from her pocket. Her hand trembled as she fingered the glass casing. Another wave of tears fought their way to the surface as she debated on whether to just push the top button. He would never know that he died. He would just stay asleep forever. Wouldn't that be more humane?

Artie appeared at her side and sat down beside her. He nuzzled his wet snout into the palm of her other hand which hung limply at her side. He gave a low groan when Sam gave no sign of acknowledgement and lay down at her feet.

"Everything Artie," Sam whispered. "They took everything."

Artie's ears perked at the sound of his name, but he didn't lift his head.

Sam stared blankly at the city as her fingers slid back and forth over the buttons. Somewhere in the city were the remnants of Sam's past. The answers had been burned to ash long ago but the framework still existed. She searched her mind for any resemblance of the missing pieces but the only thing she could see was Jordan. And Rebecca. And Cole. Their faces were scorched into her memory.

She flipped the glass casing open and pressed the middle button. Cole's eyes fluttered open. Cole's face dropped as his eyes fixed on the city. A moment later, he looked to Sam and began to sob.

"It's happening, Miss Sam," Cole said. "I can feel it happening."

"I know."

"I'm so sorry. I didn't mean to hurt ya. I would never—"

"You didn't hurt me."

A long moment of silence passed as the sky erupted in white light as tendrils of lightning scrawled through the pitch-black. Sam wrapped her hand tight around the metal device and swallowed hard. A clap of thunder broke the silence and her skin turned to gooseflesh.

"My wife," Cole said as he wiped his eyes. "I can remember my wife."

He smiled a weak, scared smile, but it was a smile nonetheless. "Oh my god," he laughed. "I can remember everything."

Sam wanted to ask if he remembered anything about Concordia. She sighed. No, she wouldn't ask him about the city. Everything she needed to know about the city had already been told to her. Evil men and women preying on the less fortunate. She wouldn't waste the few remaining moments of his life. "Tell me about your wife."

"She used to tell me that I was a hard man to deal with." He laughed nervously and ran his hand through his hair. His fingers found the metal device implanted into his skull and frowned. He stifled a sob. "I was a hard man to deal with."

Sam reached out and touched Cole's arm. He stopped rubbing the device and returned his palm to his lap. "Cole, I need you to—"

"I was born in the spring of 1997," Cole interrupted. "I fell in love with my wife in high school. Sophomore year. Fall of 2013 if I remember correctly. Name was Daphne Rose. She was a year younger than me and she was the prettiest damn girl I'd ever seen before or ever seen since. Met each other at a homecoming dance. Bet you didn't know I could dance, huh?"

Sam's hands trembled, and she took a painful breath. Tears stung at her eyes. Cole looked up to her, and she shook her head. He smiled and patted her on the leg.

"We fell in love almost at once. Hell, we were kids then. Thought we were in love. Found out that the love part comes later. When you're 16 all you care about is the physical stuff and we had our fair share of that. She got pregnant that summer and I dropped out of school to work at a printing plant. Her daddy made us get married so it'd be a proper birth. Said he didn't want no bastard grandchildren floatin' around this world. I don't expect he liked me none, but he sure did love her.

"Got married, and a few months later, we had a little girl. She died shortly after she was born. Lungs didn't develop right. Stayed on a respirator all her life." Cole paused and took a deep breath. Another crack of thunder pierced the air. "Damned shame when a kid dies. Hell, it's a shame when anyone dies. But something of that magnitude is too much for a kid to go through.

"Had a lot of anger built up inside of me after that. Started fightin' a lot. Couldn't drink in the bars but me and a couple buddies would hang out in liquor store parking lots beggin' for people to buy us booze. We'd always end up with enough, and by the end of the night, it'd always end in blows. After a few fights, nobody wanted to fight me anymore. That's when I started boxing.

"I won the golden gloves championship when I was 19 and a scout for the Olympics invited me to try out for the American team. Won a gold medal that year." Cole scratched his head. "How'd they manage to hide all these memories, Miss Sam?"

Sam shook her head.

"Anyway," Cole continued, "I decided to go pro after I got back to the states. Daphne wasn't too keen on the idea of me fighting full-time but then we got pregnant again and she seemed to care more about making sure her body was right then what I did with mine."

Sam's fingers traced the top button of the remote as her heart slammed against her chest. She knew what she needed to do. Soon, Cole would become a monster and she would have to kill him. At least this way would be painless. She hoped it would be painless. The story was making it harder though. She loved Cole all over again as he spoke and dreaded the next part of her life without him.

Cole glanced at the remote and grimaced. "Daisy Mae was born that spring, and we moved to a fixer-upper in Northwest Detroit. Daisy hung around a little longer than her sister. Made it a full year and then one day my wife went to wake her up one morning and she wasn't breathing. Doctor said she died of something called SIDS."

Sam's heart broke in two and she desperately wished that she would have just ended it while he was still asleep. No one deserved to go through this.

"Daphne wasn't the same after Daisy died. I tried to make things right again. Made a lot of money fightin' and moved her out of that junk heap in Detroit and brought her out to the coast. Got a place in San Francisco, but it didn't matter though. She was a ghost of herself. Cryin' all the time. Stopped eating and eventually I had to take her to the hospital. She never came home again. I went and saw her every day, and some were better than others. Once or twice, she even held my hand. But most of the time she just stared out the window. I went and saw her every day for 12 years. She died before the infection. Thank the gods. Doctor said it was an aneurism, but I think her heart was broken so bad that it made the rest of her body quit working. They said they found her on the floor by her bed, holding a little sweater she had knitted for our daughter."

A bolt of lightning cut through the pitch-black sky and crashed into the center of the city. It illuminated their faces for the briefest of seconds. Artie jumped to his feet and growled loudly at the darkness ahead. A moment later, the echo of thunder filled the air.

"I think when I die, I'll see her again," Cole said. His voice shook and Sam's heart plummeted into her stomach. "I'll see Daphne and she'll have the girls and she'll be normal again. She'll be happy like she was when we were in high school. Do you think the girls will remember me?"

"Yes," Sam said, fighting to keep her voice steady through the tears. "They'll remember you." She wanted to tell him how she would remember him. How she would miss him. She wanted to beg him to stay, but instead she remained silent.

"Miss Sam, if my girls would've lived...I'd have wanted them to be like you."

"Cole—"

"Don't feel bad for what you got to do. You got to get to Concordia, and you got to make them stop doing what they're doing. Me, I'll be looking down from heaven while you do it. Just remember that. And remember that I love—"

Sam pressed the top button of the remote and Cole went silent. His chin slumped onto his chest and then he fell over onto his side into the tall grass. Artie gave a low moan and then howled toward the sky.

"Cole?"

Thunder rumbled somewhere in the distance. Anxiety flooded over her as the realization of what she had done set in.

"Cole?!"

Sam hit the top button of the remote and then the middle. Her fingers pressed all of them over and over again, hoping to bring him back to life. She hadn't told him goodbye. She hadn't told him that she loved him. And now it was too late. She had killed her only friend.

She fell to her knees and draped herself over Cole's lifeless body. "Cole, I'm so sorry," she cried. "I'm so, so sorry. I didn't mean too. Please come back. Please. We'll figure something else out. I'll fix you." She shook his shoulders as she pleaded, each word growing more desperate than the last. "Please, Cole. Don't leave me alone. Please wake up. Please." She shook him as hard as she could, but her valiant giant lay as motionless as the dozens of other corpses in the field.

"No!" Sam screamed and put her head to his chest. There was no heartbeat. "Goddamn it," she cried out angrily. "Don't leave me, Cole! I need you. Please don't leave me." Her words caught in her throat and she took large panicked breaths. She was alone now. Artie lay on the ground next to Cole and licked the big man's cheek. "Please," she whispered. "Please come back to me."

The storm faded, and the world grew silent. After a while, Sam left Cole's side and found her pack through the darkness. She pulled one of the pistols from the bag and stared at the weapon for a long time. Then she lifted the pistol and pressed the cold steel barrel to her temple and wrapped her finger around the trigger.

She wanted it all to be over. She had lost everything she had ever cared about and now she was alone. If she could find the courage to squeeze the trigger, she could make it all go away. She could be back with them all in the blink of an eye. She could make the pain stop.

It's not over yet, Jordan whispered.

"I can't do it," Sam said.

Yes you can.

"I killed him, Jordan."

They killed him, Samantha. You just put him out of his misery.
The gun shook in her hand and she pressed it harder to her skull.
You're so close.
"It doesn't matter. None of it does."
Yes, it does.
"I can't do this for you, Jordan. I'm sorry."
Sam squeezed the trigger until the tension was gone. Just a little bit more and it would all be over. She took a deep breath and held it.
Don't do it for me. Don't do it for you. Do it for everyone that's left in New Hope.
Sam tried to pull the trigger but couldn't. She screamed and tears flooded down her face. She just wanted to have the strength to end the nightmare, but knew deep down that it would take more strength to see it through. The strength came with hunting down the monsters in the dark shadows of her dreams and killing them. She let the gun fall to the ground.

The storm clouds gave way and rain drizzled down in icy sheets. Sam laid down beside Cole and curled into the crook of his arm. Artie nudged his way in-between Cole and Sam and the two of them slept until morning. When she awoke, Cole's skin was ice cold, and a chill had settled into her bones. She knew the chill would never go away. She knew she would be cold inside forever.

She picked some wildflowers at the edge of the field and placed them in Cole's hand before leaving and kissed him on the top of his head. This would be the hardest part. Leaving him in this field as she had left David in her memories. She gathered the weapons that she could find and shoved them into the duffel bag. Before leaving, she knelt down in the tall grass and whispered goodbye and told Cole that she loved him. She braved a glance at the city of ash and her heart ignited with ire and rage. She spun back toward the forest. Back to the road. Artie followed but continued to look back every few feet as if checking to see if Cole was really staying.

They found the great road again and continued to the east. They walked for hours and didn't stop to eat or drink. Artie rode most of the day in the cart, only barking to get out when he had to do his business. She continued until her muscles trembled and shook and felt like they were on fire.

When darkness fell, she set up camp for the evening on the side of the road and lit a fire just large enough to keep her and the dog warm. Artie nuzzled into her arms and Sam stared at the waning fire until sleep overtook her. There was no one to take first watch. No one to keep her safe if she slept. If she died in her sleep, if an infected attacked her in the middle of the night, she would consider herself lucky. She dreamt of Cole and Jordan but neither of them spoke to her. Neither did Rebecca nor Alex or Nick. Neither did David.

In the morning, she silently packed up the campsite and gave Artie a potful of the water. He lapped it up graciously. She didn't drink any herself and chose not to eat the remainder of their food. They got back on the road and continued on their journey.

Less than an hour later, the trees on either side of the horizon disappeared and as they approached the crest of a large hill, the giant concrete wall that surrounded Concordia burst into view and Artie began to bark.

10

Sam reached the clearing and fell to her knees. The giant concrete wall stretched for miles in either direction and within, towers of glass and steel jutted toward the sky. Tears fell from her cheeks as she lifted her head to the sky. She screamed a guttural, primal scream as she raised her hands to the sun. Her throat was raw and sore, but she didn't care. She screamed again and again.

"We did it, Artie. We made it."

The dog put its two front paws on her thigh and barked again. Sam rubbed his head and more tears came. Then she collapsed to her elbows and sobbed. Her stomach contracted so hard that she fought to breathe as emotions overwhelmed her. She cried harder and all of her muscles convulsed and twitched.

Artie gave a low moan and licked her outstretched hand. She tried to calm herself and to pull herself back into a sitting position but couldn't. Her body twitched uncontrollably, and she realized that this wasn't her emotions getting the best of her. This was something else.

She steadied her breath and heard a faint whooping noise coming from somewhere in the distance. Artie growled and Sam shushed him. She tried to sit up again, couldn't and then managed to roll over on her side. Concordia towered in the distance and she gasped as a helicopter ascended from beneath the wall.

She struggled with all of her might to get up and retreat into the forest, but it was as if unseen hands were pinning her to the ground. The whooping of the copter blades grew louder as two more copters emerged. The panic ebbed and a wave of closure washed over her. This was the end. The fur on Artie's neck stood up, and the dog barked wildly.

"It's okay, Artie," Sam said. "It's almost over now."

The copters pitched forward and flew over the walls. They hovered for a moment, the three birds gleaming in the bright blue sky, and then lowered into the field in front of her. She wanted to shield her eyes from the dust as it clouded over her, but she still couldn't move. The little control she had over her muscles had faded. She closed her eyes.

Finally, the blades slowed to a stop and Sam heard doors open and footsteps on the ground. She refused to open her eyes. She couldn't move. It was over. She had fulfilled her promise to Jordan, to herself, but they had won.

"Will someone shut that fucking dog up?"

Sam's heart lurched at the sound of the familiar voice. Her eyes shot open. Prime Minister Troy was leading a group of soldiers along with a handful of men in white lab coats in her direction. Artie continued to bark and growl. Troy paused as one of the men handed him a pistol. He aimed and pulled the trigger. There was a loud yip and Artie fell silent.

"No!" Sam screamed. A surge of adrenaline coursed through her and she forced herself into a sitting position. The invisible hands weighing her down pressed against her, but she continued to move.

"I thought you said she was subdued," Troy said.

"She is, sir," another voice said.

"Does she look subdued, brainiac?"

Sam put her palm in the dirt and pushed herself to her feet. She staggered and dropped to a knee. Artie's small body sprawled across the ground, a puddle of crimson pooled underneath him. "You killed my dog," Sam said. She slid her hand up the cart and found the wooden handle of the hatchet.

Troy's lips peeled back into a wicked smile. "Indeed, Miss Albright."

"You killed my sister." She made it to her feet once more and pulled the hatchet from the cart.

"She was infected," Troy said. "Nothing personal."

"You killed Jordan." She took a labored step towards them.

"That was personal," Troy said and chuckled.

The men in white coats jotted furiously onto their clipboards. Sam picked one at random and lifted the ax into the air.

"Put the weapon down, Miss Albright. You're not going to kill an innocen—"

Sam flung the hatchet as hard as she could and it hummed through the air. The man that she aimed at looked up from his notes and his face screwed up in horror. The blade lodged into his skull and he flew backward, crashing into the ground. His body twitched for a moment and then fell still. The men in white coats gasped.

"Interesting," Troy said and stroked his thin goatee. He dug into his pocket and extracted a silver device that looked oddly like the remote control that had controlled Cole. He aimed it at her and mashed a button.

Sam grabbed for one of the guns in the cart, but Troy mashed a button on the remote before she could pull it from the bag. Sam dropped the weapon and fell to her knees. Her eyes rolled to the back of her head and the world blurred.

"Would you like us to start with the assessment?" Sam heard someone ask. The voice was distant.

"No," Troy said. "We need to play it safe. Last thing we need is her burning down another city. Wait until the man gets here. Someone get her off the ground for Christ sake. He won't take kindly if his prized little pet is all banged up." A moment later, she was being lifted in the air. And then she was sat upright.

What man? Sam thought. She tried to open her eyes, tried to move in the slightest, but couldn't. She was helpless.

A few minutes later, another whooping sound cut through the morning air. The world was still dark and blurry and the invisible hands had reclaimed control of every muscle and fiber in her being. Her heart ached for Artie and she cursed herself for not aiming the hatchet at Troy.

The whooping grew louder and the dust and wind picked up again. Then the blades cut out. Then the sounds of doors opening and closing. Then footsteps.

"What happened to Sweeney?" a new voice asked.

"What do you think?" Troy said. "This bitch has bite."

There was a long pause.

"I happened," Sam managed through gritted teeth.

Another long pause.

"Raise cognitive awareness to 50 percent," the new voice said. "Keep physical suppression set to zero."

The world appeared before Sam's eyes again. A new man stood before her. His face was familiar, and it took a moment for her to process it. And then it clicked. It was the man from the monitor. The man who'd activated the self-destruct sequence in Lost Angel. He'd fixed his hair and shaved, but Sam was sure it was him.

"Do you know who I am, Samantha?"

"You're the man from the monitor," Sam said.

He smiled. "And beyond that?"

"No."

He nodded as the men in white coats jotted feverishly on their clipboard. After a moment, he said, "My name is David. David Stanton."

Images of David, her David, flooded through her mind. The boy from the field. Her dead friend. It couldn't be. "You're dead."

David laughed. "I assure you that I'm very much the opposite. The memory you have of me is false. We've never played any games together, and I didn't die in the field. That memory, just like many other memories you possess, was developed in our lab. Think of my younger self, your memories of my younger self, as nothing more than an Easter egg in a very complex computer program." He knelt beside her and ran his fingers through her hair.

"I don't understand," Sam said.

David smiled at her. "Soon."

Sam nodded. She felt oddly at ease.

David rose to his feet. "Let's go ahead and get vitals." This was directed to the men in white. "Run a full diagnostic and begin the download sequence. We'll do a full data dump here. I don't want to bring her in the complex on this run. At least not until we know more. Daniels. Kidwell. Stand her up. Pratt, I want you to keep sights on her at all times."

The two guards lifted Sam to her feet. She wobbled but didn't fall, and then the men in white coats swarmed around her. One of the men forced a thermometer into her mouth and another wrapped a blood pressure sleeve around her arm. Two of the men had sprinted to the helicopter, and returned carrying a square white monitor strapped to metal cart with wheels. It bounced awkwardly over the uneven grass floor.

"What's with the dog?" David asked.

"It was with her," Troy answered.

"She domesticated it?"

"Seems that way."

"Interesting."

"He killed it," Sam said.

David looked down at the dog and then back to her, "Yes. Yes he did. That's very unfortunate, Samantha."

An elastic headband with wires running from it to the monitor rested on the cart. One of the men removed it and placed it around Sam's head. The other one flicked on the unit and the screen filled with a 3D image of a brain.

"I want full stats on hippocampus function and neural activity in the primary somatosensory cortex," David said. "I need a full work-up on hormone levels: serotonin, dopamine, testosterone, estrogen, the works please."

"Download stream is active." the man next to the monitor said.

David focused his attention back to Sam. "I have some questions for you. When you've answered my questions, I will answer all of yours. Does that seem fair?"

"Yes," Sam said.

"We'll start with some easy ones, okay?" His voice was comforting.

"Okay."

"Can you tell me your name?"

"Samantha Albright."

"Good. How old are you?"

"I'm 24."

"Excellent. Do you remember where you're from?"

"New Hope."

"And before that?"

Sam closed her eyes and searched for an answer. "I don't know."

"Increase memory function to five percent," David said.

Sam heard a loud humming between her ears and then a tidal wave of memories crashed into her. Images of a two-story log cabin. A rickety dock. A lake behind her house. They continued to shoot through her brain. Memories of her hometown. The old town square. Ricker's Grocery and Pharmacy.

"Try again, Sam. Where did you live before New Hope?"

"Wellspring, Oregon." The words flew out of her mouth.

"Wonderful. And can you tell me the name of your parents and of any siblings."

She combed through the new memories and then through the older ones, but there was nothing. "No."

"Increase to ten percent."

Another wave crashed into her. An image of her mother working in the flowerbed. Her father sitting at the kitchen table. And her sister. Sitting in the middle of their living room playing with her doll. Rebecca.

"No," Sam said aloud. From the depths of Sam's memory, Rebecca shrieked as she was dragged to her death. "No. This can't be right."

"Stay with me, Samantha," David said.

Image after image of Rebecca flooded her mind. Sam screamed as explosions rocketed through her brain. She snatched the headband and threw it to the ground, but the explosions continued.

"I told you to keep the physical suppression level set to zero," David said.

"It is, sir."

Sam clawed at her head as more and more of the images poured into her. She caught only glimpses, but each one stabbed at her mind. "Make it stop!" Sam shouted. "Please, make it stop. Oh, God! My brain is going to explode."

"Drop memory function back to five percent," David said. "She's overloading. Do it now!"

"The controller isn't working," one of the men in white coats said. "The memory and physical suppression chips are not responding."

"Both chips are offline," another man said. "Readings are off the chart."

The memories stopped coming, and the world slowed to a crawl. The men in white coats all wore panicked expressions, and the soldiers pawed at their holsters and drew their guns. Troy looked dumbfounded by what was going on, and David...David was within arm's reach.

Time sped up as Sam grabbed David by the collar and spun him around. She snatched the sidearm from his holster, a Remington R51 sub-compact pistol with a carbon-fiber magazine extension, and pressed the barrel to the back of his neck. A split-second later, every other pistol was aimed at her. And at David.

"My turn for questions," Sam said.

"Put down your weapon," Troy said, "you filthy little cun—"

The barrel of the gun flew from David's neck and Sam squeezed the trigger. Troy's head exploded in a mist of brain and blood. The thin man fell to his knees and then crashed into the ground. Sam pressed the hot tip of the gun to David's neck.

"Anybody else?" she asked.

No one moved.

"Tell them to lower their weapons."

"You heard her," David said steadily.

One by one the soldiers dropped their aim.

"Now tell me what's going on?" Sam demanded.

"In 2030, a group of very powerful men and women contracted the Flowers Corporation to develop a virus to wipe mankind from the face of the map. On February 19th, 2032 the RIZ-4 virus was released at the international airport in Atlanta, Georgia. It was very successful, but the results yielded more than just death."

"I know all about the infected," Sam said.

"Yes," David continued, "it yielded both dead and undead results but also it produced something else."

Sam gripped the barrel of the gun tighter. "Which was?"

"It produced an outlier group on the opposite side of the spectrum. It produced you. You're not immune from the virus, Samantha. The virus has fused with your DNA. It changed you. It made you stronger."

"I've heard this story," Sam said. "I know the how. Tell me they why."

"We discovered these results during the quarantine protocol, and a new program was initiated. The virus had caused a new subspecies of the human race to blossom. You were initially thought to be valuable because you served as a resource for creating an antivirus, but later we discovered that your group could serve different purposes. You were trained to fight the undead with hopes of someday exterminating them from our planet. When your training was complete, you were cryogenically frozen until the time was deemed appropriate to bring you back. According to your test results, Samantha, you were one of the most highly decorated students."

"Why freeze us?" Sam asked.

"The Bilderberg Group's primary initiative was survival. You were frozen until the antivirus was created. And we altered the plan due to Concordia's declining population rates. They once again tasked the Flowers Corporation with…how do I put this…fixing the world again.

"We unthawed a select group of you to run trials throughout the country. Each subgroup is given a different amount of variables with the focus on answering the most basic of questions. What makes you happy? What makes you sad? What makes you want to reproduce? Then that data is used to construct living plans for the citizens of Concordia. That is all of your purposes. To serve the citizens of our great city. And you all do it well."

"We're science experiments?" Sam asked.

"Yes."

"And your role in all this?"

"I'm the lead scientist of the Flowers Corporation."

Sam's blood boiled. "And why shouldn't I end you right here and right now, lead scientist?"

David, who had remained still until that point, stretched out his arm and signaled to the center copter. Sam tightened her grip on the gun as two men emerged from the rear: a soldier and a prisoner. A black hood veiled the prisoner's face and thick metal shackles bound his hands and feet together. Sam's heartbeat quickened. There was no one left for her in this world. No one that she cared enough about to let David go free. No one that she remembered.

"Bring him here," David commanded. The soldier shoved the prisoner with the butt of his rifle and the man shuffled forward.

"You've already taken everyone I love and care about away from me," Sam said. "No one can save you. No one will serve as a bargaining chip—"

The soldier snatched the hood from the prisoner's head and Sam's heart exploded. Underneath the black hood was her best friend, her soul mate, Jordan Riggs. His face was battered and bruised and he sported a thick, unkempt beard. He had lost weight and his bushy face was gaunt. But it was Jordan none the same.

Her grip on the pistol loosened and tears stung at her eyes. "Jordan?" Silver tape wrapped all the way around his head, and covered his mouth.

"Lower your weapon," David said. "Or I'll have him executed in front of you." His voice was cold. Emotionless.

"But…but Jordan's dead."

"It's the 24th Century, Samantha. Hearts can be healed, wounds can be patched. Now please, lower your weapon."

Sam did as he asked and David stepped away from her. The soldiers lifted their weapons in unison; a dozen automatic rifles aimed right at her. She stared into Jordan's eyes. She wanted to touch him. She wanted to lift the barrel of the Remington and kill everyone here and then make a run for it. There were 15 bullets. It was possible. Sam eyed the crowd.

"Don't even think about it, Samantha." David turned and extended his hand out. "I promise either you or him will die if you try to escape." He offered her a ghoulish grin and the image of his face on the body of midnight runner flashed through her mind. Her skin crawled at the memory.

"Why did you appear as a midnight runner in my dreams?" Sam asked.

"Hand me the gun, Samantha."

"If memories of you were just Easter eggs, then why would you—"

"Samantha, I don't have time to get into the intricacies of my program, and even if I did I believe the details would bore you. It doesn't matter why I appeared the way I did. The reasons don't concern you. All that matters is that you hand me the gun."

"Let us go," Sam said. "If you let us go, we'll stay away from here. We'll never come back."

"Now why would I do that? I want you to come back. Haven't you figured it out yet? Every time you make this journey, you place us one step closer to building the perfect human. To creating the perfect society. This is your fourth journey from New Hope and by far the most impressive one yet. You staying away from here? That's the last thing that I want."

"Please," Sam pleaded.

David shushed her. "My darling, don't be afraid. You'll wake up tomorrow and it will be like none of this ever happened. And then you'll see your sister again and Jordan. You'll see Cole again. My team has already ascertained the location of his body and is in the process of recovering him. Tomorrow he'll be good as new. "

"And then the next day you'll rip him away from me again?" Tears streamed down her cheeks. She looked to Jordan. He was so close to her. "How many times have I suffered through Jordan dying, or Rebecca? When is enough truly enough?"

"It will never be enough. It's the loss of those things that makes you fight so hard," David said. "That's why I take them away. Jordan, Rebecca, Cole, Nick, Alex. All of their deaths give you strength."

"I don't want to be strong anymore," Sam said.

"Samantha, you are perfect. You will always be strong—"

Sam lifted the barrel of the gun to her temple. David's eyes widened and his lips screwed into a frown. "I can end this right now. If I pull the trigger it all goes away. You. Troy. Concordia. All of it. Then what will you do?"

"I'll use a clone of you to run my experiments," David said. "It won't be the first time we've used them."

"But it won't be me," Sam said. "It will just be a copy. How will that affect your data? Will it be special like me? Will it fight as hard as I do? Will it be *strong*?"

David sighed. "Fine. New proposal. You put the gun down and we return you to New Hope." He shook his head and his face grew red as he continued. "Or you shoot yourself and I subject your boyfriend to the most torturous death imaginable." His voice rose until he was beet red and screaming. "I'll peel the flesh from his bones and make him eat it. I'll cut off his dick and shove it down his throat. Do you understand me, bitch? I fucking own you. I created you!"

"And if I shoot him first?" Sam asked, her voice steady. "I can shoot him and turn the gun on myself before your soldiers get off their first round and you know I can...*bitch*."

David chuckled and then his laugh grew into a fit of hysteria. There was a wild look in his eyes and Sam kept her finger firmly on the trigger. She was ready to sacrifice both Jordan and herself. They would be dead but they would be dead together. No more torture. No more journeys.

"Fine!" David yelled. He kicked the metal cart and sent the monitor flying. He took a deep breath and then another. When he spoke again his words were even and measured. "You win. You and Jordan leave here today, right now. But know that I will find you again. And when I do, I'll kill everyone you love and make you watch as I do."

"Haven't you already done that?" Sam asked.

"Leave this place," David said and turned his back toward them. "And don't come back. Daniels, release the prisoner."

"Dr. Kidwell—" Daniels started, but David interrupted.

"I said release him."

The guard's face twisted in disbelief, but he did as David commanded and unlocked the Jordan's manacles. The chains fell to the ground and Jordan pulled down the tape from around his mouth. Sam took a cautious step forward and then the two embraced each other.

She looked up at him and he bent down and kissed her. His face was sticky from the tape, but she didn't mind. She savored every second of the warm, wet perfect kiss. "You're alive," she whispered as she pulled away.

The men in white coats gathered up the gear as a couple of soldiers escorted David back toward the helicopter. A pair of ravens cawed overhead as they dipped through the morning sky together. Sam smiled. She had won. Maybe not the war, but she had won this battle.

"Sam," Jordan said, "we need to leave before it's too—"

"Sir," one of the scientists said from near the copters, "the memory suppression device just came back online."

David spun and his dark eyes gleamed in the sunlight. Sam remembered the nightmare of David turning into the midnight runner. The boy from her dreams was pure evil. She hadn't won. "Set memory suppression to 100 percent," David said at once.

Sam pulled away, her eyes wide with terror. Her mind raced with all the things she wanted to say. "Jordan, I love you."

"Charge is ready. Waiting on your signal, David."

"Remember the flowers, Sam," Jordan said. "Remember the—"

Alarms blared overhead. Sam and Rebecca huddled against the wall at the forefront of the crowd. Rebecca's wide eyes gleamed as tears spilled down her cheeks. Sam knelt down, so she was eye-level with the little girl and grasped her by the shoulders.

"What's happening?" Rebecca asked.

The vaguest of memories slipped past Sam's mind. She had been standing outside some enormous city and Jordan had been with her. She tried to hold on to it, but it disappeared into the ether of her mind. She took a deep breath. "You know what's happening," Sam said. "They've breached the walls."

"It's not a drill?"

"No. It's not a drill."

"Will everything be okay?"

"Yes…everything will be okay."

The End

CHECK OUT OTHER GREAT
ZOMBIE NOVELS

DEAD ASCENT
by Jason McPhearson

The dead have risen and they are hungry...

Grizzled war veteran turned game warden, Brayden James and a small group of survivors, fight their way through the rugged wilderness of southern Appalachia to an isolated cabin in the hope of finding sanctuary. Every terrifying step they make they are stalked by a growing mass of staggering corpses, and a raging forest fire, set by the government in hopes of containing the virus.

As all logical routes off the mountain are cut off from them, they seek the higher ground, but they soon realize there is little hope of escape when the dead walk and the world burns.

CHAOS THEORY
by Rich Restucci

The world has fallen to a relentless enemy beyond reason or mercy. With no remorse they rend the planet with tooth and nail.

One man stands against the scourge of death that consumes all.

Teamed with a genius survivalist and a teenage girl, he must flee the teeming dead, the evils of humans left unchecked, and those that would seek to use him. His best weapon to stave off the horrors of this new world? His wit.

CHECK OUT OTHER GREAT ZOMBIE NOVELS

DEAD PULSE RISING
by K. Michael Gibson

Slavering hordes of the walking dead rule the streets of Baltimore, their decaying forms shambling across the ruined city, voracious and unstoppable. The remaining survivors hide desperately, for all hope seems lost... until an armored fortress on wheels plows through the ghouls, crushing bones and decayed flesh. The vehicle stops and two men emerge from its doors, armed to the teeth and ready to cancel the apocalypse.

TOWER OF THE DEAD
by J.V. Roberts

Markus is a hardworking man that just wants a better life for his family. But when a virus sweeps through the halls of his high-rise apartment complex, those plans are put on hold. Trapped on the sixteenth floor with no hope of rescue, Markus must fight his way down to safety with his wife and young daughter in tow.

Floor by bloody floor they must battle through hordes of the hungry dead on a terrifying mission to survive the TOWER OF THE DEAD.

CHECK OUT OTHER GREAT ZOMBIE NOVELS

VACCINATION
by Phillip Tomasso

What if the H7N9 vaccination wasn't just a preventative measure against swine flu?

It seemed like the flu came out of nowhere and yet, in no time at all the government manufactured a vaccination. Were lab workers diligent, or could the virus itself have been man-made? Chase McKinney works as a dispatcher at 9-1-1. Taking emergency calls, it becomes immediately obvious that the entire city is infected with the walking dead. His first goal is to reach and save his two children.

Could the walls built by the U.S.A. to keep out illegal aliens, and the fact the Mexican government could not afford to vaccinate their citizens against the flu, make the southern border the only plausible destination for safety?

ZOMBIE, INC
by Chris Dougherty

"WELCOME! To Zombie, Inc. The United Five State Republic's leading manufacturer of zombie defense systems! In business since 2027, Zombie, Inc. puts YOU first. YOUR safety is our MAIN GOAL! Our many home defense options - from Ze Fence® to Ze Popper® to Ze Shed® - fit every need and every budget. Use Scan Code "TELL ME MORE!" for your FREE, in-home*, no obligation consultation! *Schedule your appointment with the confidence that you will NEVER HAVE TO LEAVE YOUR HOME! It isn't safe out there and we know it better than most! Our sales staff is FULLY TRAINED to handle any and all adversarial encounters with the living and the undead". Twenty-five years after the deadly plague, the United Five State Republic's most successful company, Zombie, Inc., is in trouble. Will a simple case of dwindling supply and lessening demand be the end of them or will Zombie, Inc. find a way, however unpalatable, to survive?

CHECK OUT OTHER GREAT ZOMBIE NOVELS

900 MILES
by S. Johnathan Davis

John is a killer, but that wasn't his day job before the Apocalypse.

In a harrowing 900 mile race against time to get to his wife just as the dead begin to rise, John, a business man trapped in New York, soon learns that the zombies are the least of his worries, as he sees first-hand the horror of what man is capable of with no rules, no consequences and death at every turn.

Teaming up with an ex-army pilot named Kyle, they escape New York only to stumble across a man who says that he has the key to a rumored underground stronghold called Avalon..... Will they find safety? Will they make it to Johns wife before it's too late?

Get ready to follow John and Kyle in this fast paced thriller that mixes zombie horror with gladiator style arena action!

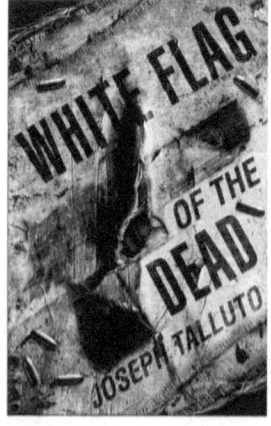

WHITE FLAG OF THE DEAD
by Joseph Talluto

Millions died when the Enillo Virus swept the earth. Millions more were lost when the victims of the plague refused to stay dead, instead rising to slaughter and feed on those left alive. For survivors like John Talon and his son Jake, they are faced with a choice: Do they submit to the dead, raising the white flag of surrender? Or do they find the will to fight, to try and hang on to the last shreds or humanity?

CHECK OUT OTHER GREAT ZOMBIE NOVELS

VACCINATION
by Phillip Tomasso

What if the H7N9 vaccination wasn't just a preventative measure against swine flu?

It seemed like the flu came out of nowhere and yet, in no time at all the government manufactured a vaccination. Were lab workers diligent, or could the virus itself have been man-made? Chase McKinney works as a dispatcher at 9-1-1. Taking emergency calls, it becomes immediately obvious that the entire city is infected with the walking dead. His first goal is to reach and save his two children.

Could the walls built by the U.S.A. to keep out illegal aliens, and the fact the Mexican government could not afford to vaccinate their citizens against the flu, make the southern border the only plausible destination for safety?

ZOMBIE, INC
by Chris Dougherty

"WELCOME! To Zombie, Inc. The United Five State Republic's leading manufacturer of zombie defense systems! In business since 2027, Zombie, Inc. puts YOU first. YOUR safety is our MAIN GOAL! Our many home defense options - from Ze Fence® to Ze Popper® to Ze Shed® - fit every need and every budget. Use Scan Code "TELL ME MORE!" for your FREE, in-home*, no obligation consultation! *Schedule your appointment with the confidence that you will NEVER HAVE TO LEAVE YOUR HOME! It isn't safe out there and we know it better than most! Our sales staff is FULLY TRAINED to handle any and all adversarial encounters with the living and the undead". Twenty-five years after the deadly plague, the United Five State Republic's most successful company, Zombie, Inc., is in trouble. Will a simple case of dwindling supply and lessening demand be the end of them or will Zombie, Inc. find a way, however unpalatable, to survive?

www.ingramcontent.com/pod-product-compliance
Lightning Source LLC
Chambersburg PA
CBHW031322170626
46807CB00002B/536